Another scream pierced the air, coming from a side room. Morgan and Two Wounds charged through the door. Morgan drew one of his pistols and slapped it hard against Private Lee Skousen's head. Skousen moaned once and fell, freeing twelve-year-old Bonnie Ashby.

Two Wounds released a shrill war cry and charged Private Vic Bowen with his knife.

"Bastards," Bowen snarled. The soldier got his revolver out and fired twice. Two Wounds jerked with the impact of the bullets, but he continued forward until he ran into Bowen.

Two Wounds made a feeble swipe at Bowen with his knife and barely nicked Bowen's neck before he fell.

"Goddamn savage," Bowen muttered as he pumped another slug into the back of Two Wounds' head. He turned to his friend saying, "Hey, Lee, look at what . . ."

After whacking Skousen on the head, Morgan had taken a couple of seconds to make sure Skousen was out, and that Bonnie Ashby was alright. He heard the gunshots and rose fast, swinging in time to see Bowen fire the *coup de grace* into Two Wounds' head.

Then Morgan fired.

SHOSHONI VENGEANCE
John Legg

ZEBRA BOOKS
KENSINGTON PUBLISHING CORP.

ZEBRA BOOKS are published by

Kensington Publishing Corp.
475 Park Avenue South
New York, NY 10016

First Printing: October, 1993

Printed in the United States of America

For Jay Watrous,
a loyal reader,
critic,
and, most importantly,
friend.

Chapter 1

Wind River Reservation
Wyoming Territory
April 1874

Orville Ashby, the agent for the Eastern Shoshoni on the huge Wind River Reservation, knelt in the mud next to Fox Head's body, shaking his head. It was going to be hell explaining this to Washakie. *As if the old warrior doesn't know already,* he thought in annoyance.

Ashby pushed to his feet, glancing up as he heard a rumble. It looked like another storm was moving in, but in this country one never could be quite certain. He nodded at the man standing on the other side of the corpse. "All right, Red Hand, take the poor bastard back to his family," he said sadly. It somehow seemed worse that the corpse had been found here in this pleasant little spot along the north fork of Sage Creek, rather than somewhere out in the desert scrubland.

The short, stocky Indian nodded in agreement. He and another Shoshoni—a massive, friendly-looking warrior named Big Horse—hoisted Fox Head's corpse and placed it in a blanket, then eased it across a horse.

Red Hand and Big Horse had found the body early that day. While Red Hand had nervously waited with the corpse, Big Horse had ridden to Camp Brown to get Ashby. Lieutenant Dexter Pomeroy, who was commander of the small force at Camp Brown, had wanted to go along, but Ashby would not allow it.

"But, dammit, Orville, this is the third one in the past couple of months."

"Jesus, Dex, I know that better than you. But you know damn well that Washakie doesn't want the army meddling in this business."

"The old bastard's not real fond of having his people killed off one at a time either."

Ashby nodded. "Just let it lie for now. I'll talk to Washakie as soon as I get back. If he wants you to bring the troops in, so be it."

"He won't allow it."

"Neither would I if I was in his position," Ashby said flatly. "Besides, what the hell can you do anyway?"

"Nothing, I guess," Pomeroy said sourly.

"Well, much as I hate the idea, I'd better hit the trail. I imagine Red Hand's crapping in his buckskins out there by himself."

"With the Arapaho out there killing off his fellow tribesmen, I suppose I don't blame him."

"Me neither. I'll be taking an extra horse for bringing the body back."

"I suppose Fox Head's family's going to want to keep the damn horse."

"Most likely. But you know Washakie'll see that it gets replaced."

"I still don't like you riding out there by yourself, Orv."

"Big Horse'll be with me."

"That'll be a big help if a war party of Arapaho comes riding over a ridge on you."

"If it was Arapaho, I don't think they'll be hanging around."

"You're being a damn fool, Orv," Pomeroy said in some annoyance. He hated this duty out here, miles from anywhere. The land for the most part was horrid, protecting the Shoshoni against the Sioux and Crow and Arapaho was demeaning, the weather was atrocious most of the time, and there was no chance whatsoever of being promoted out here. Besides, deep down he didn't like the Shoshoni—or any other Indians—very much, and it left him almost perpetually crotchety.

"Put that on my tombstone," Ashby said with a little laugh. With a distinct lack of enthusiasm, he left.

The ride to the foothills of the Wind River Mountains only took two hours. There were a few tense moments as Ashby looked around for Red Hand. Then the Shoshoni emerged from a screen of brush some yards away.

Ashby dismounted and looked around, almost as if avoiding Fox Head's body. He wasn't really, or at least not too much. He was hoping to find something that might give him a clue as to who had done this deed—and the two similar ones. He had found nothing, and so had no further reason to avoid the body.

Once the corpse was tied down to the extra horse, Ashby, Red Hand, and Big Horse headed back toward Camp Brown. Just before getting there, Ashby left the

9

two Shoshonis and kept following Sage Creek. He finally stopped in a small village spread along the creek.

Ashby could tell that word had already spread to the village. Usually the Shoshonis of Washakie's village ignored him. He was a frequent visitor and so not one to gain attention. But today they were all stopping—or at least pausing—in their work to watch his progress.

Ashby stopped at an ornately painted tepee and dismounted. A boy took his horse away as Ashby called for entrance into the lodge. A strong voice bade him enter.

Ashby went inside and sat, nodding in thanks as a young woman set a willow backrest behind him. Ashby leaned back and accepted the bowl of stew another young woman handed him. He ate a little, knowing Washakie's eyes were on him the whole time. Finally, he set the bowl aside. "You know?" he asked.

Washakie nodded solemnly. Washakie was in his late sixties or early seventies—no one knew for sure—but was still vigorous. He was tall and strong, and still walked with a straight back. His long hair flowed in a gray stream around his shoulders. He had been chief of the Eastern Shoshoni for more than a quarter century now and showed no sign of giving up the authority he had gained through strength, toughness, and bravery.

"It was Fox Head," Ashby said.

"So I was told."

"I wasn't able to learn anything more than with the last two," Ashby said apologetically.

"Something must be done, Orville," Washakie said. He had learned his first English words from mountain man Jim Bridger almost forty years ago. Bridger and the tall, striking Shoshoni became good friends. In-

10

deed, Bridger had married one of Washakie's daughters some years later. Washakie could speak English well now, though his accent was still quite thick at times.

"I know that, Washakie," Ashby said in irritation. "Trouble is, I don't know what. I can have Lieutenant Pomeroy send troops after the Arapaho." He held little hope that Washakie would accept that proposal.

"The Arapaho aren't doing these things."

"All right, then the Crow, though that doesn't seem likely, since all three killings took place on the southern side of the Wind."

"The Crow didn't do these things either."

"Then who?" Ashby asked, surprised. He and Washakie had discussed the first two murders, but they had not really addressed the matter of who had committed them. Ashby had just assumed the killers were members of one of the Shoshonis' rivals, enemies for years. The most likely perpetrators were the Arapaho, but the Crow also would have their reasons based on ages-old enmities. Now that Ashby thought about it, though, Washakie had never mentioned any possibilities.

"These things are the work of white men," Washakie said quietly.

"White men?" Ashby was incredulous. "Who? Why?"

"I don't know the answer to either question," Washakie said simply. "I only know that it's true."

"But the mutilations," Ashby protested. "All three of them had had at least one finger cut off. And both their ears. I know all Indians mutilate bodies. And I know you have your reasons for doing so," he added

11

hastily, to cut off any possible protest from Washakie. "So how can you think this was done by white men?"

Washakie looked askance at Ashby. "You just don't want to admit your people are just as bad as us savages," he said matter-of-factly.

Ashby's face flamed red, and he felt the heat of anger and embarrassment rising. Washakie's statement had hit too close to home. "Maybe," he said. It was all he would admit to. "But still, why would a white man—or white men—do it?"

"Who knows why white men do anything?" Washakie said dryly. "But look at it more closely. The Cheyenne are the ones who cut off fingers—or arms. That's their mark. No Indian people I know cut off ears. Not as a regular thing."

Ashby nodded, accepting the information. "Still, it doesn't make sense for white men to do the killing, let alone hacking up the bodies."

"It does if they want to make others believe our enemies are doing it."

"That's a point. But what would whites gain from the murders? Old enemies might be out for revenge, or to drive you off your land. Or any of a number of things. But what would whites gain from such a thing?"

"Though I have always tried to keep the People on friendly terms with the whites, there might have been times when I couldn't. But maybe the People's friendship with the white man has brought this about. Such a friendship wouldn't be good for men who might want this land for some reason."

Ashby smiled ruefully. "Most of this land isn't worth shit and you damn well know it. Not many white men're going to want it."

12

"It's not unknown for white men to hate Indians just for being Indians."

"No shit. The reverse is true, too. And it means nothing."

"Maybe nothing. Maybe they are just men who want to see Shoshoni and Arapaho killing each other."

"That wouldn't . . ." Ashby stopped, rather horrified. It was all too possible, he realized with dread. There were such men—red and white—who would love nothing more than to see people killing their "own kind." Whether they got any direct benefit out of it or not, it would, to some warped mentalities, be a worthwhile thing. As much as he hated to admit it, he knew that the white man was the more likely to stir up such a thing. It was not a matter of this particular piece of land or that particular piece of land; all they wanted was the extermination of the red man. To have two tribes killing each other off would be a rather exquisite irony.

"It's a damned devilish thought," Ashby said quietly. "But mighty damned likely."

"Yes. Mighty damn likely."

"So what're we going to do about it, Washakie? I expect that if what we think is true, they won't stop until you've gone to war with the Arapaho. Or the Crow. And we can't have you doing that. Nor can we allow any more of the Shoshoni to be killed by those savages."

"That would not be good, no."

"And I sure as hell can't have you out making war on the whites, no matter what they've done. At least until we could prove it, which we can't. But if you were to attack any white men at all, there'd be hell to pay."

"I know," Washakie said softly.

13

Ashby looked at Washakie sharply. In the several years he had known the Shoshoni chief, he had never known him to be a coward. He did not see cowardice in Washakie's eyes now, but he did notice a strong dose of fatalism. "Why not go to the army and tell them what we suspect? Hell, that's why they're here—to protect you."

"From the Arapaho and the Sioux. Not from the white man himself."

"Still, they are charged with protecting your people, especially here on your own damn land."

"I can't say why, but I know that bringing the army into this will lead only to more of my people getting killed."

Ashby was sure Washakie was right. "Maybe we should seek help from another quarter."

"What do you mean?"

"You're dead set against working with any white men?" Ashby countered. "Or just the army?"

"Depends on the white man," Washakie said reasonably. "Do you have someone in mind?"

Ashby nodded. "An old friend of mine is the U.S. marshal for Wyoming Territory. His headquarters is in Cheyenne. I could go to him for help."

"Do you trust him?"

"As much as I can anyone, I suppose."

Washakie nodded.

Chapter 2

Deputy U.S. Marshal Buck Morgan stood behind a large, fragrant sagebrush, looking down the slope at the cabin in the little gully. The several horses in a makeshift corral around one side of the cabin and a thin stream of smoke from a tin pipe on the cabin's roof were the only signs that the forlorn place was occupied.

Morgan had hoped to find the entire Spangler-Cochrane gang here, but it was beginning to look as if only some of them were in the cabin. He supposed the others were in South Pass City or Atlantic City, even though both cities were but pale imitations of their former booming selves.

Only a few years ago both cities had been roaring. South Pass City was the most populous city in the territory, and there even had been talk of making it the territorial capital. Cheyenne had won out in that, which probably was a good thing, seeing as how only a couple

15

of years later South Pass City's population was now less than a third of what it had been at the height of its gold-mining boom. There were still a few stores, saloons, and a brothel or two there. It was the same in Atlantic City. Enough to give a traveler a place to stop for some supplies, a few days' rest, or a little amusement.

The Spangler-Cochrane gang—Kevin, Jess, Avery, and Manny Spangler and Ronny, Rob, and Roger Cochrane—had had their criminal beginnings in South Pass City and Atlantic City, and they still liked to come back to the area to lay low. The dwindling of the gold mining had sent the gang farther afield in the past two years.

Morgan had been on the trail for more than a month, and he was getting tired of it. The seven outlaws always seemed to be just ahead of him. He had pushed himself and his horse hard the past two days, trying to make up time, and it finally seemed he had—only to find that the gang had split up, even if only temporarily.

It was late afternoon, and thunderheads were swirling above, as they seemed to almost every day at this time of year. Morgan hoped it wouldn't rain again. He was almost as sick of that as he was of chasing this batch of outlaws.

Morgan went back to his horse and unsaddled it. After hobbling the horse he got some jerky and his canteen, went back to the large sagebrush, and sat. He chewed on jerky and washed the leathery meat down with swallows of water, all the while keeping watch on the cabin, as well as the surrounding countryside. He sure as hell didn't want to get caught out here in the open by several returning outlaws.

Besides, he was also trying to figure out a way to approach the cabin. The land here did not offer much in the way of cover, though. It, like much of the territory he roamed on the job, was close to desert. The wheatgrass, gramma grass, and needle-and-thread grass covering the small, barren Antelope Hills southeast of South Pass City were short and often brown. With all the rain of late, it was considerably greener than usual. Still, it offered no cover, since all there was to hide behind were large sagebrushs, like the one where he was sitting.

Morgan was not fond of this land. He preferred a place where there was water and decent grass, and trees. Tall, green trees that smelled good after a nice hard rain; ones that offered shade and wood and some security. But he was here now, and he would have to deal with it. He figured he would wait until dark, then just walk on down there to the cabin and do whatever needed doing.

That was usually his way, in any case. He gave little thought to danger or his own safety. He had been told before that he was utterly fearless, and he supposed that was true. It was just the way he was. He didn't go out looking to get killed, but he rarely, if ever, backed down from a dangerous situation.

Morgan waited patiently until the sun sank over the hills to the west, and then he stood. It took a lot of standing for Morgan to reach his full six-foot-four. He checked the two .44-caliber Smith and Wessons he carried in cross-draw holsters. Then he stretched. He wanted to wait just a few more minutes for more darkness.

He started down the hill, walking in great loping strides. He looked forward to this. The Spanglers and

17

the Cochranes were a nasty bunch of men and deserved to be brought to heel. Their last several escapades, after a winter of inactivity, had been brutal and far-ranging. They had held up two trains between Rock Springs and Rawlins. A few days later they had killed two coal miners in a fight in Rock Springs, then busted up a brothel in Wamsutter, killing one of the girls. They had kidnapped three other women who worked there and dragged them north to an area of strange sand dunes. From what Morgan had been able to figure, the gang had kept the women there more than two weeks, abusing them constantly before dispatching them. A few miles east, the gang had killed a family of Cheyenne consisting of a middle-aged warrior, his younger wife, her aged mother, and two grandchildren.

They were not done yet, though word had gotten back to the U.S. marshal's office in Cheyenne and Morgan had been dispatched to hunt them down. Morgan tracked them from one place to the next, learning that they had been continuing their reign of terror. They had robbed a bank in Rock Springs, and two travelers east of town. A family trying to homestead a speck of land a few miles northwest of Rawlins was wiped out by the gang after the seven had taken their pleasure with the wife—and her nine-year-old daughter.

The gang had committed other crimes as well, but the rape of the girl was the one that had sent Morgan's rage boiling. He had picked up the outlaws' trail a few days later, with some solid leads, and that was when he began pushing himself and his horse hard. In the past three days he had had no more than four hours' sleep a night, but none of that mattered now. Not to him. All he could see in his mind was the naked, battered body of that little girl. His cool gray eyes narrowed in the darkness at the remembrance.

He stopped at the cabin door. As he had figured, the string to the latch was out. The ones inside were expecting their friends back, he assumed. He had counted on that. He eased the string forward until he heard the latch snick softly. He paused, but there was no change in the sound of talking from inside. He eased out both pistols.

With a cold, cruel smile, he kicked the door open and stepped inside, eyes sweeping the lantern-lit interior in a heartbeat. Ronny and Rog Cochrane were sitting at a rickety table; Manny Spangler was half sitting, half lying on a cot, facing the door, his back braced against the wall. Spangler wore no shirt or boots, sitting there in his dirty trousers and filthy union suit and crusty socks. All three men were drinking whiskey. The two Cochranes were shoveling beans into their mouths as well. They were fully dressed.

"Evenin', shit balls," Morgan said evenly in a deep, strong voice. Then he calmly shot Manny Spangler cleanly through the forehead. "You other two assholes're under arrest."

"What the hell'd you kill Manny like that for?" Ronny Cochrane asked. He did not seem incredulous. He was vying for time.

"Just to show you two cornholin' peckerwoods that I am of no mind to fool with you. Either you do what I tell you, when I tell you, or I'll shoot you dead just like I did your pustulant friend over there."

"Who the hell are you?" Ronny asked. He was worried now. There was absolutely no fear in this tall, hard-looking man with the star on his chest. Indeed, the marshal looked like he was out for a buggy ride with his sweetheart—except for the two big Smith and Wessons in his oversized paws.

"Deputy U.S. Marshal Buck Morgan. Now both of you ease out your pistols and toss 'em toward the back of the cabin. You with the spoon in the air, just stay the way you are. Big mouth, you first."

"But I . . ."

Morgan shot him in the face, the bullet punching a neat round hole through his right cheekbone. Ronny was slammed back out of his chair.

"All right there, shit ball," Morgan said evenly, looking at Rog Cochrane, "your turn."

Rog Cochrane was the youngest of the three Cochranes at twenty-three, according to the wanted papers out on him. Right now he looked even younger—and scared to death.

Morgan realized the young man was frightened and hoped to use that, so he waited before drilling him, which had been his first inclination. "You need a gold-embossed invite, boy?" he asked harshly.

Cochrane shook his head slowly, looking as if he thought his head might fall off if he moved it too much. He finally managed to close his mouth, which had been open in anticipation of the spoonful of beans that still dangled in midair.

"Then drop the beans and lose the pistol." He clicked back the hammer on one of his guns.

Cochrane dropped the spoon, which landed in the beans with a soft splat. He jerked his arm downward, toward his pistol, but just as quickly stopped. Then he moved his hand down ever so slowly, eased out his revolver, and held it out with two fingers on the grip.

"Fling it back behind you and then stand."

Cochrane did so. He licked his lips in fear as he looked at Morgan.

"Where's your other piece?"

"I don't . . ."

Morgan shot Cochrane in the upper right arm. "I've got no time or inclination to pussyfoot around with a shit ball like you. Not after what you did to that little girl up outside of Rawlins."

"Belly gun," Cochrane squawked.

"Get rid of it."

With his left hand, Cochrane pulled his shirt open, revealing a five-shot, .31-caliber, silver-plated Colt pocket revolver. He took it out and tossed it away.

Morgan nodded. "You got another piece on you?" he asked.

"No," Cochrane said firmly.

Morgan shrugged. "If you're lyin' to me, you'll be sorry for it."

"I ain't lyin'."

"Sit down." When Cochrane did Morgan slid away one of the Smith and Wessons. With the other lazily trained on Cochrane, Morgan checked the other two men. Both were dead. Morgan poured himself a drink at the table and gulped it down. As he set the glass down on the table, he asked, "Where're the rest of the boys?"

Cochrane hesitated, and Morgan could see in his eyes that the young outlaw was building a lie. Morgan shot him in the other arm.

"Son," Morgan said, his voice flat and firm, "you got yourself one chance to come out of this alive. And that's if you stop your bullshit. Now, where's the others?"

"South Pass City," Cochrane said hastily. "Either

21

there or Atlantic City. We was low on supplies, and I think Jess wanted himself a harlot.''

"There's some left over there?''

"Not many,'' Cochrane said with a shrug that sent a roaring blast of pain down both arms. "But there was a few last time we rode through.''

"When do you expect 'em back?''

"Tomorrow. Maybe the day after. Depends on what they find to do there.''

"You're in deep shit, boy, you know that, don't you?''

Cochrane nodded. "You gonna bring me back to Cheyenne?'' he asked.

"That's my intent. After all the shit you and your cronies pulled you'll swing sure as hell. I'd just as soon send you across the divide here and now, but I reckon boys like you are best brought to justice properly, as an example to others.''

"I don't think I'll make it,'' Cochrane said fatalistically. "And if my friends find you, you won't make it neither.''

Morgan smiled, and the coldness of it sent a wrenching blast of fear up Cochrane's spine. "We'll just see about that.''

Chapter 3

**Wind River Reservation
Wyoming Territory
April 1874**

Orville Ashby hated the journey to Cheyenne from the reservation. It was long, tedious, and blazing hot in summer, and frigid in winter. Still, the railroad made it a lot better than it could have been.

The first part was the worst. To start, there was the ride into Flat Fork, a festering sinkhole of a town just off the reservation. The place had little other purpose than to serve the soldiers from Camp Brown. Because of that, it was a town full of places of degradation. Brothels and saloons abounded, and there were precious few decent places of any kind. One of them was the station for the Hogg stage line.

Ashby boarded one of the creaking, dusty, worn stages at nine in the morning after a twelve-mile, three-hour ride from the agency quarters up near the camp. The town was just far enough from the fort to keep the soldiers from heading there too regularly or too readily, but Ashby thought it was nothing but a pack of trouble to get there when he was in a hurry.

Then there were eight days in the jolting, shuddering coach, mostly eastward and then south to Rawlins. The coach had to get across the Popo Agie, the Little Popo Agie, Twin Creek, Beaver Creak, and then the Sweetwater River. It was, Ashby had thought every time he had had to make this journey, an awful lot of water for such a dry, desolate place. It was odd to him how the land could be a virtual desert, yet there were streams and rivers crossing it. The water that flowed, though, seemed to have no effect much beyond its banks.

At last Rawlins came into view late in the afternoon—just about the time Ashby thought his spine would be driven upward by his buttocks until it poked out the top of his head. When he alit from the coach he felt like a sailor just returned from a long ocean voyage: His legs were wobbly and he had trouble walking. He made his way to the nearest hotel and slept the night through.

After a hearty breakfast in the morning Ashby boarded the train. Two days later he picked up his bag and left the train in Cheyenne. With a decidedly more cheerful air, he walked up Central Avenue to Seventeenth Street. Turning west up Seventeenth, he walked a short distance to the office of U.S. Marshal Floyd Dayton.

A tall, pudgy young man turned from a file at the sound of the door. "Can I help you?" he asked.

Ashby set his carpetbag down and brushed some of the dust off his suit coat. "I'd like to see Floyd—Marshal Dayton—please," he said quietly.

The young man pushed the file drawer closed and

turned to face Ashby. The star on his dark vest glinted dully in the sunlight streaming through a side window. He wore a pocket Colt revolver in a small, cross-draw holster on his right hip. Ashby did not think he looked much like a deputy U.S. marshal.

"Marshal Dayton's busy," the young man said. His voice was one that could be expected to come from such a man, a man whose look was soft, clean-shaven, fastidious.

Orville Ashby was not by nature a hardcase. On the other hand, he was a man who had overcome his share of adversity in life. While not much of a fighter, he was not about to be trod over by this young pup. Not after the interminable journey he had made to get here. "If you're going to lie, son," Ashby said flatly, "you had better learn to do it a lot more convincingly than that."

The deputy's eyes narrowed. "I don't take kindly to strangers calling me a liar," he said in a huff. Then he sighed. "But since you're a stranger, and one who looks like he could use himself a bit of a break, I'll overlook it for now. But you best go on now before I have to take some drastic steps." He tried to look fierce, not knowing he looked like a fool instead.

"Your arrogance is ill-directed, son," Ashby said evenly.

"Why, you cantankerous old bastard," the deputy said in disbelief. Herman Obstfelt was terribly affronted. Here he was, trying to be polite to this man, while at the same time trying to get rid of the visitor without getting Dayton involved. That would bring him up considerably in Dayton's eyes, Obstfelt figured. But this filthy stranger—who looked like he had spent two weeks sleeping in his clothes—wanted to give him

25

a hard time. Obstfelt was not about to put up with such behavior, even if it did mean working up a sweat.

"That I am," Ashby agreed. "And growing more damned cantankerous with each passing second. Now go tell Floyd that Orville Ashby's here to see him."

"I see that sterner measures are called for," Obstfelt said, cracking his knuckles. He didn't like to fight so much as he did intimidating people, which he thought he did mighty well. He was generally the only one who thought that way.

"Look, son," Ashby said in exasperation, "I'm too old for getting into scraps, and I've had a long journey. All I want to do is talk some business with the marshal and then be on my way."

"Like I said," Obstfelt noted testily, "he's not here. Now you best be on your way. I've lost my patience with you. Any more lip from you and I'll have to pitch you out into the street."

Ashby sighed. "Best get to it, then," he said wearily, "since I'm not going anywhere voluntarily."

Obstfelt grinned a little and cracked his knuckles again. He stepped forward, purpose stamped on his bright, pudgy face. A moment later he was on his seat on the floor, a hand held to a suddenly bloody nose.

"Floyd!" Ashby shouted. "Floyd, you back there?"

"What in the flying Jesus is all the ruckus about out here?" Marshal Floyd Dayton bellowed as he tore open the door of his office at the back. Then he stopped and grinned. "Orv, how're you doing?" He stepped forward, hand outstretched.

"Passable. You?"

Dayton patted his broad stomach with a hard hand. "Fat and sassy as ever," he said with a laugh. He looked down at Obstfelt, disgust flickering on his face. "Get up, boy. You look ridiculous down there."

Obstfelt got up, trying not to touch his bloody hand to his clothes. "I want to press charges against him," he said, pointing a shaky, bloody index finger at Ashby.

"For what?" Dayton asked with a low laugh.

"For assaulting a marshal. A federal marshal."

"Just for poking you in the snout?" Dayton said, laughing more. "You realize how stupid you're going to look in some court when a judge asks how this old man"—he winked at Ashby—"was able to knock a spry young feller like you on your plump ass?"

"I see nothing humorous in this," Obstfelt said stiffly.

"Oh, hell, boy, don't be so damned pompous. If you hadn't been acting so high and mighty, none of this would've happened."

"I was not acting pompous. I was . . ."

"Like hell," Dayton said, still enjoying the tableau. "I know just what you were doing. You were trying to run roughshod over Mr. Ashby here."

Obstfelt looked stricken but kept his mouth shut.

Dayton was still laughing, but it soon wound down. "Now, Herm, go clean your face up and then fetch us a bottle." He paused. "Unless you'd rather have something else, Orv?"

"Right now coffee'd be fine for me," Ashby said.

"You do look a mite overdone. Had a good trip, did you?"

"Just wonderful."

Dayton laughed again. "I bet. All right, Herm, go fetch us a pot of coffee. Might as well bring a bottle, too. There's no law I know of to prevent a man from flavoring coffee with a dose of snakebite medicine."

"Yessir," Obstfelt said dejectedly. He clumped off and out the door.

"Jesus, Floyd, where'd you ever dredge him up?"

"I needed somebody to help me with the paperwork and all that. Herman came highly recommended as a secretary. Then, damn fool that I am, I let him talk me into making him a deputy. He doesn't really do any law-enforcing, but he likes to strut around Cheyenne with his shiny badge and that little pistol of his. Impresses the ladies, I hear. Or at least a certain class of ladies."

Ashby laughed. "I guess it would. But he'd better watch his mouth around folks, or one day somebody's going to clean his plow good for him."

"He's a big boy," Dayton said with a shrug. "If he can't take care of himself, he'll have to suffer the consequences. Come on, let's go on in back and take a load off your feet." Dayton turned and walked toward the office at the rear.

Ashby grabbed his bag and followed, wondering about his friend. Floyd Dayton had put on some weight since Ashby had last seen him, and he looked mighty comfortable with city living. Not that Ashby thought there was anything wrong with that; it was just that it didn't seem to suit Dayton, or at least the Dayton that Ashby had known all along.

There was something more about Dayton, though, and Ashby couldn't quite put his finger on it. He thought it might be the fancy clothes, or the aroma of expensive toilet water that drifted on the air behind the marshal as he walked.

The two sat, Dayton behind his desk, Ashby in a plump chair in front of the desk.

"I take it you didn't come here just to pay an old

friend a visit, Orv," Dayton said, lacing his fingers behind his head.

"No, no, I sure didn't. That trip is a back-breaker. Or maybe I'm just getting old."

"I know the feeling." Dayton sighed. "Well, despite your reckless speed in getting here," he said a little sarcastically, "I figure you can wait a few more minutes."

Ashby shrugged, then asked, "Why?"

"Old friends ought to have a few minutes for visiting before getting down to business. Time for a toast, at least." He grinned. "Besides, I'd rather wait until Herm gets back here with the coffee and such so we won't have to worry about him interrupting us."

"Herm don't get here in the next two minutes, I'm liable to fall asleep sitting here."

"It's hell getting old, ain't it?"

Neither was all that old—both in their mid-forties. But each man had been through a lot in life, and that had taken its toll. Both knew that and accepted it, but both had a little trouble dealing with it. Just because they accepted it didn't mean they had to like it any.

Ashby could feel himself nodding off when Obstfelt finally bustled in, carrying a large coffeepot and two cups. He set the cups down, filled them, and then put the coffeepot on the end of the desk. From his back pocket he pulled a bottle of whiskey, which he put down on the desk in front of Dayton.

"Anything else, Marshal?" Obstfelt asked, only barely able to keep the surliness out of his voice.

"You hungry, Orv?" Dayton asked. He was enjoying himself, as he always did when he was giving Herman Obstfelt a hard time.

"I could do with a bite," Ashby said with a grin.

He managed to pull himself out of his funk a little and get into the game he could see Dayton was playing. It was true, though, that he was hungry.

"Me, too," Dayton announced. "All right, Herm, hustle on over to Clooney's and have the old bastard rustle us up a couple of steaks, taters, and whatever else to go with them."

"But . . ."

"The stalls could use mucking out," Dayton warned.

"Two steaks with all the extras coming right up." Obstfelt left, buttocks tight with anger.

Ashby grinned. "You really delight in tormenting him, don't you, Floyd?"

"I sure do," Dayton said with a laugh. "It's one of the few amusements left to me, I sometimes think."

"Seems to me it's a mighty easy target you got there."

"It sometimes does seem a little unfair, but I can't stop myself." He leaned forward and uncorked the bottle of whiskey. He poured a small amount into his coffee cup and stirred it with a chubby forefinger. "Want some?" he asked.

"Don't mind if I do," Ashby decided. He reached across the desk, took the bottle from Dayton, and then added some to his coffee. He raised his cup. "Well, cheers. Or something."

"Or something," Dayton agreed. They drank a little, and then Dayton said, "Despite whatever troubles brought you here, Orv, it's good to see you. What's it been, two years?"

"Closer to three, I think." He sipped again. "With you way out here, and me out there on that damn reservation . . ."

"Is it that bad out there?"

"It's a desolate hole," Ashby said thoughtfully. Then he grinned. "But, you know, I kind of like it out there. Most of the reservation is scrubland and desert, but not far from Camp Brown are the Wind River Mountains. God, if they aren't something to see. I try to get up there every chance I can to do some hunting and fishing."

"Sounds nice. You go with the army? Or the Indians?"

"Either. The Shoshoni're pretty nice people. Not savages like most people think. Clean, respectable, honest. I tell you, there ought to be more whites with those qualities."

"I can agree with that, even if I don't know the Shoshoni. I'll tell you, Orv, it might be nice out there, but I think I'll just stay right where I'm at. Good restaurants, a soft bed, a good selection of saloons—and brothels. Ah, the good life." He laughed.

Chapter 4

After getting what little information he could from Rog Cochrane, Morgan did what he could for Cochrane's wounds, which wasn't much. Basically he just splashed some whiskey over them—eliciting a startled hiss from Cochrane, who almost fainted when the procedure was performed on the second wound. Then he bound the wounds with a couple of dirty strips of cloth he had found on the floor.

That done, Morgan tied the outlaw up and gagged him. Then Morgan walked through the soft, warm night and got his horse and his small stock of supplies and equipment and brought them down to the cabin.

Putting the horse in the makeshift corral on the side of the cabin, he tended the animal. Fighting off the tiredness, he brought his things inside. After checking Cochrane again he cooked up a plate of beans—about all the food he found in the cabin—and ate, ignoring Cochrane's hungry eyes.

Finished eating, he relaxed a little with a cup of coffee and a rare pipe. Afterward, he forced his weariness aside and cleaned and reloaded the pistol he had used. He checked over his rifle, making sure it was fully loaded. He gathered up all the outlaws' guns he could find, as well as their ammunition and his own. He laid the guns—all loaded—and the extra ammunition on the table, ready to be grabbed if needed.

It was well after midnight when he finished. He ran a hand across his weary face. While he did not think the other outlaws would be back in the middle of the night, he decided he had better take a look around anyway. He rose and stretched. Clapping on his hat, he headed outside.

Morgan made a long, slow, careful circuit of the area, but he found nothing out of the ordinary. Still, it had taken him a couple of hours, and by the time he got back to the cabin he figured there were only a couple of hours left untill daylight. He checked Cochrane's bonds, and then poured himself some coffee.

For a bit he pondered trying to get some sleep, but he didn't know if that was safe. He opted for pouring cup after cup of coffee down his throat. It helped some, but by the time daylight came, he had to make water something awful. After doing so he made another check around the area, this one much faster.

He finally returned to the cabin and sat back to wait for the four other outlaws to return.

But the lack of rest over the past several days caught up to him and he fell asleep, snoring softly as his head slumped forward onto his chest.

Cochrane lay on the cot where Morgan had thrown him and watched the marshal warily for some time. Morgan certainly seemed to be sleeping soundly, but

Cochrane worried that the lawman was trying to fool him into trying something. Then Morgan could shoot him to death without anyone being the wiser.

After almost an hour Cochrane figured he was safe enough, and he began working to free his bonds. It was difficult—after two more hours Cochrane began to think impossible—considering that both his arms were wounded. Still, Cochrane kept at it, pausing more and more frequently as the minutes turned into hours. More than once he had to twist himself so he could bury his face in the straw tick as pain swept over him in gut-wrenching waves.

He figured it was a little past noon when he heard horses approaching the cabin. Cochrane jerked at the ropes frantically, face mashed against the mattress to keep his groans of pain quiet. But it was no use. He gave that up and instead shoved his face against the mattress time and time again, trying to force down the side of the gag a little.

The cloth budged a little, then a bit more. With a frantic look at Morgan, who was still sleeping, Cochrane rolled up onto his knees. A nail stuck out of the wall, and he slid his cheek against it several times. He tore his flesh, but finally snagged the cloth that was in his mouth. Two jerks and the gag finally came free, hanging wetly just below his lower lip.

He gasped as pain swept over him again. Then he sucked in a deep breath. "Rob!" he shouted as a warning to his brother and friends. "Raise dust outta here, boys!"

Morgan jerked awake at the shout. And he did so fully alert. Without delay, he spun, Smith and Wesson in hand, and angrily shot Cochrane through the chest. Then he jumped up and ran for the one crude window.

34

"Shit and goddamn," he snarled when he saw the four outlaws hightailing it for the ridge a hundred and fifty yards or so away. Smith and Wessons would never do for a long shot at fleeing targets, and he knew that by the time he grabbed his rifle they'd be over the ridge. He holstered his one pistol.

Teeth clenched in anger, he stomped to the cot. Cochrane was dead. "Goddamn stupid young shit ball," he muttered. He was talking as much to himself as he was to the remains of Rog Cochrane. He was enraged at himself for having fallen asleep. He finally sighed. Recriminations would do him no good, no matter who they were directed at. He turned, grabbed his rifle from the table, and went to stand in the corner near the window. That allowed him a good view of the landscape, but still kept him mostly protected.

As he stood there, he wondered if the outlaws would just keep on riding. He got his answer soon enough when a slug whistled through the window and whined off the coffeepot. Morgan did not fire back, since he had no target.

"Rog!" one of the outlaws yelled. "Rog, you still in there? Ronny? How about you? Manny?" There was a pause, then, "If any of you're alive in there, call out."

Morgan waited a few moments, then bellowed, "All three're dead. You'll be in the same condition, if you don't give yourselves up right quick."

"Who the hell are you?" an angry, arrogant voice drifted down from the ridge.

"Deputy U.S. Marshal Buck Morgan. Now give yourselves up and save us all a heap of grief."

"You really kill Manny, Ronny, and Rog?"

"All three."

"Bastard."

Morgan could see no reason to comment on that, so he said nothing.

The outlaws laid siege to the cabin all the rest of the day, firing at intervals and from slightly different locations so as not to give Morgan anything to shoot at. The shots were frequent enough to keep Morgan alert, but not enough to waste too much ammunition.

Morgan fired back on occasion, more to let the outlaws know that he was still there than for any other reason. He was grateful for the cabin's location; with all the open land between the ridge and the cabin, the outlaws could not get close enough to rush the cabin.

He did know full well, though, that the outlaws were certain to charge the cabin after dark. He figured they would do so after midnight, maybe even shortly before dawn. That would give Morgan some time to worry about being overpowered and maybe get tired, which would mean he would be less alert.

That's how Morgan figured the outlaws would reason it out, anyway. Of course, they did not know who they were dealing with here.

Morgan watched until it was too dark to see anything. Then he turned and went to the table. He tossed two Colt revolvers into his saddlebags and unloaded all the rest of the weapons. He stuck as much ammunition as he could into the saddlebags. He downed a quick cup of coffee. He had been considerably relieved earlier in the day to find that the bullet that had hit the pot had only winged the top. He had taken the time then to heat up some beans, which he had eaten while standing at the window. He did the same a couple of hours later. Now he figured he could get by without more food for the rest of the night, if need be.

36

He shut off the lantern and waited fifteen minutes. The moon provided enough light that he could see if any of the outlaws were heading for the cabin. None was.

Finally Morgan slipped out of the cabin and saddled his horse. Leaving it there, in case he had to make a run for it, he headed toward the ridge to his right. That ridge cast enough shadows that he figured he could get there without being seen.

He moved swiftly and surely, heading toward where he figured the outlaws were. He found one of them fairly quickly. The man—Morgan was not sure which one of them it was—was lying on the rim of the ridge, rifle in front of him. He was gnawing at his fingernails.

Morgan sighed. He knew it would be far easier just to put a knife in the outlaw's back and be done with it. But he was a deputy U.S. marshal, and he took his job seriously. He would have to try to arrest the man.

He marched forward and placed a foot flat against the man's back, then knelt that way. He pressed the muzzle of his Smith and Wesson against the nape of the outlaw's neck. "You're under arrest, shit ball," Morgan said quietly.

"Like hell I am," the outlaw snapped. He jerked himself up violently, shoving hard with both hands. The maneuver threw Morgan to the side a little. He fired his pistol, but the bullet just missed the outlaw's head.

The outlaw—Avery Spangler, Morgan saw now—flopped back down and then rolled away from Morgan, snatching up his rifle as he did.

Morgan shot him twice in the face, making a bloody awful mess at that range.

Morgan's hat went flying off as he heard the whine

of a bullet. He did not flinch, but he swung a little to his left, still kneeling, and fired the remaining two bullets in his Smith and Wesson at the flash of gunfire he had spotted.

Someone yelped, and there were no more gunshots. Morgan slipped the Smith and Wesson away and scuttled off a few feet to his right as he pulled the other pistol. Then he stood and moved cautiously toward where he had fired at the gun flashes.

Suddenly, he heard hoofbeats racing off. He stopped and listened for a few moments. The hoofbeats were heading away, toward South Pass City, moving fast. Still, Morgan meant to be cautious. There was no telling yet if the outlaws hadn't simply sent a couple of stolen horses running off to fool him.

Behind a rock, he found a dead outlaw—Rob Cochrane. Morgan squatted, his back against the rock, and reloaded his empty revolver. That done, he stood and moved off again.

Morgan spent several hours searching the area. He found where the outlaws had tethered their horses originally. Only one was there now. He left the horse there and continued his wary search. Shortly after midnight, he decided that the remaining outlaws had taken off. He got the one horse they had left and then went back to the two men he had killed. One at a time he threw them across the saddle. Then he walked down the slope to the cabin.

Morgan unsaddled his horse and brought his gear back into the cabin. He brought the two bodies inside and then unsaddled the other outlaw horse. Back inside, he nailed a few old boards over the window. He ate a plateful of beans and had a cup of coffee. Then he turned in.

In the morning he saddled his own horse, then tied the bodies of the outlaws across the backs of horses. Two animals were left, and Morgan set them loose. He pulled himself into the saddle and rode off, stopping when he got to where the outlaws' horses had been tied the night before. He tried to follow their trail, but it was difficult on the rocky, scrub-covered ground.

Finally, he decided to just head for South Pass City. The outlaws most likely wouldn't linger there—even if that was where they had headed—but Morgan thought someone there might have some information about the two men.

He took his time riding, not wanting to overtax any of the animals in the heat. He also was watching the ground halfheartedly, hoping to pick up the outlaws' trail. He had no luck, and an hour or so before dark he rode into South Pass City.

Morgan stopped in front of the Sherlock Hotel and dismounted, ignoring the people gathering to stare at him. He went inside the dining room portion of the hotel and took a seat.

Chapter 5

Deputy U.S. Marshal Herman Obstfelt entered the office of his boss, U.S. Marshal Floyd Dayton, after knocking. In his hand was a tray loaded with a steak dinner and all the trimmings. He held the door open for another man, who also carried a tray. The two placed the trays on the desk, one in front of Dayton, the other across the desk, near Orville Ashby, who pulled his chair closer to the desk, hunger glistening in his eyes.

"Anything else, Marshal?" Obstfelt asked tightly.

"Coffee—bring another pot. With some sugar. And we can use some more biscuits, too. Oh, and bring us a couple of those good cigars Klemmer sells."

"I hate to intrude," the other man said, "but who's payin' for all this?"

Dayton looked up at Mike Clooney and grinned a little. "Put it on the office tab. It'll be paid when I get my next check for expenses and such."

"Shit, I expected you to say that. Dammit, Marshal, I can't feed you and every goddamn criminal in the territory on your good wishes and promises. I need me some good hard cash every once in a while, dammit."

"You always get your money, Clooney," Dayton said, some of his humor dissipating.

"Yeah," Clooney admitted. "But it takes long enough." He sighed. "All right. I'll send Obstfelt here back with the coffee and sugar. He can get the cigars at his leisure, as far as I'm concerned. I'm in the restaurant business, not running a tobacco shop."

Obstfelt returned not too long after, setting a small package of cigars on the desk along with a large coffeepot and a small dish of sugar. "Anything else?" he asked, hoping he kept the annoyance out of his voice.

He hadn't, but Dayton didn't mind. "Not for now, boy, but you better stick close by just in case me and Orville here need some dessert."

After the steaks the marshal and the Indian agent decided that they did, indeed, need some dessert, so Obstfelt was dispatched to bring them another large pot of coffee plus a large helping of cherry cobbler for each.

Bloated, the two finally leaned back in their chairs. A mug of whiskey-laced coffee sat before each man and a cigar jutted jauntily out of each mouth. Once more Dayton called in Obstfelt and had the deputy clean away the supper debris. It took him several trips. On the last, Dayton said, "You can go on home now, Herm."

"Gee, thanks, Marshal," Obstfelt said sarcastically.

When Obstfelt had left Dayton looked at Ashby and asked, "Well, Orv, now that supper and all the pleasantries're out of the way, what can I do for you?"

"Someone's killing Shoshonis on the reservation, Floyd," Ashby said quietly.

"Who? And, more importantly, why?"

Ashby shrugged. "I don't know the answer to either of those questions. I wish I did."

"You have any *ideas* on who's doing it?"

"I thought it was Arapaho. They've been enemies of the Shoshoni for years, and it would seem likely."

"You don't really sound so sure of that, though," Dayton said pointedly.

"Well, the killer or killers are trying to make it look like members of a rival tribe are doing it. That's why I suspected the Arapaho. They have the hatred, and the proximity, to be able to pull something like that off."

"But . . . ?" Dayton pressed.

"But Chief Washakie suspects it's the work of white men."

"Why's he think it's white men? He hate us so much he's trying to blame everything on us?"

"No. No, nothing like that. Washakie's been invariably friendly to the white man. He's been chief more than twenty years, and never once has a Shoshoni killed a white man that anyone knows about. It's odd. Most of the other tribes don't allow one chief to rule, but for some reason the Shoshoni have allowed Washakie to do so."

"Must be one tough old bird," Dayton commented.

"He is that." Ashby paused. "There's a story about him that illustrates his toughness quite well. Seems the Blackfeet were attacking the Shoshonis regularly. The warriors wanted to send a war party against the Blackfeet to get some revenge. But Washakie told them it'd be foolish—maybe even suicidal. Well, that didn't sit

42

real well with his men, and they started making fun of him. Called him a dried-up old man who had no balls.''

"How old is he?''

"Now, about seventy, as best as anyone can figure.''

"And when did this take place?''

"Just a couple of years ago.''

Dayton looked at Ashby skeptically but said only, "Well, what happened?''

"Washakie got them to quiet down and stay home, at least for a spell. Then he disappeared.''

"Disappeared?''

Ashby nodded. "He was gone a little over a week. The young warriors were certain he had run away, and they were drumming up support for a punitive expedition against the Blackfeet when Washakie returned— with seven Blackfoot scalps.''

Dayton's eyebrows rose.

"Yes, all by himself he went to Blackfoot territory, killed seven of them, and took their scalps. Not too many of the men gave him a hard time about anything after that. There wasn't one of them who had the balls—or the ability—to do what he had done.''

"And you believe that?''

Ashby took a sip of coffee and nodded. "Yeah, I do. I've heard it from enough people—including some who can't be considered exactly good friends with Washakie—to believe it.''

Dayton nodded. "He sounds like a wild character,'' the marshal admitted. "But what's that got to do with any of this?''

"Well, you had thought he might be blaming whites simply because he hates whites. But he doesn't. And he wouldn't blame whites just for the hell of it. Nor would he allow his men to blame whites for the hell of it."

"So what made now you think it was some other Indians?" Dayton asked.

"All the bodies were mutilated."

"How?"

"All the victims' ears were cut off, as were some fingers. Two were disemboweled; rather crudely, I'd say."

"So now you're an expert on disembowelments?" Dayton asked with a grin.

Ashby shook his head, seeing no humor in the statement. "No, I wouldn't say that. But I have seen the results of an Indian battle where the bodies were mutilated, and these Shoshonis did not seem to have been done the same way. I can't really figure it out, but there was just something different about it."

"Maybe other Indians did do it but were rushed," Dayton said thoughtfully. "They hurried their job and didn't get a chance to do it right, if that's the correct term."

"What about the others, though?" Ashby countered. "The ones that did not suffer that particular mutilation?"

"Again, maybe they were pressed for time. They sliced the ears, and maybe only a finger or two, and then thought someone was coming or something. So they just kicked up the dust getting away from there."

"I suppose that could be true. But Washakie's got me more than half convinced that it wasn't Indians, in large part because of the ears. No Indians I know of cut ears off," he added, parroting Washakie. "At least, not as a regular practice."

"But why in the hell would white men do such a thing?" Dayton asked.

"Jesus, Floyd, you know the way men act. White men don't need any excuse to kill Indians. Hell, the same can be said of most Indians. Why do men—any men—do half the damn things they do? Why are men so bent on killing each other for no good reason?"

"Christ, Orv, calm down a little. I don't have the answers. I just do my job the best I can and try to treat my fellow man as good—or as bad—as he treats me."

Ashby smiled ruefully. "I was getting a little carried away there, wasn't I?" he asked rhetorically. "Anyway, I tend to believe Washakie. Being a 'savage,' as it were, he knows about mutilations far better than I do. At least with ritualistic mutilations, which is what the Indians practice."

"Ritualistic mutilations?" Dayton asked, surprised.

"Has something to do with their religion," Ashby said. "I don't really understand it, but they seem to think that if they hack up someone's body, that person'll get to the Happy Hunting Grounds in a carved-up state. Since they believe that everyone will live again after death, better to have to face an enemy who's got no arms or no eyes, or no balls—literally—than one who's got all his limbs, senses, and abilities."

"Sounds mighty damn stupid to me," Dayton commented. "But who's to say? I figure half of my beliefs'd be thought strange by others." He drained his coffee cup and leaned back, puffing quietly on his cigar for a little while. Then he leaned forward. "Whether it's whites or other Indians, why don't you go to the army? They do have troops out there for your protection, don't they?"

"Yeah, they do. Not a hell of a lot, but there're

some. They're supposed to be keeping the Shoshoni safe from the Arapaho and the Crow.''

''Then why aren't they helping find out who's committing all the murders?''

''For one, there's only fifty or sixty of them. For another, I'm not sure those idiots can find their socks if they're wearing them. But mostly, I haven't brought the army into it because Washakie's asked me not to.''

''Why the hell not?'' Dayton didn't like where this might be heading.

''He's sure that bringing in the army would only lead to more Shoshonis getting killed. I tend to agree with him.''

Dayton nodded. ''Yeah, the army does have a way of screwing things up, don't they?'' Dayton drummed his fingers on the desk. ''I don't want to,'' he finally said, ''but I guess I have to ask. What's this got to do with me?''

''I want your help.''

''I figured that. How?''

''Send me a group of deputy marshals to help find who's been doing these murders and put an end to them.''

''A group?'' Dayton said with a small laugh of derision. ''How the hell many deputies do you think I have?''

''I have no idea,'' Ashby said evenly. ''But I do know you can hire as many as you want.''

''As many as the budget'll stand is closer to the truth. And I don't have the biggest budget in the world.''

''A small group then,'' Ashby suggested hopefully. ''Half a dozen maybe?''

Dayton, who, like all U.S. marshals, was appointed by the president, didn't really want to get involved, since this was almost certain to bring controversy. He didn't know how to explain that to an old friend, though. Finally, he said, "It's really out of my jurisdiction, you know, Orv, but for an old friend, I can spare one man. That's the best I can do, Orv. Take it or leave it."

"Reckon I don't have much choice," Ashby said. "Except to bring the army in on it, and I'm not going to do that unless it's the last resort." He paused. "But I want—and Washakie, who's always been a friend to the whites wants—someone who doesn't hate Indians just for being Indians. We need someone who's strong, fearless, and used to hardships. That reservation isn't a garden spot, if you'll recall me telling you."

"I got just the man in mind," Dayton said. "He's the best I got. I'll send him out there soon's he gets free. That might be a little while, since he's after some real bastards."

"Just make it as soon as you can, Floyd. I'd like to prevent any more killings."

Chapter 6

Buck Morgan waited as long for service as he thought reasonable—perhaps three minutes. Then he said in a medium-loud voice, "If I got to get my own supper, I'm gonna leave one hell of a mess in the kitchen."

A fearful-looking woman hurried over to the table. "What can I get for you, Marshal?" she asked.

"Beefsteak, beans, biscuits, coffee," Morgan said flatly. "And don't take all night about it."

A tall, reedy older man edged into the restaurant. A cheap tin badge hung loosely from his worn vest. The pistol he carried was in a holster that flapped almost squarely over his crotch. He looked ridiculous—except for the light of determination in his faded old eyes. He shuffled to Morgan's table and sat. "I'm Fish Walters," he announced. "Marshal of South Pass City, such as it is these poor days."

"So?" Morgan was in little mood for conversation.

48

"It's my duty to ask what's with them bodies you brought in."

"They need buryin'."

"Who's gonna pay for it?"

"Sell their horses and use the money. If that ain't enough, send a bill to U.S. Marshal Floyd Dayton in Cheyenne. He'll see you get paid, I suppose."

"That ain't much comfort for those who have to do the work," Walters said calmly.

"No skin off my ass. You don't want to bury them, dump them out in the scrub somewhere. They don't deserve no better anyway. Hell, I wasn't even going to bring those shit balls in." He paused. "You know where the other two are?"

"What other two?" Walters countered.

Morgan fixed Walters with a cold, hard stare. "You might be an old coot, but you ain't that goddamn stupid."

"Don't get smart with me, sonny," Walters snapped. "I've seen a hundred smart-ass little punks like you in my many days. I'm too goddamn old to be afraid of some young snot like you."

"Maybe you are that goddamn stupid after all," Morgan mused.

"You should have more respect for your elders, sonny boy." He leaned over a little and spit into a spittoon on the floor by the table.

"Just because you're old?" Morgan asked mockingly. "You're gonna have a long goddamn wait. Now was you to give me some reason to respect you, you'd get it. But I just don't hand out my respect for the hell of it, old man."

"I really hate struttin' little bastards like you," Walters said angrily.

Morgan shrugged. "And I hate parsimonious old shits like you. Now you either shit or get off the pot, Gramps." He leaned back as the woman began setting his supper in front of him. "You want my respect, earn it. Tell me where the rest of the Spangler-Cochrane gang is."

Walters sat for some moments—long enough for Morgan to cut into his steak and began gnawing on a hunk. Finally, he said, "I ain't seen 'em since day before yesterday. They were here for a day or two, raisin' hell, as always."

"And you didn't do anything?" Morgan asked evenly.

"I might be too damn old to worry about dyin', but that don't mean I aim to commit suicide. There ain't a person in South Pass City these days that'd stand up with me against the Spanglers, the Cochranes, or any other goddamn band of cutthroats like 'em."

Morgan nodded. "I can understand that. This ain't the only town full of yellow-bellied shit balls." He swallowed. "You know where the last two got off to? They were headed in this direction when last I heard them."

Walters shook his head. "Nope. Bastards like them could be anywhere. You mind if I have a biscuit?"

"Help yourself. Coffee, too, if you like."

"I would." He turned. "Mabel, bring me a cup over here, will ya?" he shouted. A moment later the woman brought the cup, and Walters filled it. "Who were the two who got away?" he asked after a sip.

"Kevin and Jess Spangler."

"You killed the other five by yourself?"

Morgan nodded.

Walters whistled, impressed. "You must be pretty damn good, boy," he said.

"The best in the territory," Morgan said. There was no hint of boasting; he was simply stating a fact.

Walters looked askance at Morgan, who was paying Walters no mind. Walters shook his head, believing. "Anything else I can help you with, Marshal?" he asked.

"Just see if I can get a room upstairs. And see if you can have my horse tended to." He reached into a vest pocket, pulled out a ten-dollar piece, and flicked it across the table. "That ought to be more than enough for the room and the horse. The meal, too."

Walters nodded and drained his coffee cup. He stood, half-eaten biscuit in hand. "You pullin' out come mornin'?" he asked.

Morgan nodded. "Oh, one more thing, Marshal," he added. "You can ask around, see if anyone else in town has seen the Spanglers today."

"I'll do so." Walters shuffled off.

After eating Morgan went outside and got his saddlebags and rifle. Then he went into the hotel. The same woman who had waited on him in the restaurant was in the small hotel lobby.

"Sign here," she ordered, pointing with a dirty finger to a line in the ledger book. When Morgan had complied Mabel handed him a key. "Top of the stairs, back corner. We start servin' breakfast about dawn."

"And a pleasant day to you, too, ma'am," Morgan said sarcastically. He went upstairs. An hour later, Walters knocked on the door and entered when Morgan gave him leave to do so. "You learn anything?" Morgan asked.

Walters shook his head. "Nobody's seen nothin'; nobody's heard nothin'; nobody knows nothin'."

"About what I figured. Well, Marshal, I'm obliged for your efforts anyway. Now, if you don't mind, I've had a long day and I could really use some shut-eye."

Not knowing which way to go, Morgan headed for South Pass itself the next morning. In Atlantic City he stopped and asked the sheriff there if anyone had seen the Spanglers. Getting a negative response, he moved on, turning west to take the smooth, easy way across the Continental Divide.

Once through the pass, he turned his horse southwest, roughly following the course of Pacific Creek. Two days later he found himself in Farson. He got a hotel room, brought his horse to the livery, and then had a meal. After all that he began hitting saloons. There was a more than adequate number of such establishments, and Morgan had to watch his intake of liquor. He stuck to beer, and only sipped that as he tried to find out if anyone in this town had seen or heard of the Spanglers lately.

No one said he had, and Morgan was beginning to tire of the questions and the lack of positive responses. It irritated him, and that made him cantankerous. Though no one in Farson knew him, just about all could see by the look in Morgan's eye that he was not a man to be messed with.

He considered visiting one of the brothels but put it off. The best place to find out information about men like the Spanglers was in saloons. The second-best place was in a brothel. He vowed to try that avenue as soon as he made it through all the saloons in town.

52

There were only two more saloons left when he thought he had gotten a break. Two short, wiry men sitting at a back table in the Ox Blood saloon nodded when he asked his question. Interested, Morgan sat. "When did you last see them?" he asked, interest piqued, some of the tiredness dropping off him.

"Well now, who wants to know?" one asked.

"I'm Deputy U.S. Marshal Buck Morgan. Now answer the question."

"Well, now, Marshal," one said, holding up his three-quarters empty mug of beer, "I'm mighty dry here, and talkin'll need me to have a wet whistle."

Morgan felt like he would explode, but he calmed himself down. "Fair enough," he said evenly. He called over the bartender and ordered a new beer and a shot of whiskey for each of the two men. While they waited for it, Morgan asked, "What's your names, boys?"

"I'm Mark Willsey," the one who had spoken before said. "My pal here is Cliff Sloan."

The drinks arrived. "Now," Morgan said patiently, "let's hear what you boys got to say."

"Me'n Cliff're some hungry, Marshal," Willsey said with a small, insincere smile.

Morgan snapped halfway up and reached out, then grabbed Willsey by the shirtfront and jerked him most of the way across the table. "Answer my question, shit ball, or I'll shove that glass of beer so far up your ass you'll have to keep your hat on so it don't spill."

Willsey's mouth flapped and his eyes blinked rapidly.

Then someone hit Morgan with a bottle. Morgan had sensed someone coming up behind him, and just before he got hit he shoved Willsey away from him and

53

darted his head to the side. The bottle hit on his shoulder. It hurt, but it would not incapacitate him. He snapped his elbow back and hit someone in the stomach.

Not knowing what he faced behind him, Morgan dropped to the floor, turning as he did. Then he surged upward, his back knocking the table up and over. It landed on Willsey and Sloan. By the time he was standing, Morgan had one of his Smith and Wessons out. He fired once at a large, fat man who had a bottle in one hand and a pistol in the other. The fat man went down, dead.

Morgan swiftly glanced around the room. No one else seemed ready to make a move, so he spun back to face Willsey and Sloan. The latter had unlimbered his pistol, so Morgan drilled him a shot in the chest.

Willsey also had been drawing his pistol; he had it almost all the way out when Morgan killed Sloan. Willsey threw the revolver away. "Don't shoot, Marshal!" he screeched, fear stamped all over his face. "Don't shoot. I ain't got a gun no more."

Morgan grabbed Willsey's bandanna and jerked him forward. He spun, facing the room again. "You're under arrest," he announced. "Now move, unless you want to join your friend there."

As Morgan left the town marshal's office, he knew damn well that the marshal wouldn't hold Willsey any longer than Morgan was in town. Morgan didn't much care right at the moment. In a foul mood, he headed for the nearest bordello, where much of his anger dissipated in a spirited session with a tall, chubby young woman.

The next day he rode northwest. Several days later he reached Sublette's Spring. He spent the night there

54

before moving west across the trackless wastes until he came to the Green River. He saw no one until he reached a small town on the river. No one there had even so much as heard of the Spanglers. For once he was certain they were telling the truth.

He followed the river southwest, stopping at every town, farm, or ranch he spotted. Still no one had seen the Spanglers. He finally moved into the barren, arid, treacherous Bad Lands Hills. It was the kind of place men like Kevin and Jess Spangler would go to throw off a posse. But he found no trace of anyone there.

Morgan went back to the Green River and once again followed it southwest until he reached Rock Springs, where he once more got a hotel room.

He sat in a saloon that night, pondering what he should do. Since killing the three Cochranes and two of the Spanglers at the cabin near South Pass City, he had spent a little more than a month trying to find the last two Spanglers. And all he had gotten so far was a sore ass and a craw full of annoyance.

Morgan hated the idea of giving up; always did. It was especially true in this case after what this band of outlaws had done. But he knew there was no shortage of outlaws in the territory that needed to be brought to justice. And since he had heard nothing of the Spanglers at all, he thought—or maybe just hoped—that they had headed to another territory to ply their trade there. If that were true, there was always a chance that they would feel safe again one day and head back into Wyoming Territory. If they did, Buck Morgan would be waiting for them.

The next morning he boarded the train and headed east for Cheyenne.

Chapter 7

Orville Ashby looked up from his desk at the man who had entered the office and almost swallowed his tongue. He wished desperately now that he had had the sense to accept Lt. Dexter Pomeroy's offer of stationing a trooper at the door to his office. "Can I do something for you, mister?" he asked, his voice cracking.

"I'm lookin' for a Mr. Orville Ashby. That you?" The voice was deep, authoritative, rough.

"I . . . I . . ." Ashby suddenly breathed a sigh of relief when the light coming in one of the windows glinted off the star on the man's chest. "Yes. Yes, I am."

Morgan stuck out a big paw for Ashby to shake. "I'm Deputy U.S. Marshal Buck Morgan. Marshal Floyd Dayton sent me out here to help you some."

Ashby stood and shook Morgan's hand, pleased that

Morgan did not mention his sweating palm. "I've been expecting you," he said lamely. "Have a seat."

"Didn't much look like you were expectin' me," Morgan said flatly as he sat.

Ashby laughed self-consciously. "I must admit," he offered, "that you weren't quite what I expected."

"Why?"

"Well," Ashby said, licking his lips. He began to worry again. This tall, hard-eyed man had a decidedly deadly look about him. "Well, I don't know. The guns, I guess, maybe. That big knife in your boot there. The look in your . . ."

"Hell, you didn't want no pantywaist son of a bitch comin' out here, did you?" Morgan asked. His voice was not angry. "If you did, you sure didn't mention it to Floyd, or he'd never have sent a crusty bastard like me."

Ashby began to relax a little. Morgan might be deadly, but there was nothing threatening about him. At least not now. Ashby acknowledged in his mind, though, that he would not want Morgan's cool gray eyes peering too hard at him. Morgan was a man who certainly looked like he knew how to use the two ivory-handled .44-caliber Smith and Wesson revolvers he was wearing.

"No, no, I certainly didn't expect that. Indeed, now that you're here, and I know who you are, I'm decidedly relieved. I must admit, though, that you certainly gave me a fright."

"Ain't the first time I've heard that," Morgan said with a small smile. "It's my curse." He smiled again. "Or maybe my blessing. I've learned over the years that a hard look and a hard reputation can save a man like me considerable trouble."

57

"I've heard Chief Washakie say much the same thing on occasion. I'm afraid I'm just not a man who has either of those attributes. I often wish I did."

"We can't help what we are, Mr. Ashby," Morgan said quietly. "From what I figure, if you've kept the Shoshonis from goin' on the warpath over these recent troubles, you're a hell of a lot better at your job than many a man is at his own. Hell, if every man did his job as well, this world'd be a hell of a lot better place, to my way of thinkin'."

"Oh, well, I suppose so." Ashby did not sound as if he believed any of it.

"You're a married man, I take it, Mr. Ashby?" Morgan asked quietly.

"Why, yes," Ashby answered, surprised. "Yes, I am. Is it that obvious?"

Morgan shrugged. "You have kids, too?"

"Three of them. Two girls and a boy. The oldest—Bonnie—is twelve."

"And they're out here with you?"

"Yes."

"Why?"

"What do you mean 'Why,' Marshal?"

"Wouldn't it have been a hell of a lot safer—and more comfortable—to have left them in Ohio or Kentucky or wherever the hell it is back east you come here from?"

"Of course," Ashby responded, surprised again.

"Yet you brought them out here. To this desolate place. To a place where they have no others to socialize with. To a place crawling with Indians, not to mention soldiers. There's heat, bitter cold, snow to a horse's eye, dust storms, snakes, grizzlies, all kinds of dangers."

"So?" Ashby said rather defensively.

"So, you've kept them all happy, I suppose. Or at least relatively so. I can see it in your eye when you talk about them. Your wife hasn't fled back east. Nor have you given up a very difficult and trying job so that you could take them back east yourself and live in relative comfort."

"Is there a point to all of this, Marshal Morgan?" Ashby asked nervously.

"The point is, Mr. Ashby, that we all have our own talents and such. No, you're not as hard a man as me. I doubt you've ever killed a man . . ."

"No, I haven't," Ashby said flatly. He wasn't sure if he should be proud of the fact or disgusted with himself because of it.

"Yet you're every bit as tough as I am. Maybe even tougher. You have to be to do what you do. It's just a different kind of toughness is all."

"Are you married, Marshal Morgan?" Ashby asked, feeling a flush of pride in what Morgan had said. He wasn't sure that he believed it, but it felt good to hear, especially from a man like Buck Morgan.

"No," Morgan said flatly. "I was once, but it didn't take. Mostly my fault, I suppose."

Ashby suddenly wanted to know more about what had happened to drive Morgan and his wife apart, but he had enough sense to see that asking about it would only anger Morgan. The marshal seemed to have drifted off a little. He sighed. Perhaps one day he would be able to get Morgan to open up.

"Would you like a cigar, Marshal?"

Morgan nodded, trying to shake off the melancholy that had come over him.

Ashby came around the desk and handed Morgan a

fat cigar. Morgan bit off the end of it and spit it into a convenient cuspidor. He nodded his thanks as Ashby held a match out for him. Ashby went back behind his own desk and lit a cigar for himself. Blowing out a stream of smoke, he asked, "Do you know why you're here, Marshal?"

"The only thing Floyd told me was that some Shoshonis out here have gotten killed and that I was to get out here and track down the killer or killers."

Ashby explained what had happened. It didn't take long. Morgan said nothing during the agent's discourse.

"We had two more between the time I left here to talk to Marshal Dayton—an old friend of mine, by the way—and your arrival."

"And is this Chief Washakie you mentioned keeping all his warriors in check?"

Ashby nodded. "He's a tough old bastard, and there're few warriors who'll go against his word, whatever it is. Still, a few more of these murders and there's going to be hell to pay one way or another."

"I would expect," Morgan said dryly. "Well," he added after a pause, "is it too late to go talk to this Washakie?"

Ashby checked his pocket watch. "No, there's time." He stood. "I'll need a few minutes to get a horse saddled. Is your mount all right?"

"Yeah. I took it easy on him on the way out here."

"I'll be back shortly," Ashby said. "There's a bottle of rye in the bottom left-hand drawer of the desk. Though the Shoshonis are dependable, honest Indians, it doesn't pay to tempt them too much, and a bottle of whiskey sitting out in the open would sorely tempt even the strongest of them, I'm afraid."

Morgan nodded. When Ashby left Morgan got the bottle. Ignoring the glass in the drawer, he pulled the cork on the bottle and took a long, healthy swallow. He recorked the bottle and replaced it.

"It's a godforsaken place, ain't it?" Morgan said when he and Ashby were riding slowly toward Washakie's.

"It has a certain beauty—if one is willing to look for it," Ashby responded.

"I suppose. But it sure looks like the government gave the Shoshonis a shit piece of real estate for a reservation."

Ashby glanced sharply at Morgan and realized that the marshal was serious. "Have you ever heard of the government handing out a good piece of real estate to any Indians?"

"Nope. Had I been Washakie, though, I might've held out for that out there." He pointed to the snow-capped Wind River Mountains some miles away.

"I'm sure Washakie did."

"I reckon so. I can understand, too, how some Indians ain't willing to give up quietly. I'd probably be one of those renegade sons of bitches who fight until death rather than submit."

"I probably would've done exactly what Chief Washakie has done," Ashby said quietly.

Morgan laughed softly. "There's our differences again. Both strong-willed and thinkin' we're right, but going about it in completely different ways. Trouble is, it wouldn't mean a damn thing. The ones who fight're going to be dead long before the others, but those others're going to have a slow, suffocating death. Damn, it's a poor thing when a man—when a whole

61

people—have got to decide whether they want to be wiped out slow or fast.''

Ashby knew that Morgan had spoken the truth. He also knew that there was nothing more to say, so he said nothing. They rode on in silence.

An hour later they rode into Washakie's small village. Morgan took a good look around as he rode in and was surprised. There didn't seem to be a lot of destitution evident. The tepees were in good condition; the people seemed well-fed and reasonably happy. Morgan could see plenty of horses grazing to the northwest. Dogs barked, children laughed and cried and played. Unperturbed talk and bursts of laughter rang out. Morgan wondered how anyone could be happy in such a barren setting. Then again, he wondered how anyone could be happy in a teeming, foul place like New York, which he had visited once.

They stopped in front of a large painted tepee and dismounted. Two boys, each about eleven years old, ran up and took the reins to the horses. Ashby smiled. ''Hello, Yellow Wing. And to you, Rabbit Tail.''

Morgan had been a little reluctant for either of the boys to take his horse, but then he realized it would be all right. As he turned, Ashby was already calling for entrance into the tepee.

Morgan wasn't sure what to expect inside. He had never been inside an Indian lodge before. It smelled funny—not bad funny, just odd to him—and there were all kinds of things he had no clue as to what they were. At Ashby's direction he sat and leaned against some kind of backrest. Ashby did the same. Morgan kept his mouth shut, waiting to find out what would happen. He didn't figure it was his place to break the silence.

An old woman brought Morgan and Ashby bowls. Morgan lifted the horn spoon and brought it toward his mouth. He had no idea what was in the watery stew, but he'd be damned if he'd show any weakness, even if the dish was foul. To his surprise he found it wasn't bad. After a few tastes he realized it was buffalo stew. He could have used more chunks of meat in it, though.

When they finished the stew a young warrior brought out a pipe, which he handed to Washakie. The old chief took it, and the young warrior lit it. Washakie puffed for a little, blowing the smoke every which way. When the pipe was passed to Morgan, he tried to emulate Washakie, though he had no idea if he even came close. Then he handed the pipe to Ashby.

After puffing on the pipe Ashby gave it to the young warrior. Then he said, "Chief Washakie, this is Deputy U.S. Marshal Buck Morgan. Marshal, Chief Washakie."

The two men nodded and sized each other up. If Ashby had not told him, Morgan would never have believed that Washakie was somewhere around seventy years old. The Shoshoni chief was tall, or so Morgan thought, and his back was straight. He had long hair, gray now, but still full. His face was lined some, but still had a strong, determined cast to it. He had a high forehead and piercing dark eyes.

For his part, Washakie was fairly impressed with the marshal. He saw a man who was tall, strong, and rugged. Washakie thought Morgan had an honest face, and would be a man of his word. Had Morgan been born a Shoshoni, Washakie thought, he would have made a good warrior. Only time would tell, though, the old chief knew, if his initial assessment was correct.

Chapter 8

"Are you related to Charley Morgan?" Washakie asked in accented English.

Morgan was surprised, both at the question and the fact that Washakie spoke English well. He nodded. "My father's name is Charley," he said quietly.

"I thought so," Washakie said. "I knew Charley Morgan some years ago. He was a good man. You favor him in looks."

"It's an honor," Morgan said sincerely. "How'd you know him, though?"

"He was a trader among us. One of the few damn honest traders I ever knew. Most traders would steal their mother's teeth for a pinch of gold." Then Washakie laughed.

"Most merchants I know of are the same way," Morgan said, joining in the laughter. He realized he had been very tense since entering the village. The laughter had served to relax him.

Washakie finally grew serious. "Do you know why you're here?" he asked, looking at Morgan.

The marshal nodded. "Mr. Ashby explained it to me before. He told me you suspect that a white man

64

or white men is behind the murders. Why would you think such a thing?''

Washakie shrugged. "Who can know the mind of such men?'' he said flatly.

Morgan let the words sit in the air for some moments as he rolled them around in his mind. Then he nodded. "I'll accept that—for now. Mr. Ashby told me all the bodies were mutilated.''

"Yes,'' Washakie said stonily.

"They all had at least one finger and both ears cut off, right?'' Morgan pressed. "Some also were disemboweled or had limbs hacked off?''

"Yes.'' Washakie's voice was colder even than before.

"And you figure that white men committed the murders and mutilated the bodies to make it look like other Indians did it? That it?'' Morgan asked.

Washakie nodded.

"How do you figure it was whites that did it?'' Morgan asked. "Don't your people and most other Indians do such things as a matter of course?''

"I've explained all of this to you, Marshal. I . . .'' Ashby started. He stopped in a real hurry when Morgan turned a hard, unforgiving glance at him.

"I know what the hell you told me,'' Morgan said harshly. "But I want to hear it from Chief Washakie. I need all the information I can get if I'm going to catch the bastards who're doing this.''

Ashby's face flamed red, but he said nothing.

Morgan looked back at Washakie. "Well, Chief?''

"Our enemies have no reason to cut off fingers and ears. Once in a while, maybe, just for the hell of it. But on five Shoshoni? No goddamn reason.''

"I thought you did such things so that your enemies wouldn't be whole in the next world."

"This is true somewhat," Washakie said after some thought. "But the ears signify nothing. A man can still hear all right in the afterworld if he has no damn ears. A man can still fight even if he's missin' a few damn fingers."

Morgan nodded. "Let me ask you this, Chief—you got any enemies? Personal enemies, I mean. Folks that'd just as soon see you kicked out as chief."

Ashby gasped. "What kind of question is . . ."

"If you're going to be such a pain in my ass, Mr. Ashby," Morgan said icily, "then I'll just head on back to Cheyenne. I've got other work that needs doin'. So you either shut the hell up or you go outside and pace while me and Chief Washakie try to figure out what the hell's going on here."

"But . . ."

"Mr. Ashby," Washakie said quietly, "Marshal Morgan's right. If he's to find out who's killing my people, he's gonna have to ask some questions I might not like. If so, tough shit. If I didn't care who was killin' my people, I'd refuse to answer."

"Sorry," Ashby mumbled in embarrassment.

"So, Chief, you have any enemies?"

"Very few." A small smile slid across Washakie's face. "I've either killed them or outlived them, for the most part. Why?"

Morgan shrugged. "There's always the possibility that it's one of your own people."

"That's preposterous!" Ashby said.

"Is it?" Morgan countered. "Say he's got some warrior who wants to be chief somethin' awful. He kills a few of Washakie's supporters and makes it look like

66

Arapaho did it. Even if Washakie comes up with the idea—as he has—that white men are responsible for the murders, it puts Washakie in a terribly vulnerable position.''

"How?'' Ashby asked, interest rising.

"Well, if Washakie figures the Arapaho did it, he's got two choices—do nothing or go to war. If he does nothing, sooner or later this enemy will quietly foment an insurrection among the Shoshoni people and Washakie'll get ousted. If he declares war on the Arapaho, Washakie'd be almost duty-bound to lead the war party, bringing about a good chance that he'll get killed. Hell, a cunning enemy might even kill Washakie himself out there. Then he could still become the chief while praising Washakie's name to the high heavens.''

Washakie grinned.

"But what if Washakie blamed it on the white man, as he's done?'' Ashby asked.

"Well, that probably would mean that the army'd come in.'' Morgan grinned roguishly. "If someone had plotted this thing in such a way, he never would've thought that Washakie'd not go to the army to clear it up. And once the army started rooting around, there'd be all kinds of trouble. Again, the conspirator could quietly turn the people against Chief Washakie.''

"There's always people like that,'' Washakie agreed. "But I don't think that's the case here.''

"No?''

The long gray hair swung back and forth as Washakie shook his head. "If such a man existed, I would have known about it long ago.''

Morgan raised his eyebrows, then realized that Washakie was not being arrogant.

67

"I've not led my people for so many winters by bein' a damn fool, Marshal. As I have enemies, I also have friends. Many, many more friends than enemies. There is at least one who would have heard of such a plot and told me, don't you think?"

"If you know the ones who are such close friends, then your enemy would know that, too, no?" Morgan countered. "And he would avoid letting his plan reach their ears."

"When a man has many friends—including some who aren't his closest friends—it's pretty damn hard to keep such a complicated scheme quiet, ain't it?"

"That makes sense," Morgan said with a nod.

"See?" Ashby interjected. "Now don't you feel like a fool for asking such a stupid thing of someone like Chief Washakie?"

"No," Morgan said evenly.

"I would've asked the same thing," Washakie said. "Marshal Morgan might have been wrong in that thought, but it shows he's thinkin', and it shows his mind is open to the many possibilities."

"Well, I'll still keep the thought in mind, Chief," Morgan said, "though I figure you're right. That leaves us with the only other possibility—that white men did it. I'm going to ask you again, Chief, why?"

"There could be many reasons," Washakie said quietly. He stretched out his long legs and plucked idly at a piece of fringe on one of his leggings. "And many of them might not make any sense. But it wouldn't be unknown for the white man to try to cause trouble between different Indian peoples. They might have some grand motive behind it. Or maybe none at all."

"Let's hope it's not the last," Morgan said. "If it is, we might not ever be able to catch the bastards—

68

unless we catch them in the act. Let's say there is some grand plan behind it all. Any thoughts on what that might be?"

Washakie shrugged. "It could be something as simple as wanting to see two tribes killing each other off."

"That's a goddamn scary thought," Ashby said.

Washakie nodded. "That would afford many white men a good deal of amusement," he said. "But more importantly—to them—it could hasten the end of the Shoshoni people. And other people, too, like our hated enemies."

"It's like what they're doin' with the buffalo," Morgan said. "Many of the white men in power out east are of a mind that if you kill off the Indians' commissary—the buffalo—you can bring the Indians to heel."

"Yes," Washakie said sadly. "When the buffalo are gone we'll have to become farmers. I've tried to ease my people down the white man's road, but there's too much resistance. Still, I can see the slaughter of the buffalo. Soon there'll be no more. Then the Shoshoni will have to become farmers—or die."

"And anything the whites can do to hasten that day'll be looked on favorably in some circles," Morgan said. He nodded. It was a frightening thought, and one that was entirely too possible. "Yes, if a few whites could stir up trouble here, and the Shoshonis go after the Arapaho, there are those who could point and say that the Shoshoni—and the Arapaho—are still savages; that efforts by honest men like Mr. Ashby here are for naught and the Indians can't learn the white man's way. Therefore they don't deserve any land, even land as poor as this."

"Bastards," Ashby muttered, already convinced that such was what was occurring.

"No," Washakie said. "Not bastards. Just men."

Silence was allowed to grow then, to expand until it filled the smoky, crowded tepee. A young woman entered, saw the men sitting silently, and quietly made her way to the back of the lodge, where she sat next to the old woman. Her entrance caught Morgan's attention, and he could not help but keep an eye on her.

The woman was young, maybe twenty, Morgan thought, and quite attractive. She had a tall willowiness about her, which surprised Morgan a little. He had always thought Indians were dumpy and dirty and squat-looking. But Washakie—and now this young woman—had begun to change his opinion.

Morgan thought he would like to meet the woman, but then realized that such a hope was futile—and foolish. Judging by the way she had entered the lodge, she seemed to belong here, and Morgan figured that she was a young wife of Washakie's. It would make sense, Morgan thought. With Washakie's other wife so old, having a strong young woman around the lodge would be a big help to not only Washakie but his old wife as well. With an inward sigh, Morgan tried to push the young woman out of his mind—even if he would not let his sight drift off her too much.

"So, Marshal Morgan," Washakie finally said, "do you have any thoughts on how you'll catch these white devils?" He smiled a little to let Morgan know that he did not think of all white men as devils.

"Not yet. I'll need to do some cogitatin' on it. And I'd like to get out and see where the last body was found. Is that possible, Chief?"

Washakie nodded.

"We'll do that tomorrow," Ashby said. "First thing."

"There any help I can give you?" Washakie asked.

"Well, it'd probably help a whole hell of a lot if I was to have someone around who knows the country real well."

"One of the People, you mean?" Washakie asked.

Morgan nodded.

"That can be done."

"Are your people going to be willing to work with me?" Morgan asked. "After all, if you think whites're responsible for the murders, they probably think the same. And it's obvious for all to see that I'm white."

Washakie nodded. "Some—maybe even most—might be reluctant. But I figure we can find a few who'll be willin' to help. I, of course, will lend my authority to the project, which should help a little." He smiled at the last.

Morgan nodded, accepting it.

Chapter 9

"Why don't you join my family and me for supper, Marshal?" Ashby asked as the two men rode back toward the agency.

"I wouldn't want to impose, Mr. Ashby," Morgan responded quietly.

"It wouldn't be an imposition," Ashby said. Then he laughed. "Besides, your options're rather limited."

"How so?"

"Well, you could cook for yourself somewhere. Or you could eat in the soldiers' mess over at Camp Brown itself. I wouldn't recommend that," Ashby added with a laugh. "Or you could ride to Flat Fork, which I don't think'd be wise either, if you have any taste for food at all. Or see if Washakie can find someone to cook for you."

"I see," Morgan said with a chuckle. "Well, since I can't cook a lick myself, I have little liking for soldiers, I don't know where this Flat Fork is, and I don't know Washakie even as much as I do you, I reckon that supper at your house wouldn't be that unwelcome a thing. If your wife doesn't mind another mouth—and a big one at that—at the table."

72

"She won't mind," Ashby said. "If for no other reason than yours is a new face around here. She is, I'm afraid, starved for company."

"I'd expect such a thing in a place like this. After all, she wouldn't be expected to consort with the Shoshoni. Are there no other white women at Camp Brown?"

"Three: The wife of Lieutenant Pomeroy, the commander, plus the wives of two enlisted men. They're laundresses, and low sort of women."

Morgan nodded. "Speaking of the camp," he said, "is there any more to it than the little I saw on the ride in?"

"Nope. Just that small collection of pitiful stone and adobe buildings you saw. Hell, there's only about fifty men stationed there."

"And that's supposed to protect the Shoshoni?" Morgan asked skeptically.

"As far as the government's concerned, yes. They seem to be of the opinion out there that all the Indians are afraid of the blue coats, so just a show of a few men is enough to keep them in line. Pure buffalo shit, if you ask me, but no one ever does."

"The government acts the same no matter who it's dealin' with," Morgan agreed. "Bunch of shit balls back east there."

Ashby nodded, pleased to have someone of a like mind around for a change.

At Ashby's small stone house, Ashby and Morgan unsaddled their horses. "You have any grain layin' about, Mr. Ashby?" Morgan asked.

"No, but they have plenty over at the camp. I'll send someone to get some here in just a bit." He gave

73

a cursory grooming to his horse and then went inside the house.

Morgan finished tending to his horse and then hobbled the animal out back of Ashby's house. He went to the trough and, after taking off his hat and throwing it aside, dunked his head in the water. It was warm water and a little stagnant, but it felt good nonetheless.

About that time, Ashby wandered around the corner of the house. "Supper's about ready," he said as he leaned against the house's stone edge.

Morgan nodded. "You have any soap? After so long on the trail I figure I'm a mite dirty."

"Sure." He returned a minute later with a cake of strong soap and a towel.

Morgan stripped off his shirt and scooped up a pail of water, since he did not want to foul the trough. He wet his chest and arms, then scrubbed them and his face with the soap. Then came a rinse off before he finally began toweling himself dry.

As Morgan was doing so, an eight-year-old boy popped around the corner to stand next to Ashby. "Dusty," Ashby said to the boy, "this here's Deputy U.S. Marshal Buck Morgan. Marshal, my son, Dusty."

Morgan shook the boy's hand. "Pleased to meet you, son," he said.

The boy pointed to Morgan's bare chest. "Those bullet holes?" he asked with a child's innocence and honesty.

"Dusty!" Ashby said. "I'm sorry, Marshal, I . . ."

"No problem, Mr. Ashby." Morgan looked at the boy. "Yes, they are bullet holes, son," he said quietly. "And this one," he traced a long ragged scar from the side of his left breast around to just about the navel, "is from a knife."

"They hurt when you got shot? And stabbed?" Dusty asked.

"They sure as hell did."

"Did you arrest the men who did it?" Dusty asked guilelessly.

"No," Morgan answered flatly.

"Then what . . . ?"

"That's enough questions for now, Dusty," Ashby said. "The marshal's had a long journey to get here and he's hungry. We keep your ma waiting much longer and she'll be after us with a skillet or something." He grinned, not meaning it.

Morgan put on his shirt, tucked it in, then added his vest. "Ready, when you are, Mr. Ashby," he said.

"Call me Orv, Marshal. Everyone else does."

Morgan nodded. "If you call me Buck."

"Deal."

Inside the house Ashby introduced Morgan to his wife, Grace; his oldest child, Bonnie, and his youngest, Pearl, a golden-haired five-year-old.

Grace Ashby was a plainly attractive woman who was beginning to look worn. Morgan supposed she was close to forty, though she did not look quite that old. Her hair was still a rich, warm brown, though her face had crow's-feet at eyes and mouth.

"Sit, Marshal," Grace said, indicating a chair with a wave of her hand.

Morgan took a seat, a little uncomfortable in the presence of the children, the younger two of whom were staring unabashedly at him. Still, the meal looked mighty good to him. There was a platter of roasted chicken, a heaping bowl of potatoes, smaller bowls of

75

carrots and peas, a platter of fresh biscuits, a pitcher of milk, and a large pot of coffee.

"Dig in, Marshal," Grace said with a shy smile.

Morgan did so, restraining himself. With one bite of the chicken and biscuits, though, he laughed a little. "I ain't had a meal like this in a dog's age, ma'am," he said in his quiet rumble of a voice. "And I'm like to eat you out of your house and home, given half a chance."

Grace smiled and flushed with pleasure. "If I'd known such a hearty appetite was about to set at my supper table, I would've made a heap more," she said, her voice high-pitched but pleasant. "But you take your fill, Marshal. You've had a long journey and have much hard work awaiting you, if what Orv says about this awful situation is true."

"It is that, ma'am, an awful situation indeed," Morgan responded.

"Do you think you can get to the bottom of all this, Marshal?"

"Don't know, ma'am. It'll be difficult, I expect, but I hope I can learn something and put an end to these troubles."

"You ought to see his bullet holes, Ma," Dusty piped up.

Grace looked horrified, Bonnie disgusted, Ashby angry, and Pearl bewildered.

Only Morgan had retained his equanimity. "I expect your ma's not interested in my bullet holes, son," he said easily. "Nor your sisters. Women don't generally take an interest in such things. It's just the way they are, son, and we menfolk should be appreciative that they are the way they are."

Dusty wasn't sure he fully understood, but he nodded anyway. If the big hard-looking marshal said it, well, then it must be so.

"Where're you planning to stay, Marshal?" Grace asked after some silence while they all concentrated on their food.

"Hadn't really thought about it," Morgan said as he reached for another chicken leg. "Any ideas, Orv?"

"Well, I think you're stuck for that as well as for eating. You have the same basic choices—Flat Fork, Camp Brown, with Washakie, on your own. Or here."

"I couldn't stay here," Morgan said. "That'd be too big an imposition on you all. It's bad enough you've stuck your wife with having to feed a hungry old bear like me. But to sleep here? No, sir, that won't do at all."

"That wouldn't put us out, Marshal," Grace said. "You could share Dusty's room. Or, if that was inconvenient for you, we could move Dusty in with us for a time and you could have his room."

"No, ma'am, but I'm obliged for the offer. Reckon I'll just try to find myself a place to set up a camp."

"Tell you what, Buck," Ashby said. "You saw that old stone shed out back?"

Morgan nodded.

"You could stay there. I'll have a couple of soldiers come over and clean it out and put in a bunk. We've got a few other pieces of furniture stored in there that you could use."

"You sure I wouldn't be in the way?" Morgan asked.

"Not at all."

"You, ma'am?"

"We'd be delighted to have you stay there."

"Then that's where I'll hang my hat."

77

After supper Ashby said, "Dusty, run on over to Lieutenant Pomeroy's and tell him I need a couple of men to clean out the shed. Tell him to have them bring a bunk—with a ticking mattress—with them. And some grain for the marshal's horse," he added.

"Yessir." Smiling, Dusty hurried out the door. He always liked it when his father entrusted him with an important task.

The Ashby house had five rooms, a rarity in a desolate place like the Wind River Reservation. Three were bedrooms—one for Ashby and Grace, one for the two girls, and the third for Dusty. The other two rooms were the kitchen and a sitting room.

After sending Dusty on the errand Ashby led Morgan into the sitting room. He produced a cigar for himself and one for Morgan.

Grace came into the room. "More coffee, Marshal?" she asked. "Or would you prefer something stronger?"

"Coffee'll be fine, ma'am."

"Orv?"

"Coffee'll do for me, too."

They were sipping their coffee, silently puffing on the cigars, when two soldiers were escorted in. "You've got a chore for us, Mr. Ashby?" one asked. He did not look at all happy about being there, but he was a little afraid of angering the Indian agent. If he did, he knew that Ashby would report the disrespect to Lieutenant Pomeroy, and then he'd be pulling extra duty.

"Yes, Private," Ashby said as he rose. He looked at Morgan. "I'll be back in a few moments, Marshal." Then he left with the two soldiers.

Ashby returned before long. Morgan looked at him

as he sat. "All the blue coats that eager to do your bidding?" he asked with a grin.

"Some even more so," Ashby answered. He laughed.

It was well past dark when the soldiers returned. They were covered with dirt, sweat, and dust, and were puffing. "All done, Mr. Ashby," one said. He looked at Morgan. "I put a bucket of grain out back for your horse, Marshal."

"Thank you, boys," Ashby said, dismissing them.

Morgan stood. "One minute there, boys," he said quietly. When the two troopers turned to face into the room again Morgan pulled two five-dollar coins from a vest pocket and held them out. "For your efforts," he said.

The two soldiers' eyes widened as they took the proffered cash. "Thank you, sir!" both stammered as they headed out of the room.

"That was uncalled for, Marshal," Ashby said coldly when the soldiers had left. "It sets a bad precedent."

"How much do those boys make from the army? Ten, twelve dollars a month? Hell, that ain't even enough to get drunk on once. A man works hard, he deserves to get paid some. You ain't in the army, so you shouldn't be able to have them do private chores for you. But a word from you and their asses'll be in big trouble with their officers. That ain't fair."

"But that'll set . . ."

"The work they did was for me, not you," Morgan said, in tones even icier than Ashby's had been. "And I paid them out of my pocket. You still want to give me a hard time about it?"

Ashby thought about it for a moment, then grinned weakly. "No, I reckon not."

Chapter 10

Morgan watched the Shoshoni riding slowly a little ahead of him and Ashby, wondering just what the warrior thought about him. Ashby had introduced Two Wounds to Morgan that morning outside Ashby's house.

The Shoshoni was taller than Morgan had expected, though not nearly as tall as he. Two Wounds had an impassive dark face and eyes that were flat and almost black. His cheekbones protruded enough to make his cheeks look like they were being sucked inward. Two Wounds wore a fringed buckskin shirt, buckskin leggings, buckskin breechcloth, and moccasins. His hair hung in two long greasy braids wrapped in some kind of fur.

It was not a long ride to their destination, and they dismounted and tied their horses off. Not really knowing what he was looking for, Morgan knelt and looked around where the latest Shoshoni body had been found. He crab-walked around the entire site, eyes peering at the dirt and grass.

All of it seemed for naught, though, as he could discern nothing that might give him a clue. He finally rose, shaking his head in annoyance—at himself for not being able to figure out anything and at whoever had perpetrated these murders. He stood, rubbing his big, square chin, thinking. Then he swallowed some of his pride. "Can you make anything out here that might help, Two Wounds?" he asked hopefully.

The Shoshoni shrugged.

Morgan spit into the dirt. Then he glared at Two Wounds. "I'm here to help your people at Chief Washakie's request," Morgan said to the Shoshoni, stretching the truth just a bit, "whether you like it or not. Now I could go to Chief Washakie and tell him what a shit ball you're bein', but that wouldn't serve any purpose, now would it?" He paused, not sure if Two Wounds spoke any English beyond a few simple words.

Two Wounds shook his head ever so slightly.

At least the bastard understands English, Morgan thought. "On the other hand," he continued, relaxing some, "I could go tell your wife instead. I expect Shoshoni women're a lot like white women, and if that's true, I can probably talk her into bendin' your ear left and right about this. Havin' a wife naggin' your ass day in and day out might just set you on the right path."

Two Wounds's stiff face cracked a bit, and Morgan grinned slightly. Then the lawman pushed ahead, his statements growing a little broader. "Yep, I can see it now—some fat-ass old squaw doggin' your every step, squallin' about her useless shit of a husband. Hell, she'll probably be chasin' after you with an old skillet, lookin' to lay it upside your head. And you, runnin' like a buffalo calf just to get away from that old hag's constant blowin' wind, headin' . . ."

Two Wounds began laughing. "You're one funny

81

sumbitch," he said with a chuckle, using English that was heavily accented but understandable.

Morgan shrugged, but he grinned. "Now, are you going to help me?"

Two Wounds stopped laughing and looked somberly at Morgan. He was used to white men, but he had met few like Buck Morgan. The lawman was big and strong and had a dark, deadly look about him. He figured that Morgan would make a good warrior. But Two Wounds had been surprised to see that Morgan had a streak of humor in him, and that would make him a good Shoshoni. As such, Morgan was deserving of help. Two Wounds nodded. He crooked a finger at Morgan as he squatted.

Morgan knelt beside him. Two Wounds used a finger to diagram in the air just above the ground the way he had found the body and what had been done to it. Then he led Morgan to another spot, where a campfire had burned. "Five, maybe six men sat at the fire here," Two Wounds said.

"Can you tell anything about them?" Morgan asked. He was not shy about asking for help when he was in over his head.

"All are white men." Two Wounds looked at Morgan to catch the lawman's reaction.

He was disappointed. Morgan simply nodded and then asked, "How can you tell?"

Two Wounds lightly traced the faint outline of a footprint. "Boot, not moccasin," he said. "And here. And here." He pointed out several other spots.

The Shoshoni stood and walked toward a clump of brush. Morgan followed. There, they squatted again. "Horses," Two Wounds said. "White man's horses."

"Because they're shod?" Morgan asked.

Two Wounds nodded. "Shoshoni ponies don't have shoes."

"Except the ones you've stolen from whites," Morgan said flatly.

Two Wounds glared at him a moment, then decided Morgan was having a little fun at his expense. "Yes," he said with a nod.

"Still, with those boot prints over yonder, I expect these horses were used by white men." He rose and looked around. The site was in the foothills of the Wind River Mountains, and it was beautiful. Clumps of brush, plus tall pine trees and thick cottonwoods. Wind rustled leaves and branches, and the rippling of a little stream nearby gave one a feeling of peace. It was a pity, Morgan thought, that such a gruesome act had marred such serenity and beauty.

"There anything else you can tell me, Two Wounds?"

The Shoshoni shook his head. "It's been too long to learn much more."

Morgan nodded. "Though it's been even longer since the others were killed, I'd still like to see those places, Two Wounds, and see if we—you—can learn anything there."

"I can take you to those places."

"Let's go, then," Morgan said.

"I'm going to be off, if you don't mind, Buck," Ashby said. "I've got a heaping pile of paperwork to wade through. It's the worst damn thing about this job—you have to write a report every time one of your charges takes a shit."

Morgan laughed. "Same with my job." He winked. "That's why I'd rather shoot 'em and bring 'em in dead than arrest 'em."

Ashby looked up at this, shock flickering in his eyes. Then he saw the twinkle in Morgan's eyes, and he laughed. "I wish I could do something like that myself." He pulled himself into the saddle. "Well, I should be in the office, or near it, all day. I'd be obliged if you were to fill me in on what you've learned today when you get back, Buck."

Morgan nodded. "Will do—when I get back."

"What's that supposed to mean?" Ashby asked, surprised.

"Nothin' sinister. I just might have to stay out here somewhere while I look for the shit balls who've committed these murders."

Ashby nodded, relieved, and then rode off.

Morgan and Two Wounds spent the rest of the day looking over the sites of the murders. They learned little from the murder sites, other than that white men had been at two of them. The other sites held no clues; rain, wind, and animals had blurred whatever information they might have contained.

Morgan was silent as he and Two Wounds rode slowly toward Washakie's village that afternoon. He was mulling over what he had seen and learned, but no answers presented themselves. Finally, they stopped at Washakie's lodge and went inside. Morgan explained what he and Two Wounds had been up to. Some of his frustration showed through.

"Don't take it to heart, my friend," Washakie said, surprising Morgan, not only at the general tone of the words, but at the "my friend" appellation. "Things will work out."

"I'm not so sure, Chief," Morgan said with a sigh. He smiled just a little when the young woman he had seen in the lodge the last time handed him a bowl of stew. He watched her as she moved around the lodge.

"My great-granddaughter," Washakie said with a smile at Morgan.

"Not one of your wives?" Morgan asked, surprised once again. His heart suddenly seemed to be pounding harder and faster.

"No," Washakie said with a laugh. "It is good to have a young wife, it's true. And I have one. They are good for an old man. Yes. They make an old-timer like me feel like a ruttin' bull in the robes. But one that young would surely be the death of me."

The bowl of stew in Morgan's hands was forgotten now. Eyes burning with desire, he asked, "You mind if I was to come courtin' her?"

It was Washakie's turn to be surprised. Not so much that Morgan desired Cloud Woman; that had been obvious in Morgan's eyes. What did surprise Washakie was that Morgan had so formally and so stiffly asked to court the young woman. It was unlike most of the whites Washakie had met. Most of them simply wanted to buy a young woman, thinking that was the Shoshoni way or something. Buck Morgan acted more like the men in the old days, men like Blanket Chief Jim Bridger, who had married one of Washakie's daughters. He wondered where Bridger was, if he was alive, and how his daughter was.

Washakie sighed. So much thinking of the past always made him melancholy. True, he had already outlived all the friends of his youth and several wives. But he still had much to give him joy. He shook off the gloom. "You may court Cloud Woman," he said.

"What a delightful name," Morgan said. He rolled

it around his tongue a few times and decided he liked the way it felt.

"But," Washakie cautioned, "I won't allow it if Cloud Woman doesn't want your attentions."

That gave Morgan a moment's pause. Then he nodded. "I'd not want it any other way," he said honestly. "I ain't a man to force my attentions on any woman."

Washakie nodded, pleased. He had trusted Morgan right from the start; that had seemed the right thing to do. It appeared now as if his original assessment of Morgan was justified. "I'll talk to her about it tomorrow," he said.

Their talk turned to more general things, and before much longer Washakie said with a grin, "Night comes early for an old bastard like me. You can stay the night here, Buck, if you want."

"Does Cloud Woman live here with you?" Morgan asked.

Washakie nodded.

"Then I'll pass. I think it'd be too hard for me to lay there knowin' she was just across the lodge."

"I know what'd be too hard," Two Wounds suddenly said with a raucous laugh.

Morgan flamed red, but he laughed, too, accepting the jibe in the friendly nature in which it had been intended. "Guess I'll head back to Ashby's."

"Stay in my lodge," Two Wounds said, laughter finally stopping.

"You sure? I don't want to put you out any."

"I'm sure."

"Well, then," Morgan said as he stood, "I'll say good night, Chief Washakie." He followed Two Wounds to his lodge. He was surprised, though he was not sure why, when he met Night Seeker, the wife of

86

Two Wounds. Night Seeker was in her mid-twenties and quite attractive, if a little darker of skin than Morgan liked. She also seemed to be quite a pleasant young woman.

"Nice old hag, eh?" Two Wounds said with a laugh.

"Nice old hag," Morgan agreed.

Morgan and Two Wounds spent the next two days just riding around the reservation, trying to find some clues. They stayed the night out in the open. Trying to keep his mind off the possibility of courting Cloud Woman, Morgan mulled over the murders in his mind. He had found nothing to help him in his search for the outlaws.

The next day, he and Two Wounds went back to the first site they had visited. "Can you follow those tracks out of here, Two Wounds?" he asked.

Two Wounds shrugged. "It's been a while. But we won't know till we try."

The effort had proved inconclusive. There had been too much travel, too many antelope and deer, too much rain and wind for the track to stay visible. Two Wounds lost it after less than half an hour. He spent the next two hours trying to pick it up again but couldn't.

"Don't worry about it, Two Wounds," Morgan said as they headed back to Washakie's village that night. He was every bit as frustrated by the so far futile search as was Two Wounds, but he was managing to keep it under control.

Shortly before they reached the village, Morgan stopped. "I reckon I'll head back to Ashby's," he announced. "He's probably pullin' his hair out wonderin' where I am and what I've found out."

Two Wounds suddenly grinned. "Like hell," he said. "You just don't want to go back to the village 'cause you figure Cloud Woman don't want nothin' to do with you."

"Shit," Morgan muttered, but he grinned. "I'll go back to the village just to show you."

Chapter 11

Morgan awoke in a pretty good mood. Not that anyone else could really tell, with his generally stern face. Two Wounds grinned at him, still in his robes. Night Seeker grinned, too, from where she was lying half atop Two Wounds.

"I didn't know you folks was so lazy," Morgan commented drolly. "What with layin' about half the day."

"You're just jealous," Two Wounds said with a laugh.

"That I am," Morgan responded agreeably. "I'll be outside for a spell—till you're done here."

"It won't be long."

"I didn't expect it would." Laughing, Morgan poured himself some coffee and headed outside. Tin cup in hand, he wandered around the village, taking in the sights, sounds, and smells of the unfamiliar place. In his two earlier trips here he had never really had a chance to look around. He made up for that lack now.

In some ways the Shoshoni village was utterly foreign to him. But upon closer inspection he realized that maybe it wasn't all that much different from what he was used to. There were children playing and laughing, running naked through the lodges. Dogs barked and snapped and lay in the morning sun. Smoke from cookfires drifted lazily toward the sky. The village came awake much as did a white man's town, with people scurrying about. There were more women outside doing more things than he was used to, but still the general theme of new morning held true.

He was as much a curiosity to the Shoshoni as they were to him. Some of the Indians watched askance, others boldly. Most faces were either friendly or composed; only a few showed any real hostility, and those were young warriors who considered Morgan a potential competitor for the affections of the young women.

Two Wounds found Morgan after a little while. "You hungry?" the Shoshoni asked.

"Yep."

The two walked back to Two Wounds's lodge and were served food by a glowing Night Seeker. "You treat her well, my friend," Morgan said quietly to Two Wounds when Night Seeker was out of earshot.

"She's a good woman," Two Wounds agreed. When they had finished eating Two Wounds asked, "What you got in mind for today?"

Morgan shrugged. He hadn't given it much thought. He gnawed on the edges of his mustache as he pondered his next move. Finally, he asked, "How many towns are there around the reservation?"

Two Wounds seemed to be caught unawares by the question, and he had to take a little time to think about his answer. "Only two I know of. Flat Fork's closest to here. It's on the Popo Agie River, close up by the Wind River Mountains. It's a shithole, is that what you call it? It ought to be up on Badwater Creek or

90

Poison Creek. The only other place is some miles northwest, up on the other side of Wind River Canyon. Bubbling Water."

"A hot spring?" Morgan asked.

Two Wounds nodded. "Real big one. Town's not much. A few traders and such tryin' to make some money off the People, Arapaho and Crow who use it regularly." He paused. "Why are you interested in them places?"

"Well, since Washakie thinks white men are killin' your people, I'll have to look into that. Hell, you said yourself yesterday that white men were at most, if not all, the sites where Shoshoni were killed."

"You think they're ridin' here from one of the towns?"

Morgan nodded. "If they were stayin' on the reservation, someone would've seen them already. Only other whites are the soldiers. They could be the ones doin' it, and I'll keep that thought in mind, but I don't think it's them."

"Why not?" Two Wounds sounded skeptical, figuring that Morgan was turning out like all the rest of the whites—a liar. He would protect his own, and nothing more would be said about dead Shoshoni.

Morgan shrugged. "Just a hunch. It seems likely to me that if some of them were responsible, Ashby would've heard about it. Unless he's in on it, which I can't believe."

"No, Scratches Paper wouldn't do that. It wouldn't be his way."

"Scratches Paper?" Morgan asked with a laugh.

"It's fittin', don't you think?"

"Apt as hell." Morgan stretched. "Well, reckon I'd

best head off to one of those towns and see if I can find out anything.''

Two Wounds laughed. ''You just want to go there and hump some poor old woman.''

''If there're any women in those towns at all, they're probably so ugly and used up I'd rather have a go with a buffalo.''

''Ain't you gonna go see Washakie first?'' Two Wounds asked innocently.

Morgan saw the sparkle in Two Wounds's eyes. ''And just what would I go and do that for?''

''See if Cloud Woman wants to allow you to get your big white paws on her fine dark flesh.''

''You're one crude son of a bitch, ain't you?'' Morgan said with a laugh. He paused. ''Well, he did say he'd talk to her yesterday, but I don't know as if he meant it.''

''One way to find out.''

Morgan knew Two Wounds was right. So he went to Washakie's lodge. After a few perfunctory spoonfuls of the food Washakie's old wife gave him and Two Wounds, Morgan asked bluntly, ''You talked with Cloud Woman yet?''

''You're too impatient, son,'' Washakie said.

''I expect I am. But I've got a heap of things to do, most of them somewhere else.''

Washakie nodded. ''Yes, a man like you would have many things to do. I'm old and foolish to forget that.''

''Don't give me any of that poor-ol'-me shit, Washakie,'' Morgan said roughly, but he grinned.

''Found me out as a fraud, did you?''

Morgan nodded. ''Really, Chief Washakie,'' he said earnestly, ''I've got to go checking on the white man's towns just off your land, and it's going to take a heap

92

of ridin' and jawin' to try to learn anything. I'd like to know I had a reason to come back here—other than to look at your ugly old puss again.''

Washakie roared with laughter. "I like you, Buck. You're one funny sumbitch." The old warrior paused to light his small pipe. "Yes, I talked with Cloud Woman."

"And . . . ?"

"And she says she will allow the tall, furry-lipped white man to call on her now and then." He waited for laughter, or anger. He was surprised at the reaction he did get, though.

"I don't know your ways, Washakie," Morgan said solemnly, "and I ain't got time to learn them. Nor do I have time for fartin' around makin' chitchat. I need to spend some time with Cloud Woman and get to know her fast and let her get to know me. I don't have the luxury of time to waste."

"I understand," Washakie said with a nod of his gray-haired old head. "There's one problem, though."

"What's that?" Morgan asked, eyes narrowing.

"You ain't the only one wants to get his hands on Cloud Woman. Most of the others'll leave her be if they know you're callin' on her. One won't, though. Curly Bull."

"That's right, white-eyes," someone said in guttural, accented English behind Morgan.

"You allow people to just come bargin' into your lodge and insult your guests, Chief Washakie?" Morgan said, never taking his eyes off Washakie's.

"No," Washakie said flatly. "Curly Bull, you have no manners. Come sit by the fire here and we will talk as men should."

"Bah, foolish old man."

Morgan was about to rise and thump Curly Bull when Washakie rose instead. In harsh, biting terms, he snapped, "You challenge me in my own lodge?"

Two Wounds translated for Morgan.

"No," Curly Bull said hastily. "I meant no offense."

"Then sit. Take food. We will talk some."

Curly Bull sat and ate a bowl of stew. His eyes never left Morgan. When he finished the stew he tossed the bowl aside. "Cloud Woman is mine," he said flatly in poor English. "She won't go with you, white man."

"She ain't told me that, boy," Morgan responded harshly.

"Cloud Woman has no say in this," the Shoshoni boasted. "I, Curly Bull, claim her as my own. I'll give Washakie twenty horses for her. What can you give?" Curly Bull sneered.

"Somethin' all your goddamn horses can't give— respect. Respect for Cloud Woman, and respect for Washakie."

Curly Bull looked as if he had just swallowed a snake. "I challenge you. We will fight for her."

Morgan looked at Washakie. "That usual?" he asked.

Washakie shrugged. "Not really. But that doesn't mean he can't do it."

"Would it insult you if I was to take him on?"

Washakie shook his head.

"It would the other way, though?"

Washakie nodded.

"I don't mind fightin' this shit," Morgan said to Washakie, "but I'd feel some better about it if I knew it was worthwhile."

"You can't squirm out of this," Curly Bull snarled.

Morgan ignored him. "I'd be obliged, Chief, if you'd see what Cloud Woman's feelings are in all this. If she wants Crazy Bull . . ."

"*Curly* Bull," the Shoshoni snapped.

"Yeah. Whatever you say. Now, as I was sayin', if she wants shit ball there, I'm not going to waste my time fightin' him over her. But if she's willin' to accept me, well, then that's a whole 'nother story."

Washakie called to Cloud Woman, who came forward shyly. He and the woman talked quietly for a few minutes. Then Cloud Woman went back to the rear of the tepee, and Washakie looked at Morgan. "Cloud Woman says she will accept the white lawman if he wins."

Morgan nodded. "You're on, Curly Bull," he said evenly. "When you want to go about this?"

"Now."

Morgan shrugged. He rose and turned for the flap of the lodge. He had only taken one step when Curly Bull plowed into him from behind. The move pushed the two out of the tepee, pulling the flap loose.

Morgan's breath whooshed out as he hit the hard ground, belly down, and Curly Bull landed atop his back. But the landing also made them bounce, and Morgan was able to get out of Curly Bull's grasp.

He rose, warily watching Curly Bull do the same. Then Morgan pulled his two pistols and tossed them toward Two Wounds. "Hold them till I'm done with this fool," he said cockily. He turned back to face Curly Bull.

The Shoshoni was several inches shorter than Morgan but outweighed him. Curly Bull had a thick neck and bulging, muscular shoulders. His legs were short and powerful. Morgan would not underestimate him.

"You always attack folks from behind?" Morgan asked.

Curly Bull shrugged.

"Chickenshit little bastard, ain't you?"

Curly Bull charged, shoulder muscles bunched. Morgan had the thought that he would step out of the way and grab the back of Curly Bull's shirt as the Shoshoni charged by. Then he could fling the Indian down, pounce on him, and end this all.

Trouble was, Curly Bull had a full head of steam and enough weight and bulk to make that difficult, if not impossible. As Morgan stepped aside and reached out, Curly Bull plowed into him, bowling him over in a sprawl of arms, legs, and pain.

"Holy shit," Morgan murmured as he rolled a few times, unable to stop himself. Despite his silent vow he had gone ahead and thought too lightly of Curly Bull. And now the flames of pain in his chest and side reminded him of his folly.

He got up and drew in a long breath to try to settle the pain. Curly Bull had gotten to his feet and stood watching Morgan. A smirk covered the lower half of the Indian's face.

Morgan charged this time. He slammed to a stop two feet in front of Curly Bull, swung up both fists, locked them together, and then swung the flesh-and-bone club. Curly Bull's cheek skin split from the blow. A surprised Curly Bull staggered to the side.

Morgan stepped up before Curly Bull could recover and pounded him several more times with the entwined fists. Each blow hammered Curly Bull down a little more, until he was prostrate. Breathing heavily, Morgan knelt next to the Shoshoni.

"You'll leave Cloud Woman alone, eh," he said in

a harsh whisper. "At least until she decides she doesn't want me to come callin' any more. Yes?"

"Yes," Curly Bull croaked. His voice was groggy and far away.

Chapter 12

"Mr. Morgan," Two Wounds called frantically. "Buck. Get up."

Morgan threw off the cover of sleep and sat up. His chest hurt like hell and his eyes felt a little gritty. "What the hell . . . ?"

"Another body's been found," Two Wounds said, accent even thicker than usual. He was angry as well as sad.

"Shit." Morgan kicked off the covers and stood, rubbing his face. "Where?" he asked.

"Along Willow Creek, not far from Crowheart Butte."

"Crowheart Butte?" Morgan asked.

"It's a long tale. I'll tell you some time," Two Wounds said.

Night Seeker walked up and handed Morgan a tin cup of coffee. Morgan took it, nodded his thanks, and sipped it. Since it wasn't too hot, he downed the rest of it in one big swallow.

"We got time for fillin' our bellies?" Morgan asked.

Two Wounds nodded. "Lame Bear's not going anywhere," he said sourly. "But I think Rough Wolf—he found the body—won't like stayin' out there by himself.''

"I'll make it fast."

Morgan bolted down hunks of buffalo, splashing some coffee after it. By the time he finished and stepped outside into the blistering heat, Two Wounds had saddled Morgan's horse, and his own. Then the two men were off, under the hard, resentful eyes of the village.

They moved quickly, but it still allowed Morgan some time to think. After his battle with Curly Bull the day before he had spent the rest of the day with Cloud Woman. He had put off going to the towns, wanting to spend more time with Cloud Woman.

That came back to haunt him a little now. He wondered if Lame Bear would still be alive if Morgan had gone to the towns instead of making moon eyes at a beautiful young Shoshoni woman. He pushed those thoughts aside. He knew there would have been little he could have learned in the towns in half a day that could have prevented this.

His thoughts of Cloud Woman confused him all the more. He had never been struck by a woman as much as he was now by the Shoshoni. Not even when he had married.

Ivy Goodell had been an attractive young woman, too, when Morgan had begun courting her. And she had been pleasant and nice to be around. It wasn't so much that she had become a shrew after their nuptials, but she had changed in ways Morgan could not really understand. She just seemed not to want to be around him anymore. Finally Morgan just up and disappeared one day—after talking with Ivy. He told her that she could do what she wanted, tell people anything she liked. If she wanted a divorce, he told her, she could get one, using abandonment as the grounds, if that would smooth life's path for her. Morgan had no idea where Ivy was now, or what she was up to. And he really didn't care.

Still, it gave him pause. He wasn't sure he wanted to give his heart to another. Not after what had happened the last time. On the other hand, he thought with a touch of sarcasm, maybe Cloud Woman would want nothing to do with him. She had been quite reserved around him yesterday. He wasn't sure if that was because she had had second thoughts about him courting her, or if it was just that she was naturally shy.

He finally tried to ignore the thoughts and take in the landscape. He and Two Wounds were angling northwest a little, heading for the line of cottonwoods that marked the course of the Wind River. Once they reached that they followed the big river as the Wind River Valley began to narrow.

Before long, they reached the badlands, which seemed to change at every few hundred yards. While similar, they were yet different. Most were of red rock, some looking like burnt bricks. Others were flat brown, or a dusty tan.

"That Crowheart Butte out there?" Morgan asked, pointing to a low, flat chunk of light tan rock on the horizon.

"Yes," Two Wounds said.

"Tell me about it."

"What do you want to know?" Two Wounds responded, feeling a need to be contrary at the moment.

"How'd it get its name, for one thing?" Morgan said. He could understand Two Wounds's desire to not want to deal with things much at the moment. Not

100

when the weighty matter of dead Shoshoni was at hand. "The way you sounded back in the village made it seem like there was some interestin' story behind it."

Two Wounds nodded, recovering some of his normal humor and pleasantness. "You sure you want to hear another story about Washakie's prowess?" he asked with a grin.

"I sort of suspected that old coot was mixed up in this somehow. What happened?"

"It was maybe eight winters ago. Yeah, 1866, the year after you crazy white men stopped fightin' between yourselves. It was in the month you call March. The damn Crow had been given this land—*our* goddamn land—in 1851 with the Fort Laramie Treaty. Trouble was, none of us knew they had gotten a fair piece of our land. Goddamn white-eyes anyway."

Morgan glanced at him and grinned. He knew Two Wounds was just spouting off, and even had reason to.

"Once we found out that our land had been stolen from us we made a point of gettin' it back when we signed a treaty in 1863 over at Fort Bridger. Well, most of the people made a trip up there in '66, and what do we find but every goddamn Crow in the world. Campin' on our land! Bastards."

Two Wounds had to take a few moments to calm himself down some. Then he finally went on. "We weren't about to just up and leave, dammit, not because of the damn Crow. Washakie went to talk to one of their big chiefs." Sarcasm dripped from the latter word. "A dumb bastard named Big Robber. The damn name tells you what kind of man he was."

Two Wounds looked over at Morgan. "You sure you want to hear all this?" he asked.

Morgan nodded.

"Well, talkin' to those damn Crow didn't do us no good whatsoever, so we took to fightin' them. One hell of a fight it was, too. Four goddamn days! And after all that what we ended up with was a goddamn stand-off. We were in no better position than when we started. No worse, either, but we should've been able to rout those damn Crow after four days."

"One would think so, yes," Morgan said dryly. He grinned at the nasty look Two Wounds gave him.

"After all that Washakie and Big Robber called a truce and talked things over. What they came up with was to meet one on one, just the two of them." Two Wounds sounded as if he thought both chiefs were crazy.

"The two of them met on horseback at the foot of the butte there. After the first charge, though, their damn horses decided they wanted no part of such a damn-fool thing. Actually," Two Wounds added with a laugh, "when they charged each other they knocked each other off his pony. That's when the ponies decided to run like hell."

Two Wounds laughed a little, and Morgan joined him, enjoying the tale.

"Well, Washakie and Big Robber took after each other on foot, using their shields and war clubs. Took a couple of hours, or so it seemed at the time, but Washakie finally killed Big Robber. Then that crusty old bastard cut out Big Robber's heart and ate the damn thing."

"You had me believin' until the very last there, Two Wounds," Morgan said with a laugh. "You really did."

"It's true, every damn word of it. I swear."

"Now I think you're full of buffalo shit."

102

Two Wounds looked offended for a moment, then grinned. "It is all true except the last. No one knows for sure, but it seemed like Washakie ate—well, just took a bite of—that Crow's heart. Then he paraded around with it on his lance for a spell."

"That sounds a heap more plausible." He paused. "You know, just at a glance, Washakie don't look like he could do most of the things attributed to him."

"That's where a lot of men get in trouble with Washakie, that wily old bastard."

"I expect so, since there's not too many men going to look deep into Washakie's eyes and soul. I'm used to doin' such a thing, and I did it. And I saw the truth of those wild claims in his eyes."

"Maybe all white men ain't so bad after all," Two Wounds said. "Or maybe I should say that maybe all white men ain't so stupid after all."

"You don't like white men much, do you, Two Wounds?"

"Should I?" More bitterness than he had wanted crept into his voice.

Morgan shrugged. "I suppose not. Hell, there's many a white man who hates Indians—any Indians—just for bein' Indians. Guess it stands to reason that there're Indians who hate whites just for bein' whites."

"That's not what I meant, dammit," Two Wounds snapped. "And you know it." He paused. "Most whites haven't given the People much reason to like 'em. A few have—men like Orv Ashby. You. Not a hell of a lot more, though."

Morgan nodded. "Makes sense. At least you keep your eyes open to see how a man is before you condemn him."

Two Wounds's dark eyes flashed angrily. "You

make fun of me," he snapped, struggling with his English. "That ain't good."

"I ain't makin' fun of you, Two Wounds. I'm speakin' the truth. There're plenty of men—red and white—who wouldn't take the time to get to know another."

Two Wounds stopped, his anger dissipating somewhat. Then he nodded. "Yes, too many men see only a man's skin and not what kind of man he really is."

They began riding again. "So what do you think of Cloud Woman?" Two Wounds asked slyly.

"I don't think that's any of your concern," Morgan said rather stiffly.

"Oh, so the big white warrior is afraid of one little woman, eh?" Two Wounds said with a friendly smirk.

"You saw what I did to Curly Bull," Morgan growled. "I'd be happy to oblige you with the same, you keep on talking like that."

Two Wounds laughed. "You'd have to get some help. I'm not a young fool like Curly Bull."

"I'd have no trouble gettin' help," Morgan responded, fighting back a grin. "I figure Night Seeker'll be glad for the excuse to thump on a useless thing like you. I'll tell you, though, Two Wounds, I don't know why in hell a pretty young thing like Night Seeker sticks with you."

"That's easy to answer," Two Wounds said. He grabbed his crotch and almost fell off the horse, he was laughing so hard.

Morgan could think of no way to top that one, so he said nothing, though he did join in Two Wounds's laughter.

They continued riding, weaving through ragged little canyons and past jagged rock formations. The heat was stifling and the air humid and filled with mosqui-toes and gnats. The rugged badlands through which they were passing and the heat and pesty insects quickly brought a halt to the two travelers' humor.

"How much farther we got to go?" Morgan asked after a while.

"An hour. Maybe a little more or a little less."

Morgan nodded, wishing there were a faster—and easier—way of getting around in this vast, desolate land. Finally, though, Two Wounds turned them southwest, and before long they came to a rushing little stream. Morgan and Two Wounds halted to let the horses drink. Then Morgan pitched his hat aside and dunked his head in the water.

"Whoo," he shouted, coming up for air, "that feels good."

"You need to get used to livin' in the desert," Two Wounds said.

"You get used to it," Morgan said, a little irritated. "I prefer a place that's got water all the year, and trees and such. Not this godforsaken piece of hell."

Chapter 13

Lame Bear's body was stiff in death, blood clotted on the stumps of both hands where five of the ten fingers had been cut off. Coagulated blood also decorated both sides of Lame Bear's head, where his ears once were. He had been disemboweled, crudely and messily, the results tossed in a haphazard pile a few feet from the corpse. It was an altogether unpleasant sight.

Lame Bear had been young, and his friend Rough Wolf figured Lame Bear had come to Crowheart Butte to seek a vision.

Whatever humor Morgan had built up on the ride out here vanished as soon as he knelt beside the body and pulled off the blanket that Rough Wolf had placed over his friend. He rose and looked for Two Wounds.

The Shoshoni was moving slowly about the perimeter of the camp, searching for sign. Morgan walked up to him. "You find anything, Two Wounds?" he asked.

"Some," Two Wounds grunted angrily. He had not really known Lame Bear, but that didn't matter. A Shoshoni—one of the People—was dead. That mattered.

"White men again?"

Two Wounds nodded. His hatred for the whites was flaring, and at the moment he did not even want to be around Buck Morgan. He had come to like the tall, rangy lawman during their short acquaintance, but right now he just wanted to be with his own people.

"Same ones?"

Two Wounds shrugged.

Morgan grabbed the Shoshoni by the shoulder and pulled him around. "I know you don't have much likin' for white men right now, but I don't really give a shit. I want to catch the bastards who've done this as much as you. Not for the same reasons, maybe, but just as much."

"You don't know what you're talkin' about," Two Wounds hissed.

"Horseshit. But I'm not about to stand here and debate it with you. If you want me to catch these bastards, help me. If you don't want to find them, go on back to your lodge and I'll find someone else who's willing to help."

Two Wounds glared at Morgan for some moments. The hatred for Morgan—as the embodiment of all the abuses of all the white men—was as strong as anything he had ever experienced. But he had pride in his ability to control his emotions. Right now this white man could help find the men who were killing the People. That must come first. Once that was done he would address the problem of Buck Morgan.

"I'll help," Two Wounds said tightly. "Some of the prints I've seen are from the same men. Some're new."

"Let's follow them."

"Soon," Two Wounds said. "I want to look around here some more."

Morgan nodded. He was eager to be on the trail,

though he didn't know why. The condition of the body told him that the killers had been gone since sometime yesterday. Waiting a few more minutes, or even a few more hours, would make no difference in catching the men. Still, Morgan was impatient.

Morgan wandered off by himself, away from the body. He wasn't bothered by it; he had seen too many other bloody, gory scenes. But that did not mean he wanted to stand there looking at a pile of entrails covered with maggots. He pulled a thin cheroot out of his shirt pocket and lit it. Then he stood there puffing quietly, eyes wandering lazily over the countryside.

His eyes spotted something, he did not know what. It had only been a glint, or maybe just the suggestion of something. Using his peripheral vision, he tried to pick it up again, but to no avail. With a general idea of where whatever had caught his eye was, he moved slowly there, eyes sweeping the ground. Suddenly he stopped and knelt.

He reached out and picked up a button. He rolled it between his fingers. It seemed ordinary—just a plain white button from a man's shirt. It might not even be from any of the killers. But he shrugged. One never knew what might be important. He rose and stuck the button into a pants pocket.

A few minutes later Two Wounds soundlessly walked up alongside of Morgan. "Time to go," the Shoshoni said flatly.

Morgan nodded. The two trotted out of Lame Bear's little camp, leaving the Shoshoni's remains in the care of his friend Rough Wolf. Two Wounds set a fairly fast pace, and Morgan wondered if Two Wounds were following sign or just guessing which way the whites might've gone. Morgan never did find out for sure, but the trail soon faded into the rocky soil of the twisting badlands. Finally Two Wounds stopped, anger contorting his face.

"You lost it?" Morgan asked quietly.

"What the hell do you think?" Two Wounds snapped in response.

"Don't worry about it," Morgan said after a while. "I'm going to head on to the towns and see what I can find out. If white men really did all this, they'll have to show up in one of those towns sooner or later."

"After how many more of the People are killed?"

"Hopefully none, goddammit," Morgan snapped, his own anger beginning to flare. He pulled his horse's head around and rode off. Soon after, Two Wounds caught up with him, and they traveled in silence.

At Washakie's village Morgan tarried only long enough to say a few words to Cloud Woman. Then he was in the saddle and heading toward Ashby's. It was almost dark when he got there, and he was tired, hot, sweaty, dirty, and in a foul mood.

Ashby noted it all and rather calmly directed Dusty to care for Morgan's horse and Grace to reheat supper. "You want a bath first?"

Morgan shook his head. "Food first. Then a bath."

Ashby nodded, and a few minutes later, Morgan was doing serious damage to a plate of roasted pork and potatoes. Afterward, he took his time shaving, and then settled in for a short, lukewarm bath. When he was finished Ashby entered the small room Morgan was calling home. He carried a bottle of whiskey. He poured each of them a drink and then sat on the only chair in the room. Morgan was sitting on the bed.

"So, what've you learned?" Ashby asked bluntly.

"Not a hell of a lot," Morgan admitted sourly. "I'm

convinced now that white men are behind all this. Who and why, I don't know. You know we found another one today, don't you?''

Ashby nodded. "I heard. Lame Bear, wasn't it?''

"Yeah. Two Wounds found some tracks he said were the same as the ones we found where Fox Head was killed. We tried following them for a while but lost them in the badlands.''

"So what do we do now?''

"I'm going to head into Flat Fork and see if I can dredge something up.''

"You don't sound optimistic.''

"I ain't. But I don't know where else to look.''

Ashby nodded. "Well, I hope you find something soon.''

"Oh?'' Morgan asked, eyebrows raised in question.

"I can feel tension building around here. Lieutenant Pomeroy is getting itchy.''

"Scared?''

"Maybe. The main thing is that he's looking to move up in the ranks. That's his best shot of getting out of this hellhole. And to do that he needs to make a name for himself. What better way than heading off an 'Indian war'?''

"He'd kill a bunch of Arapaho just to make a name for himself?'' Morgan asked, only a little incredulous.

Ashby shrugged. "I'm not sure, to tell you the truth. He usually seems of a normal frame of mind, but he's ambitious as all hell. And there's no telling what a man like that'll do. I know he won't wait forever if these murders continue, despite what Washakie wants.''

Morgan sighed and shook his head. "I'll head into Flat Fork first thing in the mornin'.'' He finished off his cup of whiskey. "And now I'd best get some shut-eye."

Flat Fork was near about the worst sinkhole of filth and degradation Morgan had ever seen, and he had been in some mighty poor places. The place was a rancid collection of shacks and shanties stuck up haphazardly along crooked, muddy streets. Nearly every other building was a saloon, and there seemed to be few if any other kind of business. There were no hotels that Morgan could see, only one mercantile store, a hardware store, and a gunshop. He did spot a doctor's shingle on one tent structure and a rudimentary funeral home. Morgan figured those two places got plenty of use.

The air was foul with the stench of the waste and garbage that cluttered the roadways. Cooking meat from unknown animals added to the stink. The Popo Agie River was sullied with refuse.

The people that populated the festering metropolis were fitting for the place. Most looked like they would kill someone for absolutely nothing and have a chuckle while doing it. Their faces were feral, sometimes fierce, always dissipated and decidedly unfriendly. Morgan had the sudden thought that his badge was like the bull's-eye of a target.

He dismounted in front of a saloon. With a look around at the hostile, drunken faces, he headed inside. The inside of the dank den made the outside of Flat Fork look quite good by comparison. The saloon was not large, and the bar was nothing more than a narrow plank sitting on a pile of boxes at one end and a tree stump on the other. Several men snored loudly at

111

wooden tables. A few other men were drunken enough to be only dimly aware of their surroundings, but not unconscious.

Morgan stopped just inside the place to get the lay of it. He was not bothered by the stares he attracted. When he was satisfied that no one was of immediate danger to him he moved farther inside, heading for the bar. "You have any drinkable whiskey in this place?" he asked the bartender.

The man was tall and burly, but his muscle had turned to fat. He had a sweeping, wide, thick mustache and flabby, red-tinged cheeks. His clothes were filthy and the man had a disagreeable smell about him.

"I got what I got is all," the bartender said. "You want some of it?"

Morgan shrugged. "Guess it won't kill me."

The bartender slapped a dirty glass on the plank and almost filled it with whiskey. "Fifty cent."

Morgan paid him and downed the shot. When it had finally made it all the way into his stomach Morgan put the glass down. "Damn, I think I was wrong. That shit just might kill me."

"You complainin'?" the bartender asked.

"Maybe later. A question first."

"I don't answer no questions."

"I haven't even asked it yet."

"Don't matter."

"Well, let me give it a try anyway." He eased a ten-dollar gold piece out of a pocket, set it on the plank, and pushed it a little way across.

The bartender shrugged. But he reached for the coin.

Morgan kept his finger on the money. "You know any boys keen on killin' Indians?"

"I might. Why?"

"Might have some work for them."

"You're fulla shit. Lawmen don't go lookin' for nobody to go killin' Injuns."

"I don't take kindly to bein' called a liar, mister," Morgan said flatly. He was aware of the two men who had moved somewhat stealthily up behind him.

"Don't make no goddamn diff'rence to me what you like or don't. Now get your finger off that money."

"Sure," Morgan said agreeably. The finger lifted, then folded with the others until Morgan had a fist, with which he popped the bartender a good shot in the nose. Then Morgan whirled, pulling out a Smith and Wesson.

The two men froze. They were both hostile-looking men, dirty and shopworn.

"You take one more step in my direction, shit balls," Morgan said calmly, "and it'll be your last."

One started backing away, and then the other did the same, hands raised.

Morgan whipped around and slapped the barrel of his pistol against the middle of the bartender's forehead. The bartender groaned a little and dropped the shotgun.

Once more Morgan whirled, instinctively knowing that the other two men would be gunning for him again. He fired three times. One ball hit one of the men in the chest, almost dead center; another hit the second man in the right cheek and exited at the nape of his neck. The third shot hit nothing, since both men were falling when Morgan fired it.

Morgan turned slowly back to face the bartender again.

Chapter 14

The bartender's eyes crossed involuntarily when Morgan stuck the muzzle of his Smith and Wesson less than an inch from the depression between the man's eyes. Morgan thumbed back the hammer. "Are you a little more talkative now, shit ball?" Morgan asked.

The bartender licked his lips and whispered, "Yes." His eyes uncrossed but had trouble staying that way.

"Good. Now, what's your name, shit ball?"

"Herb. Herb Foster."

"Well, Mr. Foster, perhaps you'd like to tell that shit tryin' to sneak up on me that if he shoots me the hammer's going to drop and your brains—if there are any in that great, fat skull of yours—will be splattered all over yonder wall."

"Put your gun away, Marv," Foster said, his voice shaking. "Dammit, Marv, do it now!" Sweat was pouring down Foster's face now, dropping off his nose and chin to land with tiny little splats on the plank bar.

"I asked you before," Morgan said to Foster when he was fairly certain the man named Marv had backed off, "if you knew anyone who was fond of killin' Indians. You never did give me an answer. I'd be obliged if you was to answer it now.''

"Jesus, Marshal," Foster blubbered, "near every man in Flat Fork's got somethin' against Injuns. I swear they do.''

Morgan believed him. From what he had seen of this town, the place would not attract anyone with any sense or decency. "You know any that's been killin' Indians lately?''

"No, I surely don't.''

Morgan was a lot less sure this time that Foster was telling the truth, but he was no more certain that he wasn't. "You hear anything of the sort, you get word to me through Mr. Ashby, the agent for the Shoshoni. You do that, I'll remember you favorably. You don't and I learn about it, I'll come back here and drown you in your own foul whiskey. That clear?''

"Yes," Foster croaked.

"Now, I want you to squat and pick up that scatter-gun you have down there. Pick it up by the barrels. If somethin' you do makes me nervous, there's no tellin' but what my thumb might just slip off the hammer.''

"Yessir," Foster said. He did as he was told, including setting the shotgun on the plank. He breathed a large sigh of relief when Morgan's pistol left his face.

Morgan picked up the scattergun in his left hand and turned. He stood surveying the room. No one looked like he was about to make an imminent move against Morgan, but Morgan knew that most, if not all of them, would gun him down in a heartbeat, given half the chance. "Get your fat ass out here where I can see you, Foster," he said. "And bring that old bucket of whiskey you got back there.''

The bartender did as he was told.

"You Marv?" Morgan asked a man standing about twelve feet away, hand on the butt of the pistol stuck in his belt. When the man nodded Morgan said, "Ease out that pistol with your left hand and then drop it into Mr. Foster's bucket."

"You're *loco,* pal," Marv snarled.

"There's every chance I am," Morgan said agreeably. "Which is why you ought to heed what I say and do it quickly. You never can tell what a crazy man'll do, now can you?" Morgan shifted the shotgun in his left hand and braced the butt against his pelvic joint. Then he snapped both hammers back.

"No, no, I guess you can't," Marv said. He didn't look particularly worried or scared. And that bothered Morgan. Such a man was much like himself, fearless, and that meant he was dangerous.

"Then get on with it." He paused. "You do have another choice, shit ball. Pull the piece and try to gun me down. That'd show everyone how goddamn tough you are. Of course, you'd be deader than all get-out, but that's your lookout, not mine."

Marv eased his pistol out and dropped it in the bucket. "That goddamn gun cost me twenty-two dollars, and now it's ruint," he complained.

"How's it ruined?" Morgan asked, almost surprised.

"Hell, you drank some of Foster's goddamn rotgut. That shit's enough to melt the damn pistol."

Morgan nodded. "Then you best make sure later that he doesn't try to sell you that whiskey. Hell, he just might think melted-down metal and gunpowder is a flavoring."

Marv looked at Morgan in surprise. Suddenly he burst into laughter. "You got somethin' there, pal,"

116

he said, still laughing. "I'll make sure he dumps that shit on the ground." He paused. "Well, where do you want me?" he asked. He had turned pleasant, as if finally realizing that Morgan wasn't all that bad a man, and that no allegiance was really due Foster.

"Face up against the wall in back there'll do."

As Marv did as he was told, Morgan looked at another man. "The rest of you drop your pistols into the bucket—one at a time—and then go stand next to Marv back there." He waited almost patiently as the men went through the routine. When all but Foster were facing the back wall Morgan uncocked his Smith and Wesson and slid it away before moving the shotgun to his right hand. He held out his left hand. "The bucket, please."

Foster shuffled over, contemplating some heroics, like throwing the bucket at Morgan and then attacking him. Then he saw the hard, deadly gray eyes and changed his mind. He simply handed Morgan the bucket.

Morgan whapped Foster on the head with the barrels of the shotgun.

Foster sank to one knee, groaning. He held a hand to his bleeding head and looked up with hurt, hateful eyes. "What'n hell'd you go and do that fer?" he asked plaintively.

Morgan shrugged. "Just for the hell of it." Then he smiled tightly. "That, and so maybe you'll learn that next time you'll be a little friendlier to a law dog when he comes along." He turned and walked outside. He uncocked the shotgun and considered tossing it away. Then he decided to keep it. A scattergun was the perfect weapon to use in a tight spot—like being hemmed in at some saloon.

With a fast-increasing sense of impending doom he towed his horse toward the next fetid saloon. Along the way he dropped the bucket of rotgut and guns, making sure it fell on its side, where the whiskey would spill out. He looked back once to see three men fighting over the pail.

Keeping the shotgun handy, he went inside the next saloon.

Morgan choked down a rotten midday meal, figuring that he had died and gone to hell, and this day would never end. That he would forever have to walk from one horrid saloon to the next, and eat every meal for all eternity in a stinking, insect-infested shack that tried to pass itself off as a restaurant.

He was standing alongside his horse, dreading the next stop he had to make, when two soldiers rode hell-bent into town. They slowed and began looking around, searching for someone. Then one pointed in Morgan's general direction, and they both trotted over.

"You Marshal Buck Morgan?" one asked.

"I am." Morgan resisted the impulse to point out that he was the only one in Flat Fork—probably the only man within a thousand square miles—with a badge on his chest.

"Mr. Ashby's compliments, sir," the same one said. "He says you're to come back to the agency directly."

"What's the trouble?" He knew something had to be wrong. Ashby would've never sent anyone after him in Flat Fork for nothing.

"Beggin' your leave, sir," the same one said, "but Mr. Ashby's not in the habit of takin' lowly privates in the U.S. Army into his confidence."

Morgan nodded. He stuck a foot in the stirrup and pulled himself onto his horse. "Let's go," he said.

"We'll be stayin' here, sir."

Morgan looked at him askance. "What's your name, boy?" he asked.

"Lee Skousen." He nodded toward his companion. "That's Vic Bowen."

"You have permission to stay here in Flat Fork?"

"Yessir," Skousen said in sincere tones.

"Then I'm sure you won't mind any if I check with Lieutenant Pomeroy on that, eh?"

The two soldiers suddenly cast sullen, angry glances at him. Both had figured to grab a couple of drinks of whiskey and maybe a bottle for the ride back, and then to dally with one of the Cyprians. Even with all that, they could make it back to Camp Brown without raising any ruckus. Lieutenant Pomeroy wouldn't give men he trusted a hard time; that was well known at Camp Brown.

Morgan shrugged and then grinned a little. "You boys'll be a heap better off stayin' away from these hellholes," he said.

"Shit, Marshal," Skousen said, "we just wanted to wet our whistles and . . ." He suddenly turned red.

"Wanted to wet something else, too, huh?" Morgan said with a laugh. "Well, go on then, but don't you dally too much or Pomeroy'll have your ass."

"You're not gonna say nothin'?" Bowen asked.

"Not if you boys get back in a reasonable time. I don't owe any allegiance to Pomeroy. You best watch it, though, boys, while you're here. There's some mean folk stalkin' those saloons. Worse, you might just get yourself a good dose of drippin' pizzle."

"We've had the clap before, Marshal," Bowen said

with a laugh. "It ain't much fun, but it goes away after a spell."

"Suit yourselves, boys. Just remember, you ain't caught up to me in a reasonable time, I'll let Pomeroy know." He turned his horse and trotted out of Flat Fork, not looking forward to the trip.

Two and a half hours later, when Morgan was only a couple of miles from Ashby's agency, Skousen and Bowen caught up with him. Their horses were sweated and foamy. Morgan looked at the two soldiers with some annoyance. "Took you boys long enough," he said flatly.

"Well," Bowen said, beaming, "it took us a little longer'n we thought it would."

"Yeah, them women couldn't get enough of us and tried to keep us there as long as they could," Skousen added with a cocky grin.

"And now you two shit balls've run them horses into the ground. Pomeroy's likely to have your ass for treating animals that way."

"Goddamn, Marshal, you sure know how to put a damper on things," Skousen complained.

"Maybe I do. But you damn fools ought to think once in a while. So you went and dipped your wicks. Big goddamn deal. Those women'd screw a snake if the serpent paid them. You ain't nothin' special to them women. But you come out of there thinkin' you're some bull elk, crowin' and boastin'. It'd serve you right if you got a dose of the clap—and have Pomeroy assign you to muckin' out the stalls for a couple of weeks."

"Why the hell're you bein' so hard on us, Marshal?" Bowen asked, seemingly bewildered.

"I could've come straight on back and told Pomeroy

what you two shits were up to. But, no, I tried to be a decent man, let you boys have your fun a little, and then I get paid back with smart mouths and horses run into the ground."

Skousen gulped. "I never thought of it that way, Marshal," he said earnestly. "I really didn't."

"Me neither," Bowen added.

Morgan said nothing.

"Hold on there a minute, Marshal," Skousen said. When Morgan stopped Skousen said, "I know we've traded on your good nature too much already . . ."

"You sure as hell have."

". . . But I'd like to impose on you just a bit more."

"What in hell for?"

"Look, let's stop for a bit. Half hour or so. We could water the horses and rub 'em down. Then if we ride nice and easy back to the Camp, the horses won't be none the worse for wear—at least no worse than if we had ridden hard to get to Flat Fork and then hard back to the Camp with you."

"Why in hell would I go and do a thing like that?" Morgan asked evenly.

Skousen shrugged. "There really ain't a good reason for you to. I know that. But I feel bad about the way we treated you—and the horses."

"And you're afraid to get your dumb ass in trouble over this, too, ain't you?" Morgan said with a laugh.

Bowen gulped and then nodded. "You bet your ass we are . . . sir."

"Well, I can understand that." He sighed. "All right. Half an hour. No more." He paused. "And, boys, if you mess with me this time, you'll be very sorry you did."

Chapter 15

Morgan strode through the door of Ashby's office. Two men in army officers' uniforms were there, as was Two Wounds and another Shoshoni, whom Morgan did not know. A Shoshoni boy of about eleven lay on a makeshift cot.

"It's about time you got back," one of the army officers said angrily.

"It took us a while to track Marshal Morgan down, sir," Skousen said.

"Who's he?" Morgan asked, pointing to the boy. He could see that Ashby was terribly worried.

"He was Yellow Wing," Ashby said tightly.

"Was?" Morgan asked, raising his eyebrows.

"Yes, was," Ashby said, tones cold. "He died half an hour or so ago."

"He looks familiar," Morgan commented.

"He and Rabbit Tail took care of your horse, yours and Mr. Ashby's, the first time you came to Washakie's village," Two Wounds said.

"Shit," Morgan muttered. "How'd he die?"

"Old Belly there," Ashby said, pointing to the Shoshoni Morgan did not know, "found Yellow Wing, along with his father and mother. The father, Sleeping Bear, was dead and mutilated same as the others. The mother, Dawn Star, was dead and mutilated, too. Quite obscenely, I might add.'' Ashby drew in a ragged breath. He was beginning to fear that the whole reservation would explode soon unless these hideous murders stopped.

"Yellow Wing was still alive, but hurt bad. Old Belly left his wife, White Bear, with the two bodies and hurried here with Yellow Wing. Dr. Snyder tried as best he could to save the boy, but it was of no use." He paused again. "Before he died, he was able to tell us about the killers."

"Good," Morgan said. "What did he tell you?"

"You know, Marshal," Ashby said stiffly, "if you had gotten back here sooner, you could've heard it from the boy's lips yourself."

"Reckon I could've at that," Morgan said evenly. He glanced at Skousen and Bowen. The former had a smirk on his face; the latter was looking down at the floor. "But like the private said, it took awhile to track me down." He turned his gaze to Ashby. "So, what did the kid say?"

"He said white men had done it. A gang of eight or ten, he wasn't quite sure. He also said the leader of the group was a tall, burly man, with a maniacal laugh."

"Maniacal laugh?" Morgan asked, more surprised that the Shoshoni boy would have described it that way than that the outlaw did it.

"He called it a laugh like a man who has been touched by the spirits. The Shoshoni think crazy people are touched by the spirits."

Morgan nodded, understanding. "Anything else?"

"Yes," Ashby said tightly. "Yellow Wing said the son of a bitch leading the group wears a necklace . . ."

"That's not so out of place."

"This one is made of dried human ears and fingers."

Morgan's cold gray eyes narrowed. Then he nodded. "Now that I know that, it'll be easier to find him. I'll head off soon's my horse gets a little rest, grain, and water."

"No you won't," one army officer said.

"What's that?" Morgan asked, turning his harsh glare on the man.

"I said you're not going anywhere."

"And just who the hell're you?"

"Lieutenant Dexter Pomeroy," the man said proudly. He was in his early twenties, tall and thin. Fine wheat-colored hair covered his head. He had a mustache, too, but it was so fine and so light-colored that it was nearly impossible to see. Morgan could see the light of ambition in his eyes, as Ashby had mentioned.

"Well, then, listen to me, Lt. Dexter Pomeroy," Morgan said flatly. "You get in my way and I'll crush you like a bug."

"Very humorous, Marshal," Pomeroy said with a hollow laugh. "I'm the commander of Camp Brown and the Wind River Reservation. I'm the law here, Marshal, not you. You're in no position to make demands or issue orders."

Morgan's face was tight with anger, but his voice was calm and measured. "Send the doctor and the two privates outside, Lieutenant," he said.

"Why?"

"To avoid embarrassment."

Pomeroy shrugged. "Privates, head back to the Camp proper. Report to First Sergeant Bockman. Dr. Snyder, please wait outside. I'll be out shortly and we can ride back to the Camp together."

"Two Wounds," Morgan said, "I'd be obliged if you'd go see to my horse. He's been ridden hard and I'll need him again here very soon."

Two Wounds nodded. He and Old Belly headed out behind the soldiers.

When the five men had left a sneering Pomeroy turned back to face Morgan. The lawman grabbed the officer by his shirtfront and slammed him back against a stone wall and held him there.

"Now you listen to me, you pustulant little shit ball," Morgan hissed. "I aim to get the men who did this. And I neither need nor want your help. If you get in my way, I will shoot your ass dead without a second thought."

"Then you'd hang," Pomeroy blustered. He could not remember ever having been as scared as he was now. Still, he hoped to keep the others from seeing that fright.

Morgan shrugged. "You wouldn't be there to see it. That's all you have to keep in mind."

"Let him down, Buck," Ashby said wearily. "I'll see to it that the lieutenant stays here at the agency, or at the camp."

"You'll do no such thing," Pomeroy growled, forgetting his fear for a moment. "I am in charge here and . . ."

Morgan throttled him with his free hand. "The only thing you're in charge of here is your own fate. I could guarantee you didn't do anything to get in my way by killing you here and now. And let me warn you that I

125

would do it without guilt. Now, if you're willing to listen to a little sense, we might be able to solve this problem.''

Pomeroy, fear renewed and then some, nodded weakly.

Morgan pulled his hands away from Pomeroy. He pointed to a chair in front of Ashby's desk. "Sit."

Pomeroy did and then croaked, "Water."

Ashby poured him some from a pitcher and handed it to him. Pomeroy greedily gulped it down.

"Mr. Ashby told you when all this started happening that to send you and your men in would cause nothing but more trouble. The same still applies."

"Like hell," Pomeroy growled. Now that he was sitting and did not have his life being squeezed out of him, he felt far more brave. "I told Mr. Ashby that if these murders got out of hand, I and my troops would step in. Well, by God, they have gotten out of hand. By a long shot."

"Says who?" Morgan asked bluntly.

"Me."

"Yeah, and we all know you're a goddamn fool, so that means your opinion doesn't count for shit." He paused. "But let's just say you did get involved. What would you do?"

"Head on down to Flat Fork and put the town under martial law," Pomeroy boasted.

Morgan couldn't help it. He laughed, though it was devoid of humor. "You got what, fifty, maybe sixty men assigned here?"

"Sixty," Pomeroy said defensively.

"There's twice that many gunmen in Flat Fork, all of them hardened killers, and not a goddamn one who'll

126

worry for an instant at killin' a soldier—or a whole garrison of soldiers.''

''But we have arms, and cannon.''

''Except for the cannon, they've got you outgunned, Lieutenant,'' Morgan said. ''But their biggest advantage is not giving a shit. They don't care about each other, you, me, or their own goddamn sainted mothers.''

''But we are a trained, disciplined fighting force.''

''If those two shit balls you sent to get me in Flat Fork are any indication, your discipline and training are mere myth, Lieutenant. By the time you moved into ranks, half your men'd be dead or dyin'. The survivors'd get picked off one by one.'' Morgan paused to pour himself a mouthful of whiskey from the bottle on Ashby's desk.

''Besides, even if you could take over the town, how would you find the killers?''

''The leader should be easy enough to find, what with his necklace. Once we have him, we can find the others.''

''Supposin' he only wears that necklace when he heads up one of these raids?'' Morgan countered.

''Somebody'd talk,'' Pomeroy said with determination.

''Jesus, boy, you can't really be that goddamn stupid, can you?'' Morgan snapped. ''As soon as the town found out you were on your way, the place'd empty out. Come to think of it, you would be able to take over the town. Trouble is, the only ones left'd be the whores.''

''I'm afraid Marshal Morgan's right, Dex,'' Ashby said in soothing tones. ''You better let him handle this.''

"But . . ."

"Listen, Dex," Ashby snapped, angry now, too. "You'll need to keep your men ready in case the Shoshonis decide to go on the warpath. With these new murders, and knowing that the men who did it almost certainly had to come from Flat Fork, even Washakie might not be able to rein in some of the young hotheads."

"That's true, Lieutenant," Morgan offered.

"So you'll have to be ready in case that happens. If it does, you'll need to head off the Shoshonis. There's also the possibility that the Arapahos might hear that the Shoshonis think they did it, and they might plan to make war on Flat Fork or even Bubbling Water to show the Shoshonis that they were not at fault. That isn't likely, but it is a possibility."

"Neither of you is very damn convincing."

Morgan breathed in deeply and slowly blew the air out. "Lieutenant," he said slowly, "I've told you the way it's going to be. Now I've tried to be decent about it and sugar coat it some for you, but I'm tired of the bullshit. So I'll tell it to you plain just once more. You and your men are to stay out of this business, or die. It's that simple."

"Dex," Ashby interjected, "you've always been a reasonable man. You should be in this instance, too."

"But think how good this'd look on my record," Pomeroy said, a touch of whining in his voice.

"Think how it'd look on your record if you lost three-quarters of your command on a venture to make you look good," Morgan said bluntly.

Pomeroy glanced sharply at Morgan, and then nodded sadly.

"If it'll ease your mind any, Lieutenant," Morgan

said evenly, "you can take credit for the capture or killin' of these men once it's over. I don't really give a damn."

"You don't?" Ashby asked, surprised.

Morgan shook his head. "I did before today," he admitted. "I wanted to get these men and all, but it was just another job."

"And now?" Ashby prodded.

"Now it's personal. I don't hold with killin' women and children. And I don't hold with torturin' them and mutilatin' them either. Now I really want those shit balls, and there is nothing in heaven or hell or here on earth—includin' you and all your goddamn soldiers, Lieutenant—that'll stop me from findin' them. Except death. You want to stop me, Lieutenant, you'll have to put a bullet in me."

"Probably take more than one," Ashby said, *sotto voce.*

Pomeroy stared at Morgan for a few moments, then he nodded. "I'll stay out of it, Marshal—unless you get killed."

"I get killed, Lieutenant, you have my permission to hound those bastards to kingdom come." He paused a moment, thinking, then asked, "Just how the hell did Flat Fork get so far away from the camp here? Most towns like to build right outside a fort or camp."

"That's how Flat Fork began," Pomeroy said. "The first fort the army had in these parts was right next to Flat Fork. Two years later, this place was built here. The people—and it's a term I use mighty loosely when it comes to the ones down in Flat Fork—were all ready to move up this way and plant themselves here, lock, stock and barrel. But we informed them that if they moved up here, we'd train the cannon on them, and then use it, if necessary. They decided to stay where they were."

"I think they like it that way," Ashby interjected. "They can have all the lawlessness they can handle without interference from the army. Yet, being only twelve miles away, they're close enough so that the soldiers here can go down there and raise hell every payday."

Morgan nodded. "Convenient."

Chapter 16

Morgan and Two Wounds rode into Washakie's village just before dark. Two Wounds carried Yellow Wing's body. He swung off, heading for Old Belly's lodge. That Shoshoni had left Camp Brown when Two Wounds had gone to tend Morgan's horse and had ridden back to where his wife waited with the bodies of Sleeping Bear and Dawn Star. Two Wounds figured Old Belly was back, and he wanted to bring Yellow Wing there to be prepared for the funeral.

A terrible wailing gave the village an eerie cast as Morgan stopped in front of Washakie's lodge. Rabbit Tail, looking pale and upset, came up to take away his horse. Morgan nodded at the boy and gave his shoulder a soft, reassuring squeeze. "Man Above works in odd ways sometimes, boy," Morgan said softly.

Rabbit Tail nodded, but new tears were leaking from his eyes. "I will miss my friend."

"We'll all miss him, Rabbit Tail. He was a good young man, and would've been a fine warrior. But, believe me, Rabbit Tail, his death won't go unanswered."

Rabbit Tail nodded again and left with Morgan's

horse. Morgan wondered how much the boy really understood of what he had just said. Then he shrugged. It didn't matter. The boy had known that Morgan was understanding and sympathetic.

Morgan entered Washakie's roomy tepee and sat. Cloud Woman was there, as she often was. She hurried to make sure Morgan was comfortable against a willow backrest, and then to give him food. Morgan didn't really want to eat, but he remembered that he had not eaten anything since the rancid lunch in Flat Fork. The smell of the stew made him recall how hungry he was, and he ate with a fair amount of gusto.

Washakie said nothing while Morgan ate, and for some time afterward. He would let Morgan begin the talking.

Finally, Morgan said, "You know, of course?"

Washakie nodded solemnly.

"You know what the boy told Orv?"

Again the dignified nod.

"The soldier chief wants to chase after the men who've caused all the grief among the Shoshoni," Morgan said. "I've told him he'd be a damn fool to do it."

"You're full of shit," Washakie said.

"Reckon I am on that. I told him I'd kill him if he stuck his nose in this business."

"And you think you can catch these men by yourself?"

"Yes."

Washakie nodded, accepting the statement as true. "Is there anything I can do to help?" he asked.

"Keep your men from going on the war trail," Morgan said evenly. "They go out raidin', whether it's raids on whites or other Indians, the army's going to get involved, and then there'll be a lot of death. If you want to keep your people safe, or as safe as they can be, don't let them make war just now.''

"You are wise beyond your years, Buck," the old chief said. "I shall do as you ask."

"As if you hadn't thought of it yourself, eh." Morgan poured himself some coffee and then settled back again. "There's a few other things you can do, too, Washakie. For one, keep your people from going off alone. Tell your young men that if they want to seek a vision, then they can either wait or go with a group. If you don't have horse guards posted regularly now, start doin' so."

"You think they'd attack here?" Washakie asked, somewhat surprised.

"I doubt it, but there's no tellin' what those shit balls'll do," Morgan said, an edge of frustration in his voice.

"And where will you be during all this?" Washakie asked, knowing but wanting to be reassured.

"Out after them."

"You know where to find them?" Washakie asked.

"The only place they can hide out around here is Flat Fork, as far as I know. And even if not, they'll show up there sooner or later. They're the kind of men well suited to such a place."

"But you don't even know who they are or what they look like," Washakie noted.

"I know a little something about one of them."

"That's not much."

"It's a start."

"Would you like some of the warriors to go with you?" Washakie asked.

"No," Morgan said with a solid shake of his head.

"That'd only cause more trouble. If I go in there alone, even bein' a lawman, I might find one or two willin' to talk to me. I go in there with a couple of Shoshonis and there ain't a man or woman in Flat Fork that'd talk to me."

Washakie nodded. The old chief had known it all along. He had just wanted to make sure Morgan knew it, too. "Something else I can help with?" Washakie asked. "Your face tells me somethin' else bothers you."

"Yes, something troubles me. Something more than the murders. But I don't know if I should talk about it. It seems so small when compared with what's happened to the People here of late."

"If it troubles you, it is important, because if you don't find peace over it, your mind won't be on your job."

"Never thought of it that way."

"So tell me."

"Well, Washakie, I ain't sure how to go about this." His eyes drifted toward Cloud Woman. She was watching him but trying not to be seen at it. She smiled. "It's Cloud Woman," Morgan said, looking back at Washakie. "I'd like her to be mine, but I don't know how to go about it." He paused, sighing. "Makin' it worse is the fact that I don't have the time nor the patience to play at courtin' the way either of our people do." He paused again, gnawing at his mustache a little. "And I plan to hit the trail for Flat Fork tomorrow at first light."

Washakie sat nodding for a few moments, then called, "Come, granddaughter." When Cloud Woman came and sat next to him, Washakie asked in English, "Would you take this white man as a husband?"

"Yes," Cloud Woman whispered.

"Without the usual courting and rituals?" Washakie asked in Shoshoni. Again Cloud Woman answered in the affirmative. Washakie looked at Morgan. "It is usual to give a father horses for his daughter's hand."

"I have no horses, other than my own," Morgan answered frankly. "I have nothing much of anything."

"Would you be insulted if the white man pays no presents for your hand in marriage?" Washakie asked Cloud Woman in Shoshoni.

"No, grandfather."

"Then so it shall be. Find some friends and get that old lodge of mine. Raise it here near this one, you and your friends. Build a fire. Take what you need from here for your marriage bed, granddaughter. And some food."

Cloud Woman fairly beamed. At seventeen she was quite old for never having taken a husband. She had been finicky with those who had courted her, and so had driven most of them away. But her heart had turned over when she had first seen the tall, rangy, gruff-looking white man with the hair on his upper lip and the shiny badge pinned to his vest. She had never been more surprised than when he had asked to court her. She had never dreamed such a thing would be possible. And in just the few hours she had spent with him over the past several days, she had learned that she wanted him. That, too, had seemed an impossibility—until now.

Cloud Woman stood and hurried outside. Smiling, Washakie told Morgan what had just transpired. Morgan grinned a little then and asked. "So, I'm now a married man?"

"Well, not just yet. But when you have . . . dammit, what's that word . . . ?"

135

"Consummated," Morgan said helpfully.

"Yes, yes, that's the word. When you have consummated things, you'll be married."

"That wasn't very difficult."

Washakie shook his head. "Anything else?" he asked in mock exasperation.

"I think that about covers it all, Chief," Morgan said with a small chuckle. Then he grew serious again. "I'd advise you, though, to pass the word to the other bands to do what we talked about." He paused. Then he said with a sigh, "I might consider usin' some of your warriors if the outlaws head onto your land."

"We could be of great service in such a case, Buck."

"I figured you would."

They talked quietly of other things for a little while, and then Two Wounds entered the lodge.

"Everything taken care of?" Morgan asked.

Two Wounds nodded, and explained to Washakie. Then Morgan told Two Wounds what he was planning.

"I want to come," Two Wounds said flatly.

"No," Morgan said. He went through the reasons again, ending with, "I know Sleeping Bear was a good friend of yours, Two Wounds, but this is business best conducted by a white man in a white man's town. You wouldn't get ten feet inside Flat Fork before someone put a bullet through you."

Two Wounds didn't like it, but he acceded. He could do nothing else.

Morgan entered the tepee right behind Cloud Woman. It was much smaller than Washakie's and had almost nothing in it, except for a fire with a couple of cooking pots, a bed made of two heavy buffalo robes and a four-point blanket, a few boxes of Cloud Woman's possessions, and a willow backrest for Morgan.

"Are you hungry?" Cloud Woman asked shyly, her English passable.

"I ate before. At Washakie's," Morgan said. He suddenly felt like a teenager, a foolish youth who had bragged to his friends that he could do something when he knew damn well he didn't know how. It was an odd—and somewhat awkward—feeling for him.

Cloud Woman nodded, looking embarrassed. She felt as if she had been slapped. *How foolish I am,* she thought. *A woman ready for the marriage bed, but without any brains.*

Morgan suddenly realized that Cloud Woman was feeling as odd as he in this strange situation. It was expected, he knew, once he thought about it for a moment. It wasn't so much that they were unsure of being with the other sex; it was the fact that they were with a mate of another race. He knew next to nothing about the Shoshoni and their way of life. He suspected Cloud Woman knew a little more, but still not very much, about his people's ways.

Still, he knew full well that white men had been getting along with Indian women for a good many years. They, too, would work out some sort of arrangement. And it might as well start now, he told himself sternly.

"Would you think I was an old reprobate if I was to suggest we march straight on over to yonder bed and get to know each other?" he ventured.

Cloud Woman was not sure she understood all the words her new husband had said, but she got the gist of it. She smiled brightly, suddenly feeling better. She still harbored a thought or two that he might just be using her, but she hoped there was more to this night than just that.

Morgan swept her into his arms and kissed her hard. Cloud Woman responded eagerly. When they broke apart Cloud Woman was a little breathless, but she stepped back. Undoing the knots at the top of her dress over each shoulder, she watched Morgan's face as her buckskin dress fell off her, leaving her standing there in nothing but moccasins and leggings.

"Lordy, woman, but if you ain't a sight," Morgan breathed.

Smiling and proud, Cloud Woman sashayed over to the bed and sat. Morgan watched as Cloud Woman removed her leggings and moccasins. He could feel himself reacting strongly to her.

"Well?" Cloud Woman queried, sounding much more assured than she felt.

"Guess I am a mite overdressed for the occasion, ain't I?" Morgan said. He unhooked his gunbelt and set it down alongside the bed, where it would be in easy reach if he needed it. He sat and pulled out the Bowie knife stuck in his boot and jabbed it into the ground at the side of the buffalo robes. Then he pulled off the boots, stood, and removed the rest of his clothing.

Looking into Cloud Woman's smoldering dark eyes, Morgan knelt on the bed and took Cloud Woman into his arms.

Chapter 17

Saying goodbye to Cloud Woman the next morning was one of the hardest things Morgan had ever been called on to do. He wasn't sure why he had fallen in love with the beautiful young Shoshoni woman right from the start; it was sufficient, he thought, that it had happened. Now he was not so sure it had been a good idea.

Then he laughed at himself a little. Falling in love with Cloud Woman wasn't an idea at all; it was simply something that was. It had happened, catching him unawares, but there was little he could have done about it at the beginning, and there was nothing he could do about it now.

Still, knowing he was going off to make war on a bunch of savage men who butchered people for excitement did not make his leaving Cloud Woman any easier. He wished they had a week or a month to get to know each other, to explore each other, to learn each other's ways. But they didn't. They had had one night, and one night only. He would have to be satisfied with that.

He knew that in reality he did have a choice. He

could toss away his badge and ride up into the beautiful, snow-capped Wind River Mountains so nearby and lose himself with her there. But he knew that such a thing would be like a raccoon trying to wipe away the circles around his eyes. He was a lawman by choice and by desire. He could do no less than his best on whatever task he was called on to perform.

He and Cloud Woman stood in the soft new dawn behind their lodge, holding each other. They had already told each other—several dozen times, it seemed—they wished Morgan didn't have to go. Now Morgan simply said, "You heed what Washakie says to do. I don't want you goin' out by yourself for anything. You stay close to the village."

"I will."

"You better," Morgan threatened with a loving hug. "I come back here and find you've gotten yourself killed and I'm going to be one hell of an angry man."

Cloud Woman nodded and smiled up at him. "I'll be all right," she said. She knew it would do no good to tell him that she would be devastated if he went out and got himself killed, which at the moment looked likely. Such expressions would hurt him, and in turn that would hurt her. No, she figured a woman was better off keeping such things to herself.

Morgan looked up as Two Wounds, Old Belly, Big Horse, and Red Hand rode up. They stopped next to Morgan's saddled horse.

"Where're you boys headin'?" Morgan asked, sure he knew the answer.

"With you," Two Wounds said flatly.

Morgan shook his head. "No, Two Wounds. We went through this last night. Those bastards in Flat Fork'll kill all of you just for the hell of it."

"We'll ride with you to the edge of our land," Two Wounds said. "We'll wait for you there. Then we'll ride back here with you. As protection. If anyone dares attack you, they'll have to deal with the four of us."

"You give me your word you'll not go into Flat Fork?" Morgan asked, skeptical.

"We won't go into Flat Fork," Two Wounds said flatly. "Unless we hear you have died or are being held there."

"Well, let's hope that don't happen," Morgan said. "I'd hate like hell to have your deaths on my hands, too." He gave Cloud Woman one last kiss and pushed her away. "Go on, now," he said. He gave her a gentle push and swatted her buttocks lightly with his hand. He watched as she walked away. *You're a damn fool, Buck Morgan,* he told himself silently. *A great big, oversized, goddamn idiot.* He pulled himself onto his horse.

As he rode, Morgan let the anger build up in his chest again. By the time he reached Flat Fork he was in a rage, though he kept it bottled up pretty well. But every time he thought about Yellow Wing, and the boy's mother, he would come dangerously close to blowing his top.

Half a mile outside Flat Fork, he and the Shoshoni stopped. It was just before noon. "This is close enough for you boys," he said firmly. When the others nodded he moved off again, resisting the urge to turn and make sure the Shoshoni were staying put.

Morgan rode straight to Foster's saloon and dismounted. With the cocked scattergun in hand, he strolled inside. Only six men—plus Foster—were in the foul den.

Foster spotted him and looked like he had just soiled his pants. He frantically scrambled for the pistol he had gotten the previous afternoon since another shotgun was not available. He stopped his search, though, when Morgan shook his head. Foster wisely put his hands on the plank bar.

Morgan stopped alongside the near edge of the bar. He picked up a bottle sitting there and tossed it toward the back of the room. The bottle left a trail of airborne whiskey and clunked off the log wall with a dull thud.

The five patrons of the saloon looked around to see where the projectile had come from. "Now that I've got your attention," Morgan said, "I'd like to ask you shit balls if you know a man who wears a rather special necklace."

"What's the necklace look like?" one man asked, more to give someone lip than actually seeking information.

"If you have to ask that, you either don't know the man or you're a goddamn idiot."

Another man went for his gun, figuring Morgan was distracted by the first man.

Morgan fired one barrel of the scattergun. What remained of the man was not a pretty sight. "Any of you other shit balls want to make a move?" Morgan's voice was cold, hard.

Four heads shook slowly.

"Mr. Foster," Morgan said, "get your bucket."

"Ah, Jesus, Marshal," the bartender complained, "not again."

"Yes, again. And move your fat ass."

With a sigh, Foster picked up a bucket of cheap whiskey and held it out as his four living patrons deposited their firearms in the pail. A potential customer stepped inside during the procedure, saw what was going on, and quickly backed out. There were more than enough saloons in Flat Fork. A man didn't have to get himself involved in whatever was going on at one; he needed only to walk a few yards for another place.

The four men filed out, one after another. The third to leave suddenly popped up in the door again, a small belly gun in his hand. He fired once, but it went wild. Morgan let go the second blast from the scattergun and the man went down in a pile of arms, legs, blood, and entrails.

"You got any more shells for this scattergun, Foster?" Morgan asked.

Foster nodded. "In a crate back behind the bar," he said.

Morgan nodded, and caught himself just before telling Foster to get them. There was every chance that Foster had another gun under there. Morgan walked behind the plank bar and squatted, looking for the shotgun shells. And then the world crashed in on him.

Foster, seeing this as a chance—perhaps his only chance—of getting rid of this annoying marshal, as well as gaining some meager amount of vengeance, dropped his bucket and dove. He landed on the planks, resting on their wobbly supports. The planks went down with him, and it all landed on Morgan.

"Shit," Morgan managed to get out as he found himself smashed to the floor.

"I gotcha now, you pain in the ass," Foster growled as he got up and began flinging wood and other debris out of the way. He grabbed Morgan—who was still a little stunned—and slammed his back up against the log wall behind them. "I'll teach you, you goddamn irritatin' son of a bitch. Goddamn right, I will." He smashed Morgan's back up against the wall again and yet again. Then he spun in a half turn, dragging Morgan with him, and finally pitched Morgan across the room.

Morgan lost the scattergun and his hat as he bounced along the floor. He stopped against a table leg and pushed himself up. He felt shaky, but at least he was on his feet as he saw the bulky bartender charging at him.

Morgan ducked and caught Foster on his shoulder. Praying he had enough strength left, he pushed upright, shoving Foster's legs as he did. The bartender flew over Morgan and landed on his back, where he bounced.

Morgan took a few deep breaths to steady himself. He was sore, but he was fairly certain he had broken no bones nor done any serious damage to himself. He stepped up and kicked Foster in the face as the bartender tried to stand. Foster groaned and fell back.

The lawman turned and retrieved the scattergun. Then he went to where the bar had been and kicked aside debris until he found a box of shotgun shells. He grabbed a handful and stuffed the shells into a vest pocket. He did the same with the other pocket. He stuffed a few more in his pants pocket and then loaded the shotgun.

Morgan walked outside and got a pair of handcuffs he kept in his saddlebags. Then he went back inside. Foster had gotten up, but he looked weak and shaky.

"Put these on, shit ball," Morgan said, throwing the handcuffs at Foster.

"Why?" Foster asked dully.

"You're under arrest."

Foster still seemed a little stunned as he put the handcuffs on.

"Outside," Morgan ordered.

"Where're you takin' me?" Foster asked nervously as he walked outside. "There's no jail here." He was recovering some, and starting to feel a little cocky. "No law, either."

"Where I'm going to take you, there ain't a jail either, but you won't go nowhere. You got a horse?"

Foster looked scared. "At the livery."

Morgan nodded and mounted his horse. "Walk," he commanded. With scattergun in hand, butt resting against his right thigh, Morgan followed the bartender to the livery stable. There, Morgan said, "Saddle shit ball's horse, and be goddamn quick about it."

"Jesus, Marshal," the man said, "can't it wait? I'm up to my ass in work here."

"You're going to be up to your ass in your own goddamn blood, you don't have that horse saddled and out here in five minutes."

The man shivered when he looked into Morgan's cold gray eyes. "Yessir, Marshal. Right away." He hustled away. Three and a half minutes later, he came back with Foster's horse.

"Get on," Morgan said icily. When Foster had done so Morgan said, "Out. South end of town."

With a growing sense of dread, Foster got his horse moving. He was sweating as he rode, but he knew it wasn't from the heat. Or at least not totally. Having everyone stop and watch him was embarrassing, too. He was a big man, and used to keeping order in his saloon by brute force more often than not. Having these others seeing him being taken out of town in handcuffs was disheartening.

As they neared Foster's saloon, Morgan said, "Stop." He spotted a man peering cautiously into the saloon. "Hey, pard," he called. When the man looked at him Morgan said, "This here's the man who runs that shithole. And since he's here, there ain't nobody inside."

"Nobody watchin' the whiskey?" the man asked, interest sparkling in his eyes.

"Nope."

"Good gawddamn almighty," the man said. He looked as if he had struck the mother lode.

"All right, shit ball," Morgan said to Foster. "Ride on."

Foster built up a nice dose of hatred to go with his fear as he rode out of town. It wasn't bad enough he was trussed up like a Christmas turkey, but Morgan had just given everyone on Flat Fork license to raid his saloon. It wasn't very neighborly to take away a man's livelihood. And that angered him to no end. He'd get back at this marshal one way or another, he vowed.

Chapter 18

Herb Foster gave up all idea of vengeance half a mile outside of Flat Fork. There was simply no room for such thoughts amid the total, absolute terror that had suddenly clutched at his testes and robbed his spine of much of its rigidity.

"Is this one of 'em?" Two Wounds asked, pointing his bow at Foster.

Morgan shrugged. "I don't know, but I don't think so."

"Why'd you bring him out here then?"

"I figure there's a good chance he might know somethin' about the killers. So I brought him along in case he needed a little persuadin' to part with what information he might have."

Two Wounds grinned as he came right up alongside Foster and shoved his face within inches of the bartender's. He wrinkled up his nose and backed off right away. "Damn, Buck," he said, "the sumbitch's wet his pants. Goddamn if that don't beat all."

"I'm surprised he ain't shit in them," Morgan commented matter-of-factly as he dismounted. "Get down,

shit ball," he said to Foster. "Then go sit over there."
He pointed.

"We gonna work on him here?" Big Horse asked.
He sounded eager.

"No," Morgan responded. "We're too close to Flat
Fork. Those shits down there hear it, they're liable to
get drunk enough to come out here and kill some Indians."

"Damn," Big Horse muttered. He was a man with
an apropos name. He was about Morgan's height—
six-four or so—but packed thirty or forty pounds more
on his frame than Morgan did. He was a fierce and
ferocious man when he wanted to be, too. At other
times, he was like an overgrown boy. And no matter
what mood he was in, he remained something of an
enigma to Morgan.

"Why'd you stop here, then?" Two Wounds asked.

Morgan shrugged. "Just to see if anything happens.
Besides, I'm hungry."

"You're always hungry," Two Wounds said with a
laugh.

"That don't make no sense," Big Horse added.
"Not when he's full of shit." He, too, started laughing, and the others—including Morgan—quickly joined
in.

Sitting in terror nearby, Herb Foster began to think
he had come completely unhinged. Here he was, sitting
amid a pack of wild savages with a federal marshal,
and they were making jokes. It was incomprehensible.
The only explanation for all this absurdity was that he
had lost his mind, because if it was real . . . He
couldn't even contemplate that.

Half an hour later, Morgan rose and said, "Time
to ride, my friends."

"Where to?" Two Wounds asked.

"Up toward the Little Wind."

The men rode in silence, pacing their horses. As he rode, Foster still tried to make sense out of this surreal tableau in which he had found himself inserted. The Shoshoni were quite frightening, yet in another way, they seemed so . . . "normal" was the only word he could think of. They were all relatively tall, and their backs were straight. They rode like they were part of their ponies. They smelled funny, though, and seemed to be covered with grease. *They're all little better than animals,* he thought, never giving a thought to his own filthy pants and shirt and the stench of whiskey that seemed to be a permanent part of him.

Just past noon, Two Wounds, who had been riding several hundred yards ahead of the others, rode back and moved up to pace Morgan. "Someone's comin'," he said.

"Who?"

"Blue coats."

"Shit. How far?"

"Half a mile, maybe less."

Morgan nodded. "You best let me handle this, but there might be some goddamn trouble. That goddamn Pomeroy strikes me as an ass. So you and the others best stay ready. There's no tellin' but what Pomeroy might decide to get fractious."

Big Horse, who had pulled alongside, said, "I hope he does. It's been too long since I've had a good fight."

"You take some blue coat's bullet in that big fat belly of yours, you'll most likely'll change your mind on that," Morgan said. He trotted ahead so that he was in the lead.

The other riders bunched up a little closer, with Fos-

149

ter right behind Morgan, flanked by Big Horse and Red Hand. Two Wounds and Old Belly brought up the rear, hemming Foster in.

Morgan could see the cloud of dust kicked up by the soldiers. It grew closer and closer, until Morgan could see the soldiers themselves. Morgan stopped and let the troopers come to him.

Lieutenant Pomeroy held up his hand, stopping his men about twenty feet from Morgan, who was glad to see that Pomeroy had only eight men with him.

"A little out of your regular haunts, aren't you, Lieutenant?" Morgan said more than asked.

"The entire reservation is my area, Marshal. You know that as well as I do."

Morgan shrugged.

"Who's that back there?"

"A prisoner," Morgan said flatly.

"A prisoner guarded by Shoshonis? Highly irregular, I would think."

"I didn't know you could think. You've not shown any evidence of it that I've been able to see."

Pomeroy's face reddened when he heard some snickers from his men. "What's he charged with?"

"That's none of your business."

"I can make it my business."

"You can't do shit."

"Is he one of the murderers?"

"I don't think so," Morgan said honestly. "But he might have some information that'll lead me to them."

Pomeroy nodded thoughtfully. "Well, I'll just take him off your hands. I'll bring him back to the camp and interrogate . . ." He stopped and his eyes widened. "That's why you've brought him on the reservation," he said. "To have the savages torture him to extract information. Have you gone mad?"

Morgan said nothing, since he was fighting back a grin.

"Well, I'm afraid I simply can't allow that."

"Lieutenant," Morgan said, finally giving in a little to annoyance, "I am sick and tired of you and your officious bullshit. If you stayed back at the camp, like you were supposed to, we wouldn't be having this problem. But no, you had to go stickin' your nose into business that's not your affair and that you can do little about."

"If it's on the Wind River Reservation, it's my business," an angry Pomeroy insisted.

"You remember what I told you back at Ashby's?"

"Yes." Pomeroy's jaw was tight, but his eyes betrayed his worry and fear.

"Well, Lieutenant," Morgan said harshly, "you best turn you and your boys around and head back to Camp Brown." He left off the *or else,* thinking it not necessary. Despite his earlier comment, Morgan knew Pomeroy was plenty smart. It was just a matter of letting his head rule his heart. Morgan hoped Pomeroy could do it this time. Morgan had no desire to start a bloodbath. On the other hand, he could not allow Pomeroy's interference, if only for his own pride in his abilities as a lawman. Still, if even one shot were fired, this would become a bloodbath. Most of the blue coats had, Morgan figured, seen battle before; and all the Shoshoni had, too.

"When this is over, Marshal," Pomeroy finally said in a tight voice, "you'll have to answer to me."

"I'll meet you anytime, anywhere—after this is done

151

with. Until that time, keep away from me, the Sho-shonis, and Flat Fork.''

Pomeroy glared at Morgan. Then he viciously jerked his horse's head around and moved off. His men followed slowly. As Private Skousen rode by, he sneered at Morgan. The lawman leaned over a little and spit. It landed on Skousen's light blue wool pants just above the knee. Skousen's face turned livid.

When the soldiers had passed by Morgan and his group moved on. Before he went out to scout Two Wounds pulled up to Morgan. "At one point when you were talking with the soldier chief, I notice you almost smiled. Why?" Two Wounds asked.

"You remember what he had just said?"

"No. Not that I can think of."

"He accused me of bringin' Foster to the reservation here so I could have you savages torture him to get information. It's true, but what that shit ball doesn't know is that by openin' his big mouth the way he did he made our job easier."

"How?"

"Hell, Foster was ready to shit his pants as soon as he saw you. Hell, he did piss them. With Pomeroy makin' that accusation, Foster's got to be real worried. That'll soften him up if he has half a day or so to think about what you 'savages' are going to do to him."

Two Wounds grinned. "Maybe the soldier chief ain't so bad after all, hey?"

"Bullshit. He's still a goddamn idiot."

Two Wounds laughed as he galloped ahead to take his position ahead of the others. They rode on, feeling the day's heat baking their heads. Finally, about mid-afternoon, Two Wounds stopped. Morgan rode up alongside him.

"This look good?" Two Wounds asked.

Morgan nodded.

Big Horse and Old Belly began setting up a small camp. Morgan, Two Wounds, and Red Hand took care of the horses.

Foster sat leaning back against a cottonwood tree. At least at first. Fifteen minutes after arriving, Foster looked around. Everyone seemed busy, and no one was paying him any mind at all. Licking his lips, he pushed his back against the tree trunk to get up. His knees trembled with fear, but he had to get away. He sidled off, trying not to make a sound. He had no real plan, other than to get away. He would have liked to be able to get to Morgan's gear and get the key to the handcuffs, but he couldn't. He would simply have to wait until he got back to Flat Fork. Then he could have the blacksmith get them off.

A hundred yards away, Foster began to run. In moments his heart was pounding and his breath was hard to catch. A stitch started in his side. Less than a hundred yards later, he stopped running, and settled for walking. He glanced back a few times, expecting pursuit at any moment. But none seemed to be coming. He walked on with more certainty.

Breathing a little more eas he pushed on, more slowly than he wanted, but knowing that he would never be able to last if he went at any faster a pace than a medium walk. Suddenly he heard something behind him. He whirled, and then lost control of his anal sphincter when he spotted two Shoshoni bearing down on him in a rush. Mounted on their ponies, they were a terrifying sight as they yipped and howled.

The odor of feces wafted up to his nostrils and seemed to shake him out of his lethargy. He turned and began running. He did not get far before Big Horse cut in front of him. Big Horse's pony reared. The warrior let out with several "ow-ow-ows" as his pony came back to earth. Then Big Horse dropped a horsehair rope loop around Foster's neck. "You come me," he grunted. "Or me take 'um hair."

Nearby, Red Hand sat on his pony and laughed. Big Horse might be a ferocious warrior, but he had a marvelous facility for languages, plus he had an excellent education. He could speak English better than many white men could.

The two Shoshoni, mounted bareback, escorted Foster back to their camp. The overweight bartender walked between the two ponies, his face pasty white from fear.

"Took you long enough," Morgan said when the three were back in camp.

"He needed time to shit," Big Horse said with a laugh.

"In his pants, I take it," Morgan said, wrinkling his nose.

Big Horse nodded, still laughing.

"Go sit, Mr. Foster," Morgan said. "You try another stupid stunt like that and whoever catches you will break or cut off one of your body parts."

Shaking, Foster stumbled back to his tree, where he huddled, trying to climb into himself. He cried and blubbered until his nose ran and coated the lower half of his shirt.

Chapter 19

Foster looked up, a deeper terror taking hold of him. He was surprised to see Morgan standing above him with a steaming tin mug in one hand and a hunk of roasted meat on the point of a big knife in the other.

"That for me?" he asked stupidly.

Morgan nodded, and Foster took the proffered food, pulling the meat off the knife. He wiped a sleeve across his snot-smeared face and bit into the food, hungrily gobbling the half-raw meat. He finished his coffee pretty quickly and wished he hadn't. He wanted more but was too frightened to ask for it.

He watched in fear as one of the Shoshoni—the big, beefy one—came toward him. Big Horse stopped and squatted in front of Foster, his face a mask of fierceness. Then he suddenly said, "You want some more coffee?" He burst into wild laughter at the look of terror on Foster's face.

"Hey, Big Horse," Morgan yelled. "Leave the shit ball alone, dammit."

"I only asked him if he wanted some more coffee," Big Horse answered without rising. "Well, do you, shit ball?'' He laughed a little again. ''That's a funny name—shit ball. How'd you get it?''

Foster's mouth worked, but only some funny little squeaks were emitted.

Morgan strolled up. ''Go on back to the fire, Big Horse,'' he said calmly. ''You can terrify shit ball here later.''

''You're no goddamn fun at all,'' Big Horse growled, but he grinned at Morgan.

''You want more coffee?'' Morgan asked.

''Yes, please,'' Foster whispered, as if he were afraid the sky would fall on him if he spoke any louder.

Morgan took the cup, went to the fire, filled the cup, and then brought it back to Foster. ''Enjoy,'' he said evenly.

Foster looked up at Morgan, fear turning his watery eyes into great, round, dark circles. ''Why're you doin' this to me?'' he asked plaintively.

''You know goddamn well why, shit ball.'' Morgan stood staring down at the chubby bartender, almost feeling sorry for him. Then he left.

Dark came soon after, and once again Morgan walked over to Foster. He picked up the tin cup. ''Best get some sleep, shit ball,'' Morgan said. ''And for Christ's sake, don't try runnin' away again, dammit. Big Horse'll be one ugly-mad son of a bitch if he has to go chasin' you down again.''

''Well, if he kilt me, I wouldn't have to undergo your goddamn torturin' now, would I?''

''You think that if Big Horse—or any of us—had to go traipsin' after you, we'd kill you quick and fast?''

''No,'' Foster said meekly.

''Good. Now shut up and go to sleep.'' Seeing the fear in Foster's eyes increase, he added, ''You don't have to worry about these boys. They won't hurt you while you're asleep."

In the morning, Morgan brought Foster some breakfast. When the meal was over Morgan and the four Shoshoni squatted in a semicircle around Foster.

"The time's come, shit ball," Morgan said flatly. "You know what information we're lookin' for. You tell us what you know about the men we're interested in, we'll take you back to Flat Fork. If you try to give me a hard time, I'll turn you over to these Shoshoni here."

He paused to let that sink in a few moments. "Now," he continued, "they ain't near as adept at torturin' folks as the Blackfeet or the Apache—or so I've been told—but they can come up with a few ideas, I'd wager."

Foster licked his lips nervously. "I don't know much. I really don't. I swear."

Morgan shrugged. "Then tell me what little you do know."

"I can't," Foster whined.

"Why not?"

"They'll kill me sure as hell."

"And you think we won't?" Morgan asked harshly. "Let me tell you something, shit ball: If those others kill you, it'll be over quick and fast. My friends here do the job, you'll die in great pain, and it'll take a long time. I can guarantee you that."

Foster drew in a breath that shuddered and quivered both on the way in and on the way back out. "The leader of the gang that's killin' the Injuns is Del Murdock," Foster finally said in a wavering voice. "He has maybe ten men that ride with him at times."

"What's he look like?" Morgan asked. He had a

157

name now. If it was the right name, he stood a chance of making use of that snippet of information.

"He's a tall feller, Murdock is. Not quite as tall as you, maybe, but more burly. He has real clear blue eyes, and he almost always dresses in fine style. He's got a well-trimmed mustache and long, thick sideburns. But two things make him stand out—a necklace of dried human ears and fingers that he wears about all the time, and his laugh. It's crazy somehow. I don't know how else to describe it."

Morgan's face betrayed nothing, but his heart was racing. He knew now that Del Murdock was the man he was looking for. He nodded and then asked, "Do you know the names of some of the other men who ride with him?"

"A few," Foster said. He had been watching the big Indian, the one Morgan had called Big Horse, and that scared him to no end. He did not want any of the Shoshoni torturing him, most especially the vicious-looking Big Horse. So he found it easier to talk than he had thought he would.

"Give me names, and some descriptions of other members of Murdock's gang."

Foster thought a few minutes, trying to put faces to names. Then he said. "Norm Nordmeyer is closest to Murdock. Nordmeyer's the opposite of Murdock—he's real short and don't hardly weigh nothin' at all. He's a fiesty little bastard, though. He's got himself one hell of a temper."

Foster stopped. "Can I have some coffee, Marshal?" he asked quietly. "I'm parched with all this talkin'."

Morgan nodded. Over his shoulder he said, "One of you boys please get shit ball here some coffee."

158

While he waited, Morgan pulled out a thin cigar and lit it.

Red Hand gave Foster a tin mug filled with thick black coffee. Foster nodded in thanks, trying to suppress a shudder of fear at the proximity of the Indian. He took a sip as Red Hand went back to his position.

"That's better," Foster said, feeling a small sense of relief. "Other men who run with Murdock are Cliff Bagley and Henry Coates. Both are pretty nondescript sorts of fellers. You'd never be able to pick Bagley out in a crowd, and the only way you could do it with Coates is by his left eye. It points off in whatever direction it has a mind to."

Morgan nodded. "Any others?"

Foster was almost beginning to enjoy this. He had never really been the center of attention before. As a bartender, people generally took him for granted, as if he were part of the furnishings. Still, that had allowed him to overhear a lot of things that men would normally not want people to know about. Such as the names of some of Murdock's men.

"Let's see, there's Al Oberman, a big, fat feller—fatter'n me even—who has a reputation for being a sadistic man. He likes to torture people before he kills them, from what I've heard. And then there's Ward Haggerty. He looks like a damn preacher. He's always clean-shaved and scrubbed. Looks like butter wouldn't melt in his mouth. But I've heard he's also a nasty bastard, particularly when it comes to women."

Morgan nodded again. Foster knew a lot more about the marauders than he had thought the fat bartender would. "That's five," Morgan noted. "You said there were ten, maybe more. You know any others?"

"A few," Morgan said after some moments'

thought. "Let's see, there's also Roscoe Davidson. He thinks he's a dandy, what with wearing his derby and tie all the time. And Russ Quinn. Oh, but ain't he a character. Got a great big goddamn nose, enough for two or three people. And a couple new fellers. They just started runnin' with Murdock the past couple of months or so. Brothers named Spangler."

Two Wounds, sitting behind Morgan, could tell just from the sudden stiffening of Morgan's back that the names were familiar to Morgan. "You know them, Buck?" he asked.

Morgan nodded. "Couple of shit balls used to have their own outlaw enterprise down around South Pass City and thereabouts. I was huntin' them just before I come out here. I got the Spanglers' two brothers, Avery and Manny, plus another set of brothers—Ronny, Rob, and Roger Cochrane. I never could track the last two bastards down, though. Now I know why."

"You know what they look like then?" Foster asked.

Morgan shrugged. "Only from their likenesses on handbills. Any more?"

Foster shook his head as he grew frightened again. While he had been dispensing information, he had felt at least a little safe. None of the men facing him had made any move against him then. But now that he was out of information, he began to worry about his life. They might consider him useless now; he was certain he was going to be killed, after being tortured.

"They have any one place in Flat Fork where they hang their hats?" Morgan asked.

Foster shook his head again. "They frequent all the saloons—includin' mine every now and again—and whorehouses in Flat Fork." He paused, and then said thoughtfully, "You know, come to think of it, I ain't seen them in town for several days. Maybe they've ridden on.''

"They've ridden on the reservation here is where they've ridden. Those shit balls've killed three more Shoshini in the past two days.''

"Four," Old Belly said quietly from behind Morgan. "Yellow Wing, too.''

Morgan nodded, not looking back. "Four that we know of. There might be others.''

"I'm sorry," Foster said. He was sincere, but he wasn't sure if his captors knew that.

"You are sorry," Morgan said sarcastically, "that's for goddamn sure.''

"What now, Buck?" Two Wounds asked.

"I go huntin' for Del Murdock and his gang," Morgan said flatly.

"We go hunting for Del Murdock and his gang," Big Horse said. "Lame Bear was my friend. I must avenge him.''

Morgan looked back over his shoulder. Big Horse had a mean, determined set to his wide, flat face. Morgan decided he would not want to have Big Horse on his trail. Morgan nodded and looked back at Foster.

"What about him?" Red Hand asked.

Morgan knew who Red Hand was talking about. "I reckon we ought to take shit ball back to Flat Fork.''

"Why?" Big Horse growled. "That'll waste time.''

"One reason is that I promised him. For another, Murdock just might be back in Flat Fork.''

Big Horse grunted an assent, still not really liking the idea. "When do we leave?" he asked.

"Soon's we get the horses ready," Morgan said, standing.

Chapter 20

The Shoshoni waited where they had the day before while Morgan rode into Flat Fork with Foster. The bartender was still scared half out of his wits. Even though he was no longer in the company of the fearsome Shoshoni, he was almost equally afraid of Del Murdock and his men. They would kill him without a thought if they learned that he had revealed their identities to a federal lawman.

The two rode straight to the livery, where Foster left his horse. Morgan climbed down from his own horse and uncuffed Foster. "You pull anything stupid against me," Morgan warned, "and I'll come back with the Shoshonis and pay you a visit. You got that?"

Foster nodded nervously.

"Then get goin', shit ball. If you're lucky, you might have somethin' left of your saloon."

Morgan watched for a few minutes as Foster waddled swiftly down the dusty street. Then he climbed up on his horse and rode off, stopping at the first saloon he came to. He spent the best part of that day going from one saloon to another. Unlike the last time, though, now he made no pretense at drinking. He simply walked in, fired off one barrel of the scatter-gun to gain attention, and then asked loudly if anyone in the place had heard of Del Murdock, Norm Nordmeyer, Henry Coates, Al Obermann, Ward Haggerty, or Kevin and Jess Spangler. When he got a resounding response of silence he would head to the next saloon.

He got not so much as one person nodding, let alone offering information. He had hit every saloon and every bordello in Flat Fork by dusk. He was hungry, and he looked at the fetid restaurant. But he could not torture himself that much. Instead, he stopped at the mercantile.

"What can I do for you, Marshal?" a strapping young man asked.

"First off, a box of shotgun shells. Ten-gauge, double-ought buck, if you got them."

"We sure do." The young man walked off and returned a minute later with a box of shells that he placed on the counter. "Anything else?"

"You have anything to eat in here?"

The man laughed. "I see you've tried Morty's place down the street."

Morgan nodded. "Couple of days ago. My stomach still hasn't forgiven me for it."

"I know what you mean. Well, we've got jerky—both buffalo and beef; canned love apples; salted beef; bacon; beans; some antelope brought in just this mornin'; fresh apples and peaches and grapes . . . Anything strike your fancy?"

"Most of it," Morgan admitted. "Give me some beef jerky, some bacon, beans. You have any biscuits?"

"Just hardtack."

"Throw some of them in. And half a dozen apples."

As the young man began gathering up the items, he said, "We don't get many lawmen in Flat Fork, Marshal. You come to clean the place up?" He grinned.

"Only way this hellhole'd get cleaned up is to put a lucifer to it and then start from scratch."

"I agree. Definitely agree."

"You seem awfully out of place in Flat Fork, too, Mister . . . ?"

"Applegate. Alvin Applegate. Most folks call me Vin. And, yes, I do seem out of place. I feel that way more often than not, too. But I persevere."

"Don't the scum that run in this town bother you?"

"They did some when I first came here. I finally beat the shit out of a couple of them, and shot two others dead. Then I told the rest that I'd kill anyone else who messed with me. I also told them that I'd prefer to be something of a neutral spot in Flat Fork. That if opposing fellows were in here they could not fight or cause argument. They accepted that—reluctantly, I must admit, at first, but they grew more accustomed to it. I've had no real trouble with the people of Flat Fork in three years."

"You're either crazy or a nervy bastard," Morgan commented honestly.

"Perhaps a little—or a lot—of both," Applegate said with a laugh. He stopped working to look directly at Morgan. "You're a pretty nervy bastard yourself, Marshal. There's not many men who'd ride into Flat Fork alone, wearing a badge. That's an open invitation to assassination. How'd you get away with it?"

Morgan shrugged. "For one, I showed right off that I wasn't here to clean up the town, as you put it. Second, I took on several gunmen and laid them in their graves. But I think the main reason," he added with a little grin, "is the same way you got away with what you did. We just acted like we had more balls than everyone else in town."

Applegate laughed loudly as he went back to his work. "I believe you might be right about that, Marshal . . . What is your name, anyway?"

"Buck Morgan."

"You been a lawman long, Marshal?"

"Too goddamn long, I sometimes think." He thought for a moment. "Guess it's been close to ten years now."

Applegate finally stopped at the counter, a small pile of packages in front of him. "Well, that's it—unless you've forgotten something?"

"A couple of those cheroots you have there," He pointed. He put them into his shirt pocket.

"Anything more?"

Morgan grinned and pulled the top off a jar sitting on the counter. He dipped in and came up with a handful of sour balls. He dropped them on the counter. "That'll do it for certain."

When he had paid and his purchases were in a sack Morgan asked, "You know Del Murdock and his ilk?"

Applegate nodded.

"You know where I can find them?"

"That why you're here, for Murdock and his men?" Applegate countered.

Morgan nodded.

"Why?"

"That's none of your concern. Now, I asked you a question, and I'm still awaitin' an answer."

"No, I don't know where you could find them. And even if I did, I probably wouldn't tell you."

"Oh?" Morgan asked, raising his eyebrows in question.

"It's like this, Marshal," Applegate said uneasily. "When I offered this as a neutral meeting place for the many competing interests in Flat Fork, I also meant that I would stay neutral. If nobody bothers me, I'm not going to point a finger at them. Murdock's honored my position all along. I plan to honor his privacy."

"A noble attitude, Mr. Applegate," Morgan said without too much sarcasm. "I hope that it works well for you."

"It has so far, Marshal," Applegate said with a shrug. "But as for it continuing, who knows? We all do what we can."

Morgan touched the brim of his hat and then picked up his parcels. "Good day, Mr. Applegate." Morgan found that he had liked the young store owner, despite his unwillingness to provide any information. Morgan trotted out of town. Hooking up with the Shoshoni again, they rode for another two or three miles and stopped to make their camp.

"Did you learn anything in Flat Fork?" Two Wounds asked as the five men sat down to a supper of bacon, beans, and fresh antelope and rabbit the warriors had taken during the long day of waiting.

"Not a single goddamn thing. Nobody knows anything, nobody's heard anything, nobody's done anything. You'd think they were a goddamn bunch of saints." Seeing the blank looks on the Shoshonis' faces, he added, "Helpers of Man Above. They were humans so pure and wondrous that God picked them to be at his side for all times."

166

The Shoshoni nodded. Then Big Horse asked, "What do we do now?"

"Well, since I couldn't find Murdock or any of his men in Flat Fork, I expect he's not there. That means there's a good chance of him being on Shoshoni land."

"So we look for him here?" Big Horse asked. Once again there was an eagerness in his voice.'

Morgan nodded.

"That's a hell of a job, Buck," Two Wounds said. "The People have a hell of a lot of land."

Morgan looked at him and nodded. "You have any other ideas?"

"Stay near the town and wait for him to find us?" Red Hand said hopefully.

"While more of the People die?" Two Wounds said. "No."

"Even if we don't really catch them right off, if Murdock knows we're lookin' for him and his men, he might stay on the move. The more he moves around, the less chance that shit ball'll have for his deviltry."

The Shoshoni agreed. "We start in the mornin'," Two Wounds said more than asked.

Morgan nodded. He was tired from the long day, from the tension of the entire situation, so he made his good nights and went to sleep.

"How're you figurin' to do this, Buck?" Two Wounds asked in the morning over a cup of hot coffee.

"We can only cover so much land at one time, but we might as well be organized about how we go about it. I'll act as a sort of focus point, staying in the center. Two of you go out on my right flank, two on my left. Spread out as much as we think is safe and reasonable. I don't want none of you fools gettin' killed out there.

Then we just ride. We ought to be able to cover a fair piece of ground that way.''

"Why're you in the center?" Big Horse asked, unconcerned but curious.

"Because I don't know shit about trackin'. Never had the knack for it." He shrugged. It was a gift with which he had not been endowed, and wishing it different would not make it so. "You put me out on the far flank or somethin' and I'm going to miss about everything unless it up and smacks me in the face."

Big Foot rose, his face hard and set in determination. "Then let's go," he growled. "I've seen enough of the People killed already. I don't want to see no more."

Ten minutes later they pulled out. Big Horse and Two Wounds took the farthest flanks; Old Belly and Red Hand rode nearer to Morgan.

As he rode, Morgan got the feeling that he was spitting into the wind here. There was no way five men could cover the more than four thousand squares miles of the Wind River Reservation, even if ninety percent of the reservation was short grass plains or scrub desert.

Still, he pushed himself on, knowing that he had little other choice. If Murdock couldn't be found easily, at least Morgan and his four Shoshoni friends might hound him enough to get him off the reservation.

The five men headed southwesterly, angling vaguely toward the agency, the camp and the Wind River Mountains beyond. They rode slowly under the broiling blob of the sun. Sweat formed and rolled down their skin, but even the constant breeze failed to cool the men any. Morgan decided that he would hate living in this place.

The five gathered near midday to have a small meal and to talk a little. None had seen anything that would help them in their quest. On the other hand, they had not found any more bodies, either. There was something to be said in that.

They camped on the open desert that night, mostly keeping their own council. They were dismayed that they had found nothing, but they were not too discouraged. Any one with sense would know that they could not find the band of outlaws in just one day, not in the vastness of the land.

"You plan to keep ridin' in this direction, Buck?" Two Wounds asked in the morning.

"I expect so. Why?"

"We keep movin' that way, we'll hit the agency by late afternoon."

"That bother you?"

"No. Just pointin' it out."

Morgan nodded. "It might be a good idea to stop by there anyway and see if they've heard or seen anything."

Chapter 21

An hour before dark, they rode into the agency section of what passed as the army's Camp Brown. Orville Ashby came out of his office, which was next to his house, and stood, shading his eyes to watch the five men riding toward him.

"You've been gone awhile, Buck," Ashby said as Morgan dismounted and tied off his horse.

"Seems like it, but I guess it's only been what, two, three days?"

"About that. Come on in." He looked at the Shoshoni. "The trough for your horses is around back. You have food?"

Two Wounds nodded.

"Good." He and Morgan went inside the office. After Morgan had lit a cheroot and Ashby had poured them each a drink, the agent asked, "Well, Buck, do you have any news?"

"Some. None of it good. We found out who's leadin' this pack of shit balls."

"Who is it?"

"Somebody named Del Murdock. You know anything about him?"

170

Ashby shook his head. "I don't believe I've even heard the name before. How'd you find that out?"

"A bartender from Flat Fork decided to spill his guts out for us."

"And you believe him?"

Morgan nodded and finished the whiskey. "He was too terrified to lie. Besides, there were a few telltale spots where I knew something and everything that bartender said fit into it." He poured himself another shot of whiskey.

"I take it you haven't found him?"

"Not a goddamn trace."

"So what's the next step?"

"Me and the Shoshonis out there have been tryin' to methodically cover the reservation. I figured that if we couldn't find Murdock, we'd at least keep him on the move. Hopefully that'd keep them from killin' any more Shoshonis."

"It's too late for that," Ashby muttered.

Morgan's tired eyes snapped to alertness. Spotting Ashby's grim look, he asked, "Another one?"

Ashby nodded. "A young couple and their newborn. All dead, all carved up."

"Jesus goddamn Christ," Morgan snarled. Anger surged through him, building with each pulse beat. He polished off the whiskey and then dropped the cheroot in the glass, where it hissed for a moment. He rose. "Get me some rations—bacon, beans, jerky, hardtack, and coffee. Enough to last me and four Shoshonis a couple, three days."

"Where're you goin'?" Ashby asked.

"Where the hell do you think I'm going? Where'd it happen?"

"You don't think you'll find anything there, do you?"

"Tell me where it happened, you bastard, or I'll beat it out of you."

Ashby blanched, but nodded. "In the little neck of land where Pevah Creek enters the south fork of Sage Creek."

Morgan nodded curtly.

"What's your rush, Buck?" Ashby asked. "This happened a couple of days ago. There's no need for such haste."

"Like hell there ain't. It means there's a good chance Murdock is still on the reservation somewhere. Besides, I want to get out of here before that shit ball Pomeroy sticks his nose in here."

Ashby smiled a little. "I heard you and he had a little run-in the other day."

Morgan nodded. "Dumb bastard," he muttered. "Well," he added, "can you get me those supplies?"

Ashby nodded curtly. "Of course. You want a mule for packin'?"

"No, just divide it among several sacks. We can each take a little. I don't want any more distractions or baggage than's absolutely necessary."

"You'll be out back with the horses?"

"Yeah."

While tending the horses, Morgan explained what had happened and what his plan was.

"I think we should spend the night at Washakie's village," Big Horse suggested when Morgan was finished talking.

"Why?" Morgan asked, eager to be on the move. "We're not gonna find anything at night."

"True, but if we go out there now, we'll be right

172

there to take a look at things as soon as the sun comes up.''

''Somebody in the village might have something to tell us.''

Morgan looked sharply at the big Shoshoni. ''You just want to go back there so you can hump your woman,'' he said in accusatory tones.

''And if I do?''

''Dammit, Big Horse. A young warrior was killed. And a woman and a newborn little child.''

''I know these things.''

''Then how can you think of humpin' knowin' what happened to some of the People?''

''If I thought we'd catch them right off, I'd ride forever if need be to do so. But we won't catch 'em tonight. Tomorrow neither.''

Two Wounds walked up to Morgan and threw an arm around the lawman's shoulders. ''A night in the robes with Cloud Woman would do you much good, my friend,'' he said quietly. ''It's good for a man to be with his woman. Tomorrow we'll ride to where the white devils did their work.''

Morgan nodded, accepting it. He still would have preferred riding straight to the murder scene and so get a jump on this in the morning. But he also knew this was all weighing very heavily on him and that he probably would not be thinking too clearly when he would most need to. He and the four Shoshoni rode out half an hour later, heading northwest.

They rode into the village sometime after dark, but it seemed the whole village came alive to greet them. Many of the Shoshoni were rambling on about the latest murders while trying to ask a hundred questions of the men who had just returned.

173

Morgan bulled his way through the crowd. Cloud Woman waited for him just outside their lodge. He slid out of the saddle and grabbed her in his arms. He kissed her hard, and then swung her around.

"I must see to your horse," she said laughingly when he put her feet on the ground again.

"The hell with the horse," Morgan growled. He was suddenly very intensely grateful that Big Horse had suggested they return to the village. He wanted Cloud Woman desperately. He had not realized until this minute how much he missed her and wanted her.

"But . . ."

"Hush," he whispered, covering her lips with his. Then he swept her into his arms and barged into the lodge, thankful he had not knocked it down. In minutes they were on the robe bed and thrashing happily.

Afterward, he stood and rearranged his clothing.

"Where are you going, my husband?" Cloud Woman asked. She was not really worried, but she did want him back in her bed, even if only for sleeping. She loved this tall, strange man with his white skin. She had been shocked when she had really looked at his naked form for the first time. His face and hands, and even his arms, were weathered and browned from the sun. But the rest of him reminded her of a new snowfall—just a bountiful expanse of absolute white. But none of that mattered. She loved Marshal Buck Morgan and wanted him close to her as much as possible.

"Out to tend my horse."

"That is woman's work," Cloud Woman said sternly. She stood up and her dress, which Morgan had merely shoved up as high as necessary fell into place. "I will go."

"That ain't woman's work, Cloud Woman," he said.

"Here it is. Now go lay down. You need sleep. You'll need to be fresh in the morning."

Morgan stood looking at her for a few moments, pleased at what he saw. Then he nodded. He was asleep by the time Cloud Woman returned. She shucked her dress, leggings, and moccasins, and then slid carefully into the robes beside Morgan. She rested her small head on Morgan's outstretched right arm. She sighed and fell asleep.

Cloud Woman awoke before Morgan in the morning. She smiled when she saw his face so near to hers. It mattered little to her that his face was covered with stubble and that he snored a little. She kissed the tip of his nose. Morgan shuffled a little but did not awaken. So she did it again. When she got the same response she decided that the third try would be her last. If he did not respond then, she would get up and build up the fire in preparation for their morning meal.

She was disappointed when she got almost no response this time. With a sigh of regret at the lost opportunity, she rolled over and shoved aside the robes. Just as she was getting up, Morgan suddenly grabbed a handful of her naked buttocks.

"Where're you goin', woman?" he asked, voice still rough with the dregs of sleep.

She whooped with surprise, then rolled back over until she was half atop him. "Nowhere, my husband." Interest and desire burned in her coal-black eyes.

Cloud Woman finally got to rebuilding the fire, but she had to rush the meal. Big Horse and the others would be along soon, she knew, coming to get Morgan.

The lawman had barely gulped down some buffalo meat and two cups of coffee before he heard Two Wounds and Big Horse yelling at him to come out.

While Morgan had been eating, Cloud Woman had run outside to saddle Morgan's horse in the dark and then bring it around to the front of the lodge. Big Horse and the others were calling for Morgan.

"Go tell that lazy husband of yours to come out here and greet the day," Big Horse said to Cloud Woman in Shoshoni. He was smiling, though. "Tell him it is a good day, and that good things await him."

"Christ," Morgan grumbled good-naturedly as he stepped outside, "are you always this goddamn noisy in the mornings? No wonder your woman throws you out most times." He kissed Cloud Woman and climbed into the saddle.

They pushed their horses some, wanting to make as much distance as possible before dawn arose. Daybreak caught them still on the trail, but very soon afterward, they reached the spot where the killings had taken place. It was evident from the signs on the ground what had happened here.

The Shoshoni moved about, their well-trained eyes covering the ground, looking for any scrap of information the land might yield to them.

Morgan knelt where he figured the woman had died. Visions of a young Shoshoni woman—one looking suspiciously like Cloud Woman—and her baby being brutally murdered floated before his eyes. His fists clenched and he ground his teeth together as he battled the avalanche of rage that was close to destroying him.

He rose and turned, heading swiftly toward his horse. Even Big Horse, that massive warrior, was taken aback by the look on Morgan's face. As he and Two

Wounds mounted their ponies next to each other, Big Horse said quietly in Shoshoni, "There's death in that white man's eyes. He'll have blood before the sun goes down."

A little frightened, Two Wounds nodded. He and his three Shoshoni companions kicked their ponies into a trot to catch up to Morgan.

Two Wounds pulled up alongside Morgan. "Slow down, my friend," he yelled above the rushing wind.

Morgan shook his head.

"You won't help nobody if you kill your horse and get put afoot. Take your time. They can't get away from us."

Morgan looked at Two Wounds as if he had never seen the Shoshoni before. Then the light of recognition came to his eyes, if only a little. He nodded and slowed his horse.

Chapter 22

Near noon, Two Wounds, who had been riding far out ahead of the others, following the sign they had picked up that morning at the murder sight, trotted up to Morgan.

"You know where this sign is headin', don't you, Buck?" he asked.

Morgan nodded tightly. "Flat Fork. It's the only place men like Murdock can go."

"I counted eight, maybe nine horses."

"So?"

"So, if they get to Flat Fork, you'll be alone against eight, nine, maybe even ten men. Like you said, me and the others can't help you much in there." He had thought about that often since Morgan had first mentioned it. Two Wounds had been insulted at first, but then he had forced himself to look at it rationally. When he could see it clearly he realized that Morgan was right. The Shoshoni wouldn't get more than a dozen yards into the town before they'd all be blasted into oblivion. And even if that didn't happen, there would be no way the evil populace of Flat Fork would talk to a man like Morgan when that man was accompanied

178

by four Shoshoni. In either case, it would seriously endanger Morgan, as well as Two Wounds and his three fellow Shoshoni.

"I've been alone before. Against odds that big, too," Morgan answered flatly.

"This is no time to be a hero, Buck," Two Wounds said urgently. The Shoshoni had come to have a lot of respect for the white lawman, and he would hate to see him killed.

Morgan shrugged. "There's no choice."

"Go to the soldier chief and have him send some blue coats with you."

"No."

"Why?"

"I don't trust that soldier chief in the least. I think he's an ambitious, conniving little ball of shit who'll trample anyone who gets in his path on the way to attaining higher rank and glory."

"Can you call other lawmen like you?"

Morgan shook his head. "That's one thing I did consider. But it's impossible. The only place I could get such help is from my own office down in Cheyenne. But the U.S. marshal there, Floyd Dayton, doesn't have enough deputies to go around as it is. And even if he did, it'd be weeks before we could get anyone up here."

"There's the singing wire and the iron horse."

"Yeah, I could wire Floyd from the agency. That wouldn't take too much doing. But even if he could find the deputies, he'd have to round them all up. Hell, we just don't sit in an office down there drinkin' coffee. Once he did that, he could send them by train to Rock Springs or Rawlins. Then they'd have to ride the rest of the way up here. That's almost a week by itself."

"So you're just gonna go into Flat Fork by yourself and get killed, is that it?"

Morgan smiled in self-deprecation. "Maybe you best make up a death song for me."

"Fool," Two Wounds snapped. He turned and raced out ahead again. He went back to following the outlaws' tracks, doing so all the way to Flat Fork. He stopped on a very low rise about one hundred fifty yards from the edge of town, and sat there on his pony, waiting for the others to catch up to him.

While waiting, he saw a puff of smoke, and at almost the same instant, he saw a bullet kick up dust a few feet to his left. Moments later he heard the report of the rifle. Shaking his head in annoyance, he backed up some and dismounted. This way he could keep an eye on the town, yet be out of rifle range.

Finally, the others were there. "See anything?" Morgan asked.

"Just one fool who took a shot at me."

"Friendly folks down there, ain't they?"

"You sure you don't want us to go there with you Buck?" Big Horse asked.

"I'm sure. There's no reason for you to place yourself in such danger."

"We can go at night," Old Belly offered. "Then we wouldn't be such easy targets."

"Thanks, Old Belly," Morgan said. "But no. Besides, if somethin' happens to me, you boys'll still be around to catch the rest of those shit balls."

"You watch yourself down there, my friend," Two Wounds said, clapping a hand on Morgan's shoulder.

Morgan nodded. "Thanks, Two Wounds." He rode down the low ridge toward the town. He rode down the main—well, only—street, a well-abused thorough-fare that reeked with the flotsam and jetsam of a town.

He stopped in front of Foster's saloon and went in-side, shotgun at the ready. "Where's Foster?" he asked the bartender.

"Gone to parts unknown. Sold me the place for next to nothin' and skedaddled."

"When?"

"Couple of days ago. He told some wild story of being taken away by some goddamn law dog and then bein' scared shitless by a bunch of Shoshoni. And . . ." He finally spotted the star on Morgan's vest. "Oh, Jesus," he muttered, throwing away his cigar, "you're the one, ain't you? He wasn't lyin', was he?"

"Shut up," Morgan commanded sharply. When the man did, Morgan asked, "You seen Del Murdock or any of his outlaw friends?"

Still scared to death, the bartender shook his head.

"Keep your mouth shut about me bein' here," Morgan said sternly, "or you'll get what Foster did." He turned and left.

As he rode down the street, he noticed that Vin Applegate's mercantile store was a mess. The two small windows in the place were gone, leaving behind only jagged edges. On a hunch, Morgan stopped and went inside. Broken bottles and jars were scattered all over, piles of clothes were torn, and a few looked like some-one had tried to set them afire. Penny candies were strewn all over. Shovels lay on the floor, handles sawed in half.

"Jesus, Vin, what the hell happened, here?" Morgan asked.

The young store owner turned his angry glare on

Morgan. "Some of the boys decided they'd wreck my store.

"Why? I thought you had a pretty good truce with them."

"I did. But that was before they saw me talkin' to you."

"You sayin' this was my fault?" Morgan asked, surprised and just a touch angry.

"Maybe I am," Applegate snapped.

"There's a lot of folks worse off than you are, Mr. Applegate. Believe me."

"But my store is wrecked. Everything I owned was tied up in this store."

"You know who did it?"

"Sure. Del Murdock and his bunch."

"When did it happen?"

"Early this morning."

"I've been following his tracks since just after dawn. I figure he actually got back here sometime yesterday."

Applegate nodded. "Just before dark. It took him a while, I guess, to find out I had been talkin' to a lawman. He wouldn't accept my telling him that you'd just come in to buy some goods and supplies."

Morgan nodded. "Do you have any idea of where I followed him from?" He leaned the scattergun against a barrel that had once contained flour and pulled out a cigar.

"Can't say as I do." Applegate's frustration was beginning to get the better of him. "Look, Marshal Morgan, I've got a real mess on my hands here, as you can plainly see. I don't have the time nor the inclination for chitchat."

"Just shut your yap and listen for a few minutes," Morgan snapped after he lit his cheroot. "You heard anything of what's been happening over on Shoshoni land?" he asked.

"Yeah," Applegate answered with a shrug. "So, a few Shoshonis have gotten killed by some Arapahos. What's the big deal?"

"Who told you Arapaho were doin' it?"

Applegate shrugged again. "It's common knowledge."

"It's also complete and utter bullshit," Morgan said coldly.

"What?" Applegate said, startled. "If not . . . then who . . . ?"

"White men wanting it to look like Indians were doing it."

"No white man'd go through . . ." He stopped, eyes widening in realization. "Murdock and his men?" he asked, almost incredulous.

Morgan nodded. "Where the hell do you think he got that goddamn necklace of his?"

"He told most people he bought it from some Mexican trader down in the border country."

Morgan shook his head.

"Look, Marshal, like I said, I've got a damn lot of work to get done here. Is there some point to all this? I mean, I don't give a damn that Murdock's been killing Indians, no matter what kind they are."

"In following his tracks I started out at the place he had left his last victims."

Applegate shrugged again, uninterested.

"He and his men killed three Shoshonis this time. A warrior, his young wife, and their two-day-old baby. Then they proceeded to butcher the corpses."

"Oh, sweet Jesus," Applegate groaned, as if in pain. When he looked at Morgan there were tears in his eyes. "This isn't the first time he's killed women or kids, is it, Marshal?"

Morgan only shook his head.

Applegate sighed, leaning against his broom as he thought things over. Finally he stood. "You're right, Marshal, there's a lot of folks a hell of a lot worse off than I am. And, by Christ, it's time for a little justice. I think Murdock rode out of town just after he and his boys busted up my place. But some of his boys were down in the Bighorn Saloon, an ill dive of a place if ever I saw one."

"I've been in there," Morgan said. "It doesn't seem any worse than any of the other saloons in Flat Fork."

"I suppose you're right," Applegate said, smiling weakly.

"I was wonderin', Mr. Applegate," Morgan said offhandedly, "If you might not like to come along and help me arrest whatever miscreants we find over at this Bighorn Saloon."

Applegate thought it over for a bit, then shook his head. "I'd like to go, Marshal, but I'm not much of a gunman. A fistfight, yeah, I'd go with you, sure. But this looks like it's going to be a gunbattle, and I aim to stay out of such things. Besides, I figure to still live here in Flat Fork, which means I'll have to deal with the scoundrels who call this place home."

"It seems odd that you'd still want to live here, Mr. Applegate."

"I didn't say I *wanted* to stay here in Flat Fork, Marshal," Applegate said wearily. "I said I figure I would. Like I told you before, everything I owned was tied up in this store. I don't have the money to go anywhere else, no matter how much I might want to."

Morgan nodded. "I understand. I half figured you'd

184

turn me down, but I wanted to offer you a chance to get some measure of revenge against those who did this to you." He waved his hand around the wreckage of Applegate's store.

"It's revenge enough for my timid soul to point out where some of the bastards are."

Morgan nodded. He started to leave, but turned back when Applegate called him.

"Just wait a minute, Marshal," Applegate said. He dropped his broom and then hurried to where his counter used to stand. Only parts of it were left. He rummaged around a little and came up with a small .31-caliber Colt pocket pistol. "Here, take this," Applegate said. "Use it for a belly gun. Just in case."

Morgan took the small pistol and nodded thanks. He checked it to make sure it was loaded and pulled out one of the five shells in the five-shot pistol. "I've got no desire to shoot my nuts off," he said flatly. He stuffed the pistol into the waistband of his trousers, inside his shirt.

"You have enough shells for that scattergun?"

Morgan nodded. "Obliged, Mr. Applegate," he said. He turned and headed outside.

Chapter 23

Morgan rode slowly down the street and stopped in front of the Bighorn Saloon. He dismounted and looked around. He had drawn quite an audience, though no one seemed ready to threaten him—yet. He checked the shotgun and his two Smith and Wessons. With a slightly sardonic grin, he headed for the door of the saloon.

He eased inside and stopped just to the side door. He was glad there were only seven—including the bartender—in the wretched place. Four of them were Murdock's men. He recognized Henry Coates, Cliff Bagley, Roscoe Davidson, and Russ Quinn.

Morgan fired the shotgun in the air. "You," he said, pointing to the bartender, "come out from behind there. And bring a bucket of water. You other shit balls stay right where you are for now. When the bartender gets out here I want you and you," he pointed to the two men who were not members of Murdock's gang as far as he knew, "to drop your weapons in the bucket. Then get the hell out. Then you other four dump your pistols in the bucket and go line up against yonder wall." Once more he pointed.

"What the hell's all this about, Marshal?" Davidson asked.

"You and the three shit balls with you are under arrest," Morgan said flatly.

The four started to laugh. "You ain't serious, now, are you, Marshal?" Davidson asked in wonder.

The bartender had come out from behind the bar. The two patrons who had been told to leave hurriedly stood, dropped their pistols into the pail, and then practically ran outside.

"Yessir, I am serious," Morgan said as he pulled the empty shell from the scattergun and replaced it. He snapped the weapon closed and pulled back the hammers. "Now, you boys can do like I said. One at a time. Why don't you take the first honors, Mr. Bagley, since you're the closest to the bartender."

Still laughing, Bagley rose and started walking toward the bartender. Two feet away, he went for his Colt. The other three men began yanking out their pistols at the same time.

Without hesitation, Morgan fired the scattergun at Bagley. The outlaw went down, as did the bartender. Not sure but that he hadn't gotten a full load of buckshot into Bagley, Morgan let loose the other barrel, hitting Bagley again.

Morgan felt a hammer blow to his stomach, and he was shoved back by the blast. He fell, managing to keep a hold of the shotgun. Another bullet kicked up dirt from the floor inches to his side. He rolled until he was behind the giant keg that made up part of the Bighorn Saloon's bar.

Morgan quickly pulled out the two spent shells and rammed two more home. He snapped the shotgun closed and cocked it. Then he popped straight up, shotgun butt to his shoulder, and fired twice. Just before dropping behind cover again, he saw that he had hit Quinn. He also noticed that neither the bartender nor Bagley had moved.

Figuring he did not have time to reload the shotgun again, he dropped it to the floor and pulled out one of his two Smith and Wessons. He decided to check around the side of the barrel rather than over the top. He was glad he did, too, since two bullets clunked into the log wall of the saloon, directly behind where he had fired from moments before.

The outlaws had ducked behind tables, and it looked as if things were going to be something of a standoff for a while. That did not bode well for Morgan. Pain radiated from his abdomen, and he figured he was a goner if he didn't get out of there soon and find some help. That still might not save him, but it was better than not doing anything.

Seeing that the ''bar''—one much like the one Foster had used—had a screen of dark cloth across the empty spot between the two kegs holding the bar up, he put his Smith and Wesson away, retrieved his shotgun, and reloaded it. Then he began slinking across the floor toward the other side of the bar. He suddenly froze when he heard something just around the side of the bar. Then he nodded.

He slithered back until he was about centered on the open space between the two kegs. Then he squiggled into the space. He held his breath, trying to catch sounds while at the same time trying to see through the cloth a little. He thought he could see two of the outlaws behind tables. He wasn't sure of that, but he would have to take the chance that he was right.

He heard a sound and then another. Suddenly he

rolled—out through the hanging piece of cloth. He rose up onto one knee, shotgun against his shoulder. He fired both barrels at a tabletop that was at right angles to the floor.

He threw the scattergun away and dove to his left. He hit harder than he expected and bounced off a table. He was slow getting to his feet, but when he did he had the Smith and Wesson in hand. A bullet punched him in the shoulder, knocking him back a step.

Morgan recovered his balance and fired twice at Davidson, who was at the far side of the bar. Morgan noted that at least one, and maybe both, shots had hit Davidson in the head. He figured he wouldn't have any more trouble from him. He looked around, a little worried about the two men who had hidden behind tables. He saw no movement from there, though. If they were dead, or at least incapacitated, then Morgan figured he only had one more man to contend with—and that one was now behind the bar.

Morgan saw a little movement from the keg on his side of the bar. He took the chance and fired. He was rewarded with a yell of pain.

"You son of a bitch!" the outlaw behind the bar bellowed. "You shot off my heel, you bastard."

"I'll shoot off somethin' else, you don't quit this foolishness, shit ball."

"You just wait, you son-of-a-bitch bastard."

"I got time." Actually, Morgan didn't think he had much time at all. His stomach hurt like hellfire, and his shoulder was bleeding pretty well. He got no response from the outlaw, though he thought he caught a tiny movement behind the curtain. He wasn't sure, though, and did not fire.

189

Suddenly, Coates popped up from the far end of the bar. He had a pistol in each hand. He fired steadily as he hobbled for the door.

Morgan let him run out of ammunition before he stood and calmly fired the last two shots in the Smith and Wesson. Both hit Coates in the back of the head, adding to his momentum. Coates landed on his face in the dirt.

Morgan reloaded the Smith and Wesson and shoved it back into his holster. He walked over and picked up the shotgun and reloaded that, too. Then he looked down at his stomach. There was no blood, which surprised him. He pulled his shirt out of his pants. With it came broken bits of the pocket pistol Applegate had given him. He spotted the .44-caliber slug that had hit him. He shook his head, amazed. He pulled out the rest of that pistol and threw it away.

Then he went to check on the bodies. All four outlaws were dead, as was the bartender. Morgan felt a little sorry about that, but not much. Any man who willingly chose to run such a foul bar in such a festering boil of a town couldn't be all good, Morgan figured.

Morgan stepped over to the bar, such as it was, and found an unbroken bottle. He poured some down his throat. With shotgun in hand, he headed outside and stopped.

"Any of you other pustulant shit balls want some of this?" he roared, holding up the shotgun.

No one answered in the affirmative. "Then you tell Del Murdock that I'm Deputy U.S. Marshal Buck Morgan, and I'm coming after him. When I find him—and rest assured, folks, I will find him—I'm going to give him a dose of his own goddamn medicine. That shit ball will know what that means."

"You'll never find him," someone from the crowd yelled.

"There ain't a place he can hide from me. It might take me years, but I'll find him. You tell him."

Morgan mounted his horse and began riding slowly toward the south end of town. There was a sharp pain his left shoulder, near the original one. About the same time that he realized he had been hit again, he heard the gun firing. He whirled and spotted the thick cloud of powder smoke swirling around one man.

The man raised his pistol again when Morgan yelled to his horse. The animal bolted forward, going full out in half a dozen paces. the man fired, but the bullet did not hit Morgan.

Morgan still bore down on the man, who suddenly turned and tried to run. But he got nowhere against the solid wall of people. With Morgan almost on them, the crowd began to part, backing away toward the side of the street.

The man who had fired the gun had finally found a little avenue for escape, and he fled down it with Morgan in pursuit. A dozen paces on, Morgan edged past the man and then swung his horse to the right. The man slammed into the animal and then fell flat on his back in the street.

"By rights, I ought to arrest you, you back-shootin' little shit ball," Morgan said icily. "But I've got neither the time nor the inclination for it. But I'd best make sure you learned your lesson."

"I have, I have!" the man screeched. He was still groggy, but he knew he was in serious trouble.

"I'm not so sure of that!" Morgan lowered the shotgun and fired.

The man screamed when his right leg shattered.

"Next time it'll be your face," Morgan said flatly, leaving no room for doubt as to his sincerity. He reloaded the scattergun and then trotted out of town. As he passed Applegate's store, Applegate was standing outside. The store owner smiled a little and waved.

Morgan touched the brim of his hat at Applegate and kept right on going. Despite his brave front, though, Morgan felt as weak as a babe when he reached his friends. He almost fell off his horse, but Big Horse caught him and eased him down onto the scrubby grass. He was barely conscious.

"We better get him back to the camp. Or the agency. They have a medicine healer there," Old Belly said.

"I don't trust those white men," Two Wounds said flatly.

"Neither do I," Big Horse agreed. "We'll take him to Cloud Woman. Two Wounds, you ride for the agency. Tell Orv to have the medicine healer come to Washakie's village."

Two Wounds nodded. He jumped on his pony and sped off.

Big Horse got on his war horse—a big-chested, sturdy animal, one that a man as big as Big Horse needed—and then took Morgan when Old Belly and Red Hand held him up. Big Horse settled Morgan in front of him and held him in place with beefy arms.

"This ain't necessary," Morgan said weakly.

"Bullshit," Big Horse said nonchalantly.

Morgan nodded and slumped against the big Shoshoni.

Big Horse and his companions arrived at Washakie's village about midmorning. The whole village turned out to watch as Morgan was eased out of Big Horse's powerful grip and carried into Cloud Woman's lodge. Moments later, the band's medicine man, No Blood, entered the lodge and began performing his rituals.

It wasn't until the afternoon that Dr. Snyder arrived—with an escort consisting of Lt. Dexter Pomeroy, a man with a second lieutenant's insignia on his shoulders, and six soldiers. The Shoshoni suddenly melted into their lodges, watching with weary eyes as the armed soldiers dismounted and surrounded Morgan's tepee.

The Shoshoni did not like this one little bit. They would find no comfort in knowing that the soldiers were far more frightened than they. There was something utterly terrifying to the soldiers about standing amid so many Indians, even if a majority of them were women and children.

Chapter 24

Snyder, Pomeroy, and the other army officers entered the lodge a little worried. None had been inside an Indian lodge, and they did not know what to expect.

Snyder was seriously affronted by No Blood. "Get him the hell out of here," the physician ordered, pointing to No Blood.

Big Horse glared at Snyder, who was not paying any attention as he knelt beside Morgan. Big Horse shrugged. "Come, grandfather," he said in his own language, taking No Blood's arm, "we must go. The blue coat chief and the blue coat medicine healer don't want us here."

No Blood started to protest, but Two Wounds, who had brought Snyder and Pomeroy to the village, said in Shoshoni, "No arguments. Buck is chief among his people, and we must let his people help him."

No Blood did not like it, but he knew both Big Horse and Two Wounds were right. With a sigh of annoyance—brought on by the rapidly dying customs of his people—he left. Big Horse and Two Wounds, though, stayed in the lodge.

Snyder examined the wounds. He nearly jumped

when Morgan said calmly, "Neither bullet's still in there, Doctor."

"You let me determine that, son. That's my job." An examination proved that there were, indeed, no bullets in either wound, though a few fragments remained. Snyder removed those, then poured antiseptic in both wounds.

Morgan hissed at the latter, but he said nothing otherwise.

Finally Snyder bandaged Morgan and stood. "We'll make arrangements to get you to Camp Brown right away, Marshal," the physician said.

"No thanks, Doctor," Morgan said flatly.

"Come now, Marshal," Snyder said condescendingly. "You can't recuperate properly in such a place. There's filth all around. Look at this place."

"This is my home now, Doctor," Morgan said harshly. "And I'd be obliged if you didn't denigrate it."

"Christ, Morgan," Pomeroy snapped, "come to your senses, man. If you want to poke one of these savage females now and again, there's no one going to stop you. But to claim that this . . . this hovel is your home is quite preposterous."

"Eat shit, Lieutenant,"Morgan said calmly. "Now get the hell out of my home."

"Enough, Marshal," Pomeroy said pompously. "You are hereby ordered to return to Camp Brown by whatever means I—and Dr. Snyder—deem appropriate."

"Order, my ass. Get the hell out of here before I get up and throw you out."

Pomeroy smirked. "You'd have considerable trouble in your condition. However, not wanting to exceed my bounds, I have brought something for you to see." He pulled a sheet of paper from his blouse pocket and held it out.

Wondering what trouble this was, Morgan unfolded the sheet and read to himself.

"Well, dammit," Ashby said, "what does it say?"

"It says I'm placed under the command of Lieutenant Shit Ball there. It supposedly comes from U.S. Marshal Floyd Dayton."

"I don't believe it," Ashby said sharply. He took the paper from Morgan and read it himself. "Oh, my Lord. I would never have expected Floyd to do something like this."

"He wouldn't,"Morgan said flatly. "If you'll notice, that's a telegrapher's translation—or what's supposed to be a translation—of telegraph code. There's no more proof that this's real than we'd have if you said you had run from here to the agency in three minutes."

"You'll have your proof, damn you," Pomeroy snarled. "Soon, dammit. But until then, you will obey that wire."

"In a pig's ass," Morgan said with a strong laugh.

"I see," Pomeroy said, fighting to restrain his temper, "you want to do this the hard way. I had planned to allow Dr. Snyder to return here with an ambulance to bring you back to Camp Brown, but since you insist on being troublesome, we'll take you back now, whichever way we can."

"You won't do any goddamn such thing," Morgan said calmly.

"Oh, is that right? Well, as soon as we are ready to leave, I'll have my troops in here to pick you up and drag you to Camp Brown if need be."

"No you won't," Big Horse interjected.

"Are you addressing me, you savage?" Pomeroy asked. He was furious.

"As a matter of fact I am, you putrefying bag of wind. And if even one of your soldiers sticks his nose in here, every one of them here—including you and the pustulant doctor there—will die."

Pomeroy was stunned, not by the threat but by the very refined language. He did not, could not, know that Big Horse had found out about his affinity for languages when he was being educated in Saint Louis. His adopted father, an old trader Washakie had known for years, had brought him to the white man's city, and for six years Big Horse—or Benny Horse, as he was known there—became educated in the white man's ways. After the six years he had chucked it all and returned to his people, where he quickly showed as much affinity for the bow and lance as he had for languages.

Despite being stunned, Pomeroy figured that the Shoshoni meant what he had said. He had only six troopers with him against several dozen warriors. "All right, then," he finally said stiffly, "we'll leave here for now. But I'm telling you now, for all to hear, Morgan, that I am taking over this case of the Shoshoni murders."

"All you're going to do is get a lot of people killed. Most of them innocents," Morgan said.

"I don't believe that. You have no proof to back up such statements. You never did. It was solely your arrogance. Your arrogance wouldn't let you allow another man to win at something you had chosen to win for yourself."

"Lieutenant, your desire for promotion and for getting out of this hellhole is admirable. Yes, indeed, it is. But it don't mean a damn thing to me. I'm here to get the shit balls who're killin' Shoshoni and either arrest them or kill them. It doesn't make much of a difference. But unlike you, I ain't lookin' for glory or medals."

"You insufferable son of a bitch," Pomeroy hissed.

"Lieutenant," Morgan said wearily, "I'm full fed up with you and your bullshit. Now get the hell out of my home before Big Horse throws you out."

Pomeroy's face was livid; he looked as if he would explode at any moment. Then he turned on his heel, leaving Snyder and the other officer behind. Those in the lodge could hear him shouting, "Mount up, men! Let's ride."

Snyder looked at Morgan. "I could care for you better back at the camp, Marshal," he said.

"I know. But this is my home, and I feel most comfortable here now."

"Well, then, this is good-bye, since I certainly do not intend to traipse up here and sit amongst these savages just to treat your wounds."

"I've been shot before, Doctor. I made it through those times and I'll damn well make it through this one, too. Now you best be on your way before Lieutenant Pomeroy takes you behind the woodshed."

"Pomeroy was right, Marshal. You are an insufferable son of a bitch," Snyder said before he left in a huff.

The other officer, who had said not a word, though he had watched all the proceedings with great interest, left, too.

"You best go with him, Orv," Morgan said to Ashby.

The agent shrugged. "Some of the Shoshoni'll give me an escort back if need be."

"Are many white men like that?" Two Wounds asked, pointing toward the flap of the tepee. He was rather in awe of the foolishness of the white men who had just left.

"Too damn many of them," Big Horse answered.

"He's got that right," Morgan added. He sighed. "I'm obliged to you two for gettin' me back here before I died."

Big Horse squatted next to Morgan. "You would've done the same for me or Two Wounds."

"I probably would have," Morgan said with a nod. "And then you'd be thankin' me instead of the other way around." He suddenly grinned. "Of course, if it'd been you, me and Two Wounds would've had a devil of a time gettin' your fat carcass back here."

Big Horse laughed, but then turned pensive. "You know, Buck," he said musingly, "one of the reasons I came back to the People was because I didn't see what I liked of white men. Not to say that the People are perfect, but white men seem to need hatred and duplicity the same way they need air. Or at least most white men do. You, my friend, are an exception. One hell of an exception. I'm glad to call you my friend."

"Same here," Two Wounds piped in. "I don't know those many fancy-ass words that Big Horse uses, but I think I know what he means, and I agree with him."

Morgan smiled. "Thanks." He looked at Ashby. "Who the hell was the other blue coat?" he asked.

"Second Lieutenant Virgil Whitehill. He just arrived a couple of days ago."

"Know anything about him?"

Ashby shook his head. "Not much. He seems a reasonable man, but then again, so does Pomeroy on occasion. He's quiet, but I think he's noting everything that crosses his path. I think he's got Pomeroy a little nervous.''

"Why? Pomeroy wants out of here in the worst way.''

"Pomeroy wants out of here in the best way. Being relieved of duty for reassignment with no heroics to his credits will keep him a first lieutenant for another decade, maybe more.''

Morgan nodded. "Well, maybe you best keep an eye on him for a while.''

"I intend to.''

"Now,'' Morgan said with a tired sigh, "I best get some shut-eye.''

Big Horse, Two Wounds, and Ashby went outside and stopped to savor the night. It was warm but not oppressively so, and a gentle wind caressed them.

"Do you think that wire Pomeroy showed you was real?'' Big Horse asked Ashby.

The agent shook his head. "It's not real,'' he said flatly.

"Anything you can do to prove that?''

"I think so. I'll look into it as soon as I get back to the agency.''

"You want an escort back now?'' Two Wounds asked.

"I suppose so. I'd just as soon stay the night here, but I don't like leavin' my wife and kids alone.''

"You never can tell with all those blue coats around,'' Big Horse said, tongue in cheek.

"Despite your sarcasm, Big Horse, those're true words. Well, we better get moving.''

Inside, Morgan slept like the dead for almost a full

twenty-four hours. He ate a little and then, since it was night, he went back to sleep.

He felt pretty good the next morning, and he asked Big Horse and Two Wounds to come to see him. When they arrived and settled in Morgan said, "I want you two to go to the agency and tell Orv to watch his ass. I don't trust that shit ball Pomeroy, and I'm pretty sure he'll pull something."

"It's already done," Big Horse said. "He's smarter than you think."

"Yeah, I suppose he is. He say anything about that piece of paper?"

"Said he was sure it was phony and that he had an idea for proving it."

Morgan nodded.

"One other thing, Buck," Big Horse said. "He asked us to send a couple of men to the agency to watch over his wife and kids. Said he trusted the People more than he did the army."

"Smart."

"I thought so."

"He say why?"

Big Horse nodded. He picked a piece of meat out of the cooking pot and popped it in his mouth. His eyes did a merry little dance when his tongue announced to him just how hot the meat was. It took more than a minute for him to recover.

In the meantime, Two Wounds, laughing, said, "Agent Ashby said he needs to go to some city. A real one, not Flat Fork. I think it has something to do with that paper."

Morgan nodded. "Who're you going to ask to go on the watch down there?"

"I thought me and Big Horse," Two Wounds said.

201

Morgan shook his head. "I'd feel better knowin' you were here. I don't know what Murdock will hear about the ruckus over in Flat Fork the other day, but he might be a little emboldened and try some more raidin' out here."

"Good thought," Big Horse said. "We'll have Red Hand and Old Belly watch over Mr. Ashby's family. They're both friendly enough, and are known to his family."

"Sounds good."

Chapter 25

Morgan recovered quickly, and within a few days he was feeling almost his old self. The bruise remained on his abdomen, but the pain was gone. His shoulder was still very stiff and sore and would be for some time, but after a few days it was well enough to use.

Six days after being brought back to Washakie's village, Morgan felt the itch to move on. "You heard anything from Orv yet, Two Wounds?" he asked.

The Shoshoni shook his head. It was plain he was worried about the agent.

"Let's say me, you, and Big Horse mosey on down there and see what's going on?"

Both Shoshoni nodded.

"Somethin' doesn't seem right," Morgan said as he, Big Horse, and Two Wounds moved slowly toward Ashby's house.

"Like what?" Big Horse asked.

Morgan shrugged. "I don't know. Things don't *seem* right is all. Those horses over there don't belong to Orv, nor to Old Belly or Red Hand." He stopped his horse and sat there, thinking. Then he nodded. "Maybe I'm as crazy as a bedbug, but I'm sure something's wrong at Orv's house."

"So, what do you want to do about it?" Two Wounds asked.

"Big Horse, how about you ride on around back of the house and come on it that way. Two Wounds and I'll come on the front just like usual."

"Don't matter to me," Big Horse said. He moved off, heading toward his right so that he could come up from the back side of the house, past the small stone cabin Morgan had used ever so briefly when he had arrived here.

"You think there's trouble, Buck?" Two Wounds asked.

"Hell if I know. I don't see any sign of trouble, really. I don't hear any . . ."

A scream tore through the air. It was faint, since it was coming from inside the house.

Morgan and Two Wounds kicked their horses into a run. Morgan could see that Big Horse had done the same. The two were off their horses before the animals had fully stopped, and they ran for the house. Morgan jerked the door open, and only after he had rushed inside did he realize he could be walking into a bullet. But it was too late to worry now.

Inside the dim house, he almost tripped over two bodies. He jammed to a stop and knelt. "Shit," he breathed.

"Who is it?" Two Wounds asked, looming over Morgan.

"Old Belly," he said flatly. "I'd wager the other's Red Hand."

Another scream pierced the air, coming from a side

204

room. Morgan and Two Wounds charged through the door to the room. Without stopping, Morgan drew one of his pistols and slapped it hard against Private Lee Skousen's head. Skousen moaned once and slumped sideways, then fell, freeing twelve-year-old Bonnie Ashby, whom he had pinned to the tabletop with his body.

As Morgan was hitting Skousen, Private Vic Bowen looked up from where he was attempting to ravish Grace Ashby. "Bastards," he snarled as he went for his pistol.

Two Wounds released a shrill, short war cry, and then jumped toward Bowen. The Shoshoni had dropped his pistol when he ran into the room, so he pulled his knife as he charged at Bowen. The soldier got his revolver out and fired twice. Two Wounds jerked with the impact of the bullets, but he continued forward until he ran into Bowen. The soldier fired again, with the muzzle of his Colt against Two Wounds's shirt.

Two Wounds made a feeble swipe at Bowen with his knife and barely nicked Bowen's neck before he fell.

"Goddamn savage," Bowen muttered as he pumped another slug into the back of the prone Two Wound's head. He began turning toward his friend, saying, "Hey, Lee, look at what I . . ."

After whacking Skousen on the head Morgan had taken a couple of seconds to make sure Skousen was out, and then to see that Bonnie Ashby was all right. He heard two gunshots and he rose fast, swinging around in time to see Bowen fire the *coup de grace* into Two Wound's head.

Morgan's eyes bulged as a burst of rage assaulted his veins, making it hard to see for a moment. Then

Bowen began turning, calling to his friend. Morgan fired.

Two bullets in the brain, within half an inch of each other, put a swift end to Bowen.

Morgan stood there for a moment, almost shaking in his fury. Grace and Bonnie moved tentatively, straightening their clothing. They were afraid of Morgan while at the same time knowing that he was the only reason they were alive and unsullied. Still, one look at the absolute rage stamped on Morgan's face and one thought of the bloody efficiency of Morgan's killing, and the woman and the girl became afraid.

Morgan began to return to normal. The rage was not gone, nor was the grief. The two emotions entwined inside him, sitting there, letting Morgan work through his anger and grief while at the same time letting him do what needed to be done.

He drew in a breath and let it out slowly. "You two all right?" he asked.

Grace and Bonnie looked at each other and then nodded. "Yes, Marshal," Grace said with considerable dignity. "Thanks to you."

Morgan shrugged. "Where's the two youngsters?" he suddenly asked.

"I don't know," Grace said, worry for her children overriding the mortification at the way she looked.

"They're here," Big Horse said in his quiet, booming voice as he shepherded Dusty and Pearl Ashby ahead of him. He spotted the bodies and swung the children around. "Wait outside, little ones," he said. The only sign of his rage was the darkening of his eyes. Otherwise, he seemed as jovial as he had been a moment ago.

"See to your children, ma'am," Morgan said to Grace. "Go. We'll clean up in here."

When the Ashbys were gone Big Horse said, "What happened?"

Morgan explained it in a flat, deadly voice.

While Morgan talked, Big Horse went to look at Two Wounds. Then he was back to stand next to Morgan.

When Morgan finished his narration he asked, "Where were the youngsters?"

"A couple of blue coats were holding them in the kitchen," he said nonchalantly.

Morgan looked sharply at his big friend. "And these blue coats no longer live, is that it?"

"They bled well," Big Horse said with a shrug. "But they died poorly."

Skousen groaned. Big Horse looked at him, the light of expectation in his eyes. He pulled his knife. With a small but vicious smile on his lips, he moved toward Skousen.

Morgan grabbed one of Big Horse's arms. "No," he said quietly.

"What?" Big Horse asked, stopping and looking angrily at Morgan.

"I want him alive."

"He deserves to die."

"No doubt about that."

"So what's the trouble?" Big Horse asked harshly. "You suddenly get faint of heart with all the blood?"

"You know better than to say something that goddamn stupid, Big Horse." He sighed. Big Horse could not see it, but Morgan had at least as much desire as Big Horse had to kill Skousen.

"Then why?"

207

"There's more to this than is obvious," Morgan said flatly. "It doesn't make any sense for anyone—even a shit ball as dumb as Skousen—to try what he and his cronies did here today. There's got to be a reason. There's got to be."

"Suppose there ain't?" Big Horse demanded. "Then what?"

"Well, if we figure that out, and he had no reason other than he thought to come over here and cause trouble, I'll give him to you."

Big Horse nodded, satisfied if not happy.

Morgan walked outside and got a pair of handcuffs from his saddlebags. Back inside, Skousen was showing signs of life. Morgan handcuffed him, hands behind his back. Then he hauled Skousen up into a roughly sitting position.

With a sigh, Morgan reloaded his pistol and then headed out of the room again. He found the Ashbys in the sitting room. "You still all right?" he asked.

Grace nodded. She was pasty and shaken, but Morgan could see in her face that she was not going to give in to all this.

"You know where your husband is?" Morgan asked.

"He said he was going to one of Hogg's stage stations up the way. Not the one in Flat Fork. That's all I know."

Morgan nodded and returned to the dining room, where the gunfight had taken place. Big Horse wasn't there, but he returned a few minutes later. "Where've you been?" Morgan asked.

"Takin' out the garbage." He pointed to where Bowen's body had been.

Morgan nodded. "From the kitchen, too?"

"Yes." He looked at Skousen, but directed his question at Morgan. "What do we do about him?"

"See if he'd like to chat."

"I can encourage him." Big Horse sounded a mite too eager.

"Later." Morgan wandered over to where Skousen was sitting on the floor, back against the wall. A stream of blood meandered down his face from a bloody knot on his head. "Howdy, Private," Morgan said almost congenially. "Looks like you and your boys were about ready to have yourselves quite a time here."

"Go shit up a tree, Marshal."

"Your attitude could use a mite of improvement, shit ball," Morgan said without the rancor that ate at his insides. "You think up this harebrained scheme yourself? Or did you have someone else help out?"

"I ain't tellin' you a damn thing, you skunk-pokin' son of a bitch. You've got no power over me."

"That so?"

"Yeah, asshole. You just wait till Lieutenant Pomeroy gets wind of this. You'll be one sorry son of a bitch then."

"You see that big, mean-looking Indian over there?" Morgan asked in calm, reasoned tones. When Skousen nodded Morgan said, "He's real eager for me to turn you over to him. Despite his education in white schools back east, he's still basically a savage at heart. And he would love to carve you into teeny-weeny pieces."

"He won't get nothin' from me," Skousen said, trying through bravado to impress or worry Morgan.

"You aren't that tough, shit ball. So quit tryin' to prove you're a big man. You're not. Now, suppose you tell me which one of your idiot friends thought all this up."

Skousen thought about it for a while. He held no loyalty for anyone and could see no reason not to speak. However, he was absolutely certain that the big mean-looking Shoshoni would kill him as soon as Morgan and the Shoshoni figured they had all the information they could get from him. In addition, if he kept his mouth shut, the army would probably get him out of this predicament.

"I don't think so, Marshal," Skousen said, trying to sound sincere. "Principles, you know." Skousen never saw the knife. He just knew that Morgan had moved very fast and that a moment later blood was streaming down his face and his forehead hurt. He looked at the bloody blade of the big knife Morgan held in his hand.

"How's that for principles, shit ball?"

Skousen was suddenly very, very frightened. He was sure Morgan was utterly mad. But he still did not want to reveal any secrets. He licked his dry lips. "What'm I gonna get outta all this if I tell you?" he asked.

"I'll turn you over to the army." Seeing the look of hope that sprang into Skousen's eyes, he added. "It might not be to Pomeroy, though. Wherever I turn you over will have to be willing to court-martial you."

"Court-martial me? For what?"

Morgan reared back and hit Skousen with a big, hard fist. Skousen screamed when he felt the bones around his left eye socket break. The scream, though, seemed to wake Morgan up again. He rose. "Let's take him back to the village, Big Horse," he said. "There's been enough bloodshed here for one day, and I don't want Orv's family being subjected to our tryin' to persuade shit ball here to talk to us."

Big Horse nodded.

Chapter 26

Big Horse was tying Old Belly's corpse across the back of Old Belly's horse when he spotted riders heading toward the house. He walked inside to where Morgan was talking with Ashby's family. "Someone's coming, Buck."

"Who?"

Big Horse shrugged. "Blue coats, I suppose."

Morgan nodded and rose. When he turned to head for the door he saw Big Horse standing there with a silly grin on his big, broad face. And the Shoshoni was waving at Ashby's two youngest children. They were enjoying the performance.

Morgan and Big Horse went outside and stood on the porch, watching the riders, who were close enough now that Morgan could tell that they were soldiers, and that there were only four of them.

Lieutenant Dexter Pomeroy and his three men stopped and dismounted, looking at the three Shoshoni corpses on the ponies. Pomeroy walked up the three porch steps and stopped, eyes on the bodies of the three soldiers.

"What in all that's holy is this?" he asked, his arm movement encompassing the house and bodies.

"Bodies," Morgan said sarcastically.

Pomeroy's eyes blazed fire when they looked at Morgan, who was unfazed. "What the hell happened?"

Morgan explained it perfunctorily. He finished by saying, "I'm going to recommend to Marshal Dayton that your command at this post be investigated most thoroughly."

"You bastard," Pomeroy hissed. "You insufferable, rotten, chicken-poking bastard. The goddman puking bastard Shoshoni have just started a war by attacking and killing three U.S. soldiers, plus beating another one into unconsciousness, and you have the gall, the goddamn audacity, to tell me that you want me investigated? Jesus goddamn Christ, man, you're absolutely mad."

"You got things backward, shit ball," Morgan said, straining to keep his anger in check. "It was the soldiers who started this war. Old Belly and Red Hand would've seen nothing wrong in letting some of your soldiers in the house. And when they did, they were attacked and killed. Then your upstanding troops— scum that they are—tried to rape a woman and a twelve-year-old girl. God knows what they would've done to the two littler ones. Then when Two Wounds tried to stop those shit balls from attacking the Ashby women, he was killed, too."

Morgan realized he was getting almost as carried away as Pomeroy had been, and he reined himself in some. "Now, I don't know if you had a hand in any of this, but if you did, I swear that I will track you down no matter where you go, no matter how long it

212

takes. Now, you best go on back to your fort before you really piss me off.''

Pomeroy blinked several times, as if not believing anything that was happening around him. Then, in a tight, cracking voice, he said, "You and the savage there"—he pointed to Big Horse—"are under military arrest. You have flaunted army rules and regulations, continually provoked me, and now have killed three of my troops. You'll be thrown in the guardhouse until I can arrange a trial, after which you both will hang. I can't have savages like you two disrupt the peaceful functioning of Camp Brown. Nor can I allow you to stir up trouble amongst the tribes of savages in the area. I can't have you getting in the way of things, tracking across the reservation chasing men who've done nothing more than try to . . . help things along, shall we say . . . aiding my command in the performance of its divine and rightful duties. . . .'' He suddenly stopped, knowing he had said too much already.

Pomeroy was almost rabid, so Morgan stepped up and popped him a shot in the face, knocking him off the porch.

Pomeroy scrambled up. "Arrest them!" Pomeroy screeched, his face the color of a ripe tomato. "Kill them! Shoot them down. Now! That's an order.''

Morgan noticed that Lt. Virgil Whitehill had waved a hand, indicating that the two nervous troopers do nothing.

"Do what I say, damn you! Damn you!''

Whitehill moved up to him. "This is not the time for arresting people, Lieutenant," he said soothingly. "They have friends to take back to their village. We have men who must be buried. There is much to be done. We can worry about the marshal here another time."

Whitehill winked at Morgan when he said the latter, surprising Morgan. But the lawman nodded once.

"Come on now, Lieutenant," Whitehill said again.

Pomeroy nodded and allowed himself to be turned. Suddenly, he stopped and spun back. "Where's Private Skousen, you son of a bitch?"

"Inside. He's under arrest."

"You have no authority to arrest a soldier."

"Yes, I do." Actually, Morgan wasn't nearly as sure of that as he sounded, but he was not about to give up his prisoner.

"Where're you going to keep him?" Pomeroy said, growing cocky again. "We have the only jail in the whole of the reservation."

"I've got a better one at my disposal. A place where you and your shit balls can't get to him."

"Oh, yeah?" Pomeroy said in disbelief. "And where is this wondrous guardhouse?"

"Washakie's village."

Pomeroy's eyes widened. "No. Absolutely not. The army won't permit it. I won't permit it, goddammit!"

"I don't recall askin' your permission," Morgan said flatly. "Nor the army's. You don't like it, tough shit. Now, I'd advise you to get the hell out of my sight before you join Skousen in chains under the watchful eyes of the Shoshonis."

"You haven't seen or heard the last of me, Marshal, you bastard. I'll get you for this humiliation. You mark my words good, you smug son of a bitch. I'll have your balls in a bottle."

"Be the first pair you ever had," Morgan said.

Big Horse laughed uproariously, his joy heightened by the look of choler on Pomeroy's face.

Pomeroy turned and walked stiffly to his horse. He mounted and jerked the animal's head around viciously. Then he stabbed his spurs deep into the horse's side and galloped. His two troopers followed him.

Whitehill hung back a moment. "I didn't mean most of that crap I said there, Marshal," he said in a melodious voice, one that was almost too pretty for a man. "I don't know just what the hell's going on around here, but until I find out, I don't aim to take sides."

Morgan nodded. "A small word of advice. Until you do take a side, I'd watch my back when I was around Pomeroy."

"I've been doing that since the day I arrived here. By the way, Marshal, what's your name? I never did learn it last week out in the Shoshoni village."

"Buck Morgan."

"Lieutenant Virgil Whitehill."

Morgan nodded. "You ever need information about what's going on around here, come to me. Or anybody but Pomeroy and the men under his command."

"I'll do that." He nodded and turned, then raced off after Pomeroy and the two soldiers.

As he and Morgan watched the soldiers, Big Horse said, "We've got a problem, Buck. We can't trust Pomeroy as far as I could throw this house. So I think it unwise to leave the Ashbys here unattended. Not while Orv is gone."

"I've been wonderin' what to do with them myself. I've got an idea, though I don't know if it's a good one or not."

"What is it?"

"Come on inside."

215

Grace Ashby and her children were in the kitchen now that Big Horse had dragged the two bodies out and cleaned up most of the blood. Mother and daughter were making a pie, and Morgan figured it was as good a way as any to work out of their terror and shame.

"If I might have a few words with you, ma'am," Morgan said quietly.

Grace stopped what she was doing and nervously wiped her hands on her apron. Her eyes gave away her fear, but she was doing quite well at keeping her upset from her children. "All right," she said quietly. "Children, Marshal Morgan and I will be in the sitting room. You two young ones listen to Bonnie."

A few minutes later, Grace was seated in the parlor. She burst into tears almost immediately. As she dabbed at them with the hem of her apron, she said, "I'm sorry, Marshal. All this sobbing and such. It's not like me."

"It's perfectly understandable, ma'am," Morgan said calmly. "You've been through a real rough time here. There's no shame in letting out some of your worries and such."

"Thank you, Marshal," Grace said, gaining control of herself. "Now, what was it you needed to see me about?" She was all business now, composed if not serene.

"I think you and the youngsters'll be a lot safer in Washakie's village."

"Oh, dear me, no," she said. "I couldn't leave my home. Besides, I'm sure we'll be safe here now. The soldiers won't bother us any more."

"Ma'am," Morgan said urgently. "you're in more danger now than you were when those four showed up today. Lieutenant Pomeroy has, I think, gone 'round the bend, and can't be trusted.''

"Oh, that doesn't sound like Lieutenant Pomeroy. He's a gentlemen.''

"Mrs. Ashby, Lieutenant Pomeroy is livin' close to mania. There's no tellin' what he'll do.'' He paused. "I'm not advocating that you live in the village forever, just till Orv gets back. Then you and he can figure out what you want to do.''

"But I don't want to put the Indians out any,'' she said guilessly.

Morgan had been squatting in front of Grace's chair. Now he stood. "Why don't you see how the youngers're doin', Big Horse?'' he said.

Big Horse looked at him skeptically. Then he nodded. It had taken him only a moment to realize that Grace Ashby simply did not want to live with the Shoshoni; that despite her several years of living on the reservation she did not know the People and thought them below her. Oh, not consciously, of course, but it was there all the same. She accepted Old Belly and Red Hand as guards for her and her children, but to live among them, eat with them—that was too much for a patronizing person.

Big Horse figured that Morgan would have to have her air some of that to get her to agree. And it would be better for all concerned if Big Horse—one of the people who would be discussed—were not there.

"Ma'am,'' Morgan said as Big Horse left the room, "I know what you're feeling about this. I really do. I'd never been in an Indian village before I got here. Now, by golly, I'm married to one of them.'' He smiled, but her shocked look wiped the grin off in a hurry.

"Let me try this one more time, Mrs. Ashby. I don't

217

give a hoot how patronizing you feel about those people, or how much better than them you think you are. With Orv gone, it seems to be my responsibility to keep you safe. And I think that right now the only way I can do that is to take you out to Washakie's."

"I've not been so insulted, Marshal Morgan," Grace said stiffly. "I'm not patronizing toward those people. And I don't think them below me."

"Yes, you do. It's most likely not purposeful, but it's a fact nonetheless. You see them as either savages or as children of a kind. You can't see the wisdom, their abilities, their humor, and their love. They are much like any other people. They love each other and sometimes fight each other. They love their children and want what's best for them."

"No, they don't," Grace interrupted. "We have offered them every opportunity for education, to learn to become farmers, to have churches and schools built. But they will have nothing to do with it."

Morgan smiled a little. "That's what *you* think is best for them. Not what *they* think is best for them." He sighed. "Put the Shoshonis out of your mind a minute. Think back an hour or so ago. About those soldiers. You've been around soldiers long enough to know that a good many are scum dredged up in the slums of big cities in the east. Or just come off the boats from Europe. They're not saints. Neither are the Shoshonis, but at least you can deal with them."

"I can't be sure of that, Marshal." Still, she thought back to the attack. She could still feel Bowen's hand clawing at her bodice and running up inside her dress to touch her most private flesh. She could still smell the soldier's foul breath and see the several blackened teeth leering over her. She could feel his hard insistence

218

pressing against her. And she could hear the other soldier fairly slavering over her daughter. She felt a new rush of the shame, fear, and disgust she had felt then.

"But I'll give it a try," she said firmly.

"Good."

"When will we leave?"

"Soon's we get ready. I suggest you leave a note for Orv so he knows where we are. Don't make it too long, and don't tell him what went on here today. You can tell him that face to face."

"Oh, I could never do that, Marshal," Grace whispered. "I just couldn't."

"Yes, you can, and you will—when the time is right. Orv is a better man than you're givin' him credit for bein'."

Chapter 27

The ride back to Washakie's village had never seemed longer to Morgan, mainly because it gave him too much time to think. And those thoughts generally were on the Shoshoni.

It was still startling to him that he had taken so easily to the Shoshoni. Granted, they were a generally open and friendly lot, but the reason he was here could have turned the Shoshoni against him right from the beginning. But that had not happened. They had accepted him first off, though he thought at the time that he could see some reserve in them. That was understandable. But as their acceptance of him grew, he in turn came to like and admire the Shoshoni more.

And now here he was, in the Wind River area just under a month, and he had a wife, and two great friends in Big Horse and Washakie. He had even lost another great friend with Two Wounds's death.

He wondered how Night Seeker would deal with the death of her husband. The two had been together a long time—ten years or more. A month ago, Morgan would have figured that Night Seeker would not miss Two Wounds all that much. He would have figured that they had married simply for convenience, and that she would be glad she was shed of him. Now he knew that was not so. For all he knew, they might have married for convenience's sake, but even if they had, they had come to love each other over the years they had spent together.

Morgan was glad that Big Horse would be the one to break the news to Night Seeker—if the news needed to be broken. With this entourage, the deaths would be known before they even got to the village. Still, Morgan was glad he would not have to face Night Seeker.

Morgan thought about Big Horse. The Shoshoni warrior was an enigma at best. Far more educated than most whites, he yet had returned to live with his people in a primitive, sometimes savage existence. Once he considered it, though, he figured that it wasn't much more primitive and certainly no more savage than that of his own people.

Morgan liked Big Horse considerably; had almost from the start. He enjoyed the big warrior's humor, and there was no other man Morgan would rather have at his side in battle. Big Horse was as violent a man as Morgan had ever seen, too, but at the same time he was highly compassionate and friendly with children. All the youngsters Morgan had seen—red and white— took to the Shoshoni immediately. It was almost uncanny. Even now, Dusty and Pearl Ashby were riding at the end of the entourage, breathing in the dust, just so they could ride on either side of Big Horse.

What really startled Morgan about Big Horse was the Shoshoni's ability to change from one thing to another in the blink of an eye. One moment he could be a vicious, ultimate warrior bent on killing, as he had in the Ashby home not long ago, and the next moment he would be playing with the Ashby children. He could swing from being a fun-loving, playful man almost immediately to an orator in any one of five languages.

Morgan wondered if perhaps Big Horse hadn't been foolish in coming back to the Shoshoni. With his intelligence, education, and natural gifts, he could have gone far in the white man's world. Something like that made sense to Morgan. The lawman had tried to see it from Big Horse's standpoint, but that made even less sense. Surely a man as intelligent and educated as Big Horse must see what was happening to all Indian peoples, including the Shoshoni. Morgan had asked him about that once.

"A man does what he is called on to do," Big Horse had replied.

"You think it was your fate to return to the People?"

Big Horse nodded. "Something like that."

"But can't you see that the Shoshoni way of life is threatened? That it won't last another fifty years, at best?"

"Of course," Big Horse said matter-of-factly. "But what better way to prepare the People for living with the white man when the white man takes over all the Shoshoni land?"

"You living here and maybe dying in a futile battle to preserve the old ways will prepare the People for living with the whites?" Morgan asked, angry at himself for not understanding. "That makes no goddamn sense at all."

"Dying for such a cause doesn't make any sense." He sat back and fired up a small clay pipe. "But I don't intend to die." He smiled in self-deprecation.

222

"No, Buck," he said, forestalling any protest from Morgan, "I'm not thinking I'm some kind of god or something. I had a vision, though, and in that vision I don't die, no matter how many men come to fight me."

Morgan nodded. "So that's why you're such a crazy bastard in a fight, eh?"

"Yes." Big Horse paused. "You are the same, my friend."

"I've never had some damn stupid vision," Morgan said defensively.

"It doesn't matter," Big Horse said evenly. "I have seen it in your eyes. You wade into battle with a self-assurance that few men possess. You are utterly fearless and ruthlessly, relentlessly efficient. As a warrior I can see in you that you know inside that you won't die."

"I think you're crazy as a bedbug, Big Horse," Morgan said. Now, though, thinking of that conversation while he and the others were heading back to Washakie's village, he suspected that Big Horse was more than half right.

He sighed and partly turned in the saddle to look back. Grace and Bonnie Ashby rode just behind him, side by side. Then came a still handcuffed Private Lee Skousen, who still looked stunned by the fractured eye socket and the clubbing Morgan had given him. Behind him rode Big Horse, with one of the Ashby children on each side. He also held the rope to three ponies bearing their grim cargo.

"Shit," Morgan muttered as he looked forward again. He would miss Two Wounds, who had become perhaps his closest friend among the Shoshoni. Closer even than Big Horse. It was almost odd that such a thing would happen. Neither man had been particularly impressed with the other when they first had met. Each had seen the other as an enemy of sorts. Both had been wary and cautious, like two dogs sniffing at each other to determine their place.

But somewhere along the way they had lost their suspicion of each other. Morgan was not sure when that had started to happen, but he thought it could be that morning he had left Two Wounds's lodge so that Two Wounds and Night Seeker could make love. It had shown Morgan that Indian people weren't all that different from whites in some ways. And, in the ways the Shoshoni were different, more than a few were better than what he was used to. Like Night Seeker's lack of shame in wanting to make love with her husband. Morgan could not picture a white woman—a proper white woman—doing that. Not for all the money in the world. He supposed there might be some, but he had never run across them.

Morgan also thought now that that time was when he began looking at Shoshoni in general as good people. They were warm and friendly, for the most part; open and giving; they adored their children, showering much more affection on them than most whites did with their children.

Two Wounds had been all those things and more. He had a bawdy, often outright vulgar sense of humor, though he also could be very contemplative at times. He clearly loved his wife and children and was well-respected by the other warriors. Despite that, or possibly because of it, he had been of great help not only to Morgan, but also to Washakie, in keeping the warriors from going to war over the killings here. He would be sorely missed by the Shoshoni.

Morgan would miss him, too, but one could never tell it from his demeanor. He was as calm of expression as anyone ever saw him. But down inside sat his grief, a hard knot of rage and loss sitting in the dark waiting for release. Then it would grow into a ferocious beast that would rule its master for a time, before the master could reassert himself.

Morgan was thankful that he had Cloud Woman now. She would help ease the hurt and sense of loss. His marriage to the young Shoshoni woman was another source of astonishment, though once he considered it, he realized that just about everything he had seen, heard, or felt since coming out here amazed him.

Morgan would have bet a gold mine a month ago that he would never marry again. Not after his experience with his wife—or maybe she was his former wife by now—Ivy. And if someone had told him that he would have an Indian wife, he would have shot the man, since someone that mentally deranged could not be left alive to roam the earth and possibly procreate. Yet after only a few days, and fewer words between them, Morgan suddenly found himself married, albeit Shoshoni-style. Such a thing would never hold up in a court of law, but then again, he didn't really give a damn. He loved Cloud Woman; had no question about that in his head or in his heart. He was equally sure that she reciprocated in kind.

It was, however, he would admit to himself, still strange between them. While Cloud Woman spoke English, she was hard to understand when she did. He, on the other hand, spoke no Shoshoni. He had tried to learn a few words here and there, but things had been much too hectic. The only one patient enough to be a teacher was Big Horse, and he was not too inclined to take on such a poor student as Morgan.

Morgan and Cloud Woman managed to communicate quite well despite their being hampered by a language problem. Cloud Woman was all Morgan could want in a woman. She was well-educated in all the womanly arts: was a fine cook; did beadwork better than anyone else Morgan had seen in the village; she was a willing bed partner, one who gave back as good as she got; she was quiet and retiring when it was proper, but she had a spark in her that would flair into flame now and again.

Morgan was fairly certain that one of the reasons he loved Cloud Woman was that she accepted him as he was. Any white woman he had ever met had hinted that if she was to marry him, then he would have to change considerably. He was too violent, a man who killed people for his living. Such was not conducive to settling down to have a home and family. But Cloud Woman, who was used to living amid warriors, had no such trouble. Indeed, she was quite proud of him for it. He was a warrior in her eyes as much as any other man in the village. She had no concerns about marrying a man who lived by the gun and the knife.

He hoped he met her specifications as well as she did his. He had never considered himself particularly handsome, and he usually saw himself as all arms and legs. But Cloud Woman had hinted that such thoughts were incorrect, and who was he to correct his wife in such matters? And as a warrior, he knew she was satisfied with him. But he still worried on occasion if he was providing for her the way he should; and if he was meeting her needs. He supposed that she would let him know if he weren't.

As he began seeing the first signs that they were approaching Washakie's village, Morgan's thoughts turned to the old chief. He felt a certain kinship with Washakie, and he figured that was due to Washakie having known his father. It gave them a bond.

Washakie was, Morgan thought, some character. The lawman believed the stories about Washakie's prowess. Maybe not in total, but he was sure that most of those stories were true. Like Big Horse, Washakie could go from one thing to another swiftly. He was at once a fearless warrior and a friend to white men; full of wisdom and full of mischief; solemn, yet nearly always with a glint of humor in his eyes.

It was going to be hellacious to have to sit there and explain to Washakie how he had lost three warriors from his band in a place in which they were supposed to have been safe. No, that would not be a good time at all. But Morgan was never one to shirk his duty, no matter how onerous that duty might be. He would do it, for sure; he wouldn't even try to pawn it off on someone else. That didn't mean he had to like it though.

Chapter 28

"We've got a peck of troubles, Buck," Big Horse said as the procession stopped not far from Washakie's village.

"What makes you think that?" Morgan asked.

"Hear that noise?"

"That wailin'?"

"Yes. The People are wailing in grief. It means there's been death in the village. It might be only that some old man died in his sleep, but the way things've been going around here lately . . ." Big Horse raised and lowered his wide shoulders.

"Well, hell, let's go see what it is." Morgan was fatalistic about it. There was only so much a man could do, and one of them was not changing what had already occurred. One might affect the future with whatever decisions one made, but the past was the past.

"One of us should go in there first and smooth things, especially if there's been trouble. We don't want Mrs. Ashby and her youngsters to get set upon if something's happened in there."

"Good point. You best go, though. Even as welcome as I've been made this past month or so, I'm still not one of the People."

Big Horse nodded. "I had thought the same. You'll be all right here by yourself?"

"Sure. Why wouldn't I be?"

"You'll be left with a woman, three kids, a prisoner, and three bodies."

"I'll be fine. You go on. We'll follow in a few minutes."

Morgan watched as Big Horse trotted off, his long, unfettered hair flying out behind him. Finally Morgan turned and said, "Let's go."

"I ain't movin'," Skousen announced. The facial and head wounds had eased their paining somewhat, and Skousen was feeling defiant.

Morgan trotted back and stopped alongside Skousen, their horses nose to tail on opposite sides. He pulled his rope off his saddlehorn and quickly fashioned a noose.

"Hey, goddammit, what the hell're you doin'?" Skousen demanded as Morgan placed the noose over Skousen's head and let it settle on the soldier's shoulders.

Morgan leaned over, until his mouth almost touched Skousen's ear. "Watch your language, shit ball," he said softly. "There's women and youngsters around."

"I don't give a good goddamn what . . ."

Morgan turned his horse and walked it away. The noose tightened on Skousen's neck and then pulled him off the horse. Morgan stopped and looked back. "You got a choice, sh . . ." He caught himself. "You have a choice, Private. You can walk, or I can drag you. It don't matter to me which one."

"I want to ride," Skousen insisted.

"That's not one of the choices." He turned and began to move off.

"Wait, goddammit!" Skousen shrieked. "Let me get up!"

Morgan stopped. "Best make it quick."

"It'd go a heap faster if you was to come down here and help me."

"I don't help shit balls," Morgan said. He looked at Grace Ashby. "Sorry, ma'am."

Grace nodded and even put forth a small, weak smile. "As offensive as such language is, Marshal Morgan, it does seem to describe that miserable creature," she said quietly.

Morgan nodded and rode off, moving slowly enough for Skousen to keep up, but not slow enough that he had much room to pull something.

Grace and her children were white-knuckled with fear as they entered the village. The only Indians they had ever seen up close had been at the agency. It was different now, Grace figured, because her family was in the Shoshonis' home. She found she was almost as curious as she was frightened as she watched the Shoshoni women who were watching her and her family. It was an odd situation.

Big Horse came trotting up on his pony. "It's bad, Buck," he said. "Murdock and his men—apparently he rounded up a mess of new ones—roared through the village this morning. They killed three and run off a bunch of horses."

"Who?" Morgan croaked, his mouth and throat suddenly dry with worry.

"Cloud Woman wasn't one of those killed, Buck," he said, knowing how his friend must be feeling.

"Now, let's get the Ashbys into your lodge and then go to the council Washakie's having."

Morgan nodded. "What about shit ball back there?"

"Hell with it, we'll bring him with us." He smiled tightly. "I don't think he'll be much of a bother," he added dryly.

"I suppose not. What's the attitude of the People?"

"What do you mean?" When Morgan indicated the Ashbys with a move of his head Big Horse nodded. "It's all right, I think. There're a few hotheads who want to cause trouble, but most of the People know that Orv had nothing to do with it. With Orv's family under our protection—and I expect Washakie's too, once he's told of it—they'll be safe."

Morgan nodded. "Best get going then."

They rode to Morgan's lodge. Morgan figured that Cloud Woman must have been watching; she burst out of the tepee the moment Morgan came into her sight. He slid off his horse and swept her up in his arms and kissed her hard and deeply.

"I missed you, woman," Morgan said when they finally parted.

"And I missed you, husband." Then she hesitantly asked, "Who are the others?"

"All but the blue coat are Mr. Ashby's family. They'll be stayin' with us for a spell." He didn't need to ask, but he did anyway. "If that's all right with you."

"Yes, yes," she said. "Come," she said to Grace, who had gotten gingerly off her horse. "We go inside and you have food. You be safe here."

Grace smiled weakly, still scared half to death.

"Mrs. Ashby," Morgan said, "this is my wife, Cloud Woman." The two women smiled at each other.

"The others are Bonnie, Dusty, and Pearl," Morgan said to Cloud Woman.

She nodded. "Come," she said again. "It's all right."

Grace looked at Morgan, worried and scared.

"Go on in, Mrs. Ashby," Morgan said. "You'll be safe here. Nobody'll bother you."

"How can you be so sure of that?" Grace asked. "I heard what Big Horse said about some people getting killed here. And I know it was done by a white man. Won't these people treat my family poorly because we are white?"

"No, ma'am," Morgan said. "A few might think to do that, but the majority won't allow it."

"I don't know. I really don't." She very much regretted having agreed to this wild scheme. Here she was in the midst of a band of bloodthirsty savages, ones whose anger had been pumped up to great heights by the raid of white men on the village. It was insane, she thought now, to have come along.

"I'll guarantee your safety, ma'am," Big Horse said. "Marshal Morgan might be new to our village and to our ways, and because of that some of the People might not listen so closely to him. But they will to me, and if anyone here wants to harm you, he'll have to get through me—and Buck—first."

Grace looked up into the big Shoshoni's eyes, wanting to believe, but too afraid to. Then she nodded. She had no choice anyway, and she knew that. Perhaps things would get better. After all, no one had made any move to hurt her—so far—and the stares of the Shoshoni women and children certainly were understandable. She was as foreign to these people as they were to her.

232

Leaving Skousen under Big Horse's watchful eyes, Morgan held the flap open. Cloud Woman entered, followed by Grace, Bonnie, Pearl, and Dusty. Morgan went into the lodge. "Our humble home," Morgan said quietly, taking his hat off. He twirled it is his hands as he spoke. "There are enough buffalo robes and blankets around for you folks to make yourselves beds. The cooking pot is usually on the fire, but if you're of a mind to make something different and the ingredients are here, have at it."

He looked from one pale white face to the next. Grace still looked terrified; Bonnie a little less so. The two younger ones looked interested, as if they were having some great adventure, which to them it was, in a way.

"Cloud Woman doesn't speak English very well, ma'am, but you can usually understand her. You can make yourself understood, too, by speaking slowly. If you need anything, want anything, whatever, let Cloud Woman know. I'd stay inside mostly, if I was you, at least till things settle down."

"Have no fear of that, Marshal," Grace said with a wan smile. "I have no intentions of going anywhere."

"Good. I wouldn't think too much of getting a lot of company for a bit, visitors who come and say they need to talk to Cloud Woman. The Shoshonis are very interested in seeing you and touching you. Cloud Woman won't let them bother you too much. She will have to go out for a little, to tend to my horse, but she'll be right out behind the lodge."

Morgan put his hat back on. "Now, ma'am, business calls." He headed outside.

Morgan and Big Horse, towing a frightened, worried, and wounded Private Lee Skousen, went to Was-

233

hakie's lodge. The tepee was crowded, with perhaps two dozen warriors trying to find a little space. The talking stopped as all eyes turned to the new arrivals.

"Sit, shit ball," Morgan said, pushing on one of Skousen's shoulders. He squatted on Skousen's left; Big Horse on Skousen's right.

"We're glad you're here," Washakie said in Shoshoni. Big Horse translated quietly for Morgan. "These are dark times for the People. And we look to you, Buck, to help us."

"We don't need his help," Curly Bull said.

Washakie just glared at the warrior. "What do you have to say?"

"Not much I can say," Morgan noted. Again Big Horse translated. "We know who's done all these things, and I even got some of the men who ride with him. But there won't be any safety on Shoshoni land until they're caught and dealt with."

"Are you going to do this?" Washakie asked.

"Yes." It was flat, hard. "And the sooner I leave, the better it'll be."

"That's because you're afraid to stay here," Curly Bull sneered. He stood and faced Morgan.

The lawman also rose. "I kicked your ass once before, shit ball, and I'll do it again if you keep pushing me."

"Enough!" Washakie snapped. "This is no time for friends to be fighting among themselves."

"He's no goddamn friend of mine," Curly Bull snapped.

"Perhaps that's true," Washakie went on calmly, "but Marshal Morgan is a friend to the People, and we shouldn't forget that."

"What kind of friend is this white man?" Curly Bull

demanded, his voice thick with sarcasm. "He comes to help us, or so he says, but what has he done? Nothing. Many of the People have died since he came to bring his strong white man's medicine to our land."

"And what have you done, shit ball?" Morgan said calmly. "You have been asked to help, but have turned us down. You do nothing but sit here on your ass and mock other men's medicine when you have none of your own."

"Sit down, Curly Bull," Washakie said harshly. When the young warrior turned his determined face on the old chief, Washakie stood. "I will challenge you," Washakie said.

"That's not necessary," Curly Bull muttered. Then he sat.

Washakie and Morgan also sat again. "How many will go with Morgan?" Washakie asked.

Most of the hands in the tepee went up. Washakie nodded. "It is good."

"No, it's not, Washakie," Morgan said. "Your men will be of more use to the People here. They must stay in the village to protect their families. And others' families."

"But what will you do? Go alone?"

"No," Big Horse said. "He will not go alone. I will go with my friend."

"No, Big Horse," Morgan said. "You're needed here."

"Two Wounds was my great friend, too, Buck," Big Horse said simply. "You're not the only one who wants to avenge his death."

Morgan could not argue with that, so he just nodded, accepting.

"Take others too," Washakie said. "At least some."

Morgan and Big Horse looked at each other and shrugged. Neither knew who should come along and who should stay.

"I want to go," Rough Wolf said, standing. "I found the body of my friend Lame Bear, and I have a black heart to the men who killed him."

Big Horse nodded once. "That is all," he said with authority.

Chapter 29

Morgan and Big Horse took Skousen down toward the stream. Morgan unhooked the handcuffs and, with Big Horse's help, put them on again—this time with Skousen's arms backward around a tree. Skousen's legs were straight out ahead of him at a slight angle.

"What the hell're you doing to me, goddammit?" Skousen roared. "Goddammit, let me go."

Morgan came around to the front of the tree again and squatted in front of Skousen. The soldier tried to kick Morgan in the groin but could get no leverage, and Morgan's quick hand flattening Skousen's leg prevented the maneuver.

"I see you like to hit a man where it hurts, eh, shit ball?" Morgan said in cold tones. He slid the large Bowie knife out of the sheath in his right boot. He idly flipped the knife by the handle. The blade struck into the ground between Skousen's legs. Skousen could not close his legs, since Morgan was between them. Skousen began to sweat.

Morgan pulled out the knife and flicked it again. This time it stuck quivering in the ground less than half a foot from Skousen's crotch. He did it once more, a little closer. Then a fourth time. When the knife landed that time the back of the blade brushed Skousen's uniform trousers.

Morgan pulled the knife out and flipped it up in the air and caught it on the way down. "Now, Private Shit Ball, there's quite a bit you have to account for, and right now I'm not really predisposed to haulin' you all the way back to Cheyenne. However, should you show some willingness to tell me things I want to know, my humor might improve, and then you might even get to Cheyenne."

"I ain't tellin' you shit, you son of a bitch," Skousen snarled. "I told you that before, you dumb bastard."

Morgan spit tobacco juice, hitting Skousen in his left eye—the one with the broken orbit. "I do believe you're showin' a less-than-helpful attitude, shit ball," he said. "Now let me tell you a couple of things. One, if you don't answer my questions, you'll die. Second, if you die, it will be a long and painful experience for you. Now I don't think you're nearly so tough as you like to play pretend at." Morgan was surprised that the soldier had retained much of his fire despite the broken bones and the knot on his head. Morgan paused and sighed, as if he was dealing with a recalcitrant child. "I suppose you might need a little . . . shall we say . . . encouragement to loosen your tongue."

"Do what you need to, ass wipe. You're not going to get anything from me."

Morgan nodded. "If that's the way you want it." He thought of jabbing a thumb against the fractured bone around Skousen's eye, but for reasons even he could not fathom, he decided against that. "Big Horse, please remove shit ball's boots." When that was done

Morgan said calmly, "Big Horse, you have a choice to make. You either cut off a couple of toes or you can break shit ball's foot in as many place as you can."

"Damn, that's a hard choice," Big Horse said. He seemed almost cheerful. "How's about if I do one to one foot and the other to the other?"

"I suppose that'd be all right."

Skousen sat there, thinking his captors were lunatics. "It's not going to work, asshole," he said with bravado. "Neither of you is gonna do any such thing. And I . . ."

Skousen suddenly screamed. Since he had heard no sound of breaking bones Morgan assumed Big Horse had opted to start with a couple of amputations.

"I only sliced off the three small ones," Big Horse said. "You want the rest off?"

"That's up to shit ball here." He spit tobacco juice again. This time it splashed on the front of Skousen's cotton army shirt. "Well, shit ball, are you going to talk? Or shall I have Big Horse perform some more surgery?"

Tears were running from Skousen's eyes and his face was screwed up tight with pain.

"You haven't answered me yet, shit ball," Morgan said quietly, calmly.

"Wait," Skousen said, whispered. He suspected that if he talked too loudly, his other toes would fall off. "I'll talk." He groaned. "Jesus, my foot. Goddammit."

"You get to talkin', the sooner you'll be gettin' that foot treated."

"What . . . What the hell do you wanna know, for Christ's sake?" Some shock was setting in, and to Skousen it seemed as if the pain—all the pain—had

239

lessened a little. He began breathing a little more comfortably.

"I asked you before who came up with that harebrained scheme to take unwelcome actions with Mrs. Ashby and her daughter. I'd still like an answer."

"Lieutenant Pomeroy."

For some reason Morgan was not surprised.

"Why? What the hell would that accomplish?"

"I ain't sure, since I wasn't privy to all the lieutenant's secrets, of course."

"Don't go pushin' your luck with me, shit ball," Morgan warned.

"Well, dammit, it's true. A lieutenant in the U.S. Army just don't confide in low-class enlisted men. He might pick us for some dirty work, but he sure as shit ain't gonna explain his grand scheme."

"And you didn't ask him what this was all about?"

Skousen shook his head. "Nope. He says I got a job for you, I go do the job. I get some extra money and maybe some extra privileges, and that keeps me happy."

That was plausible enough. If Pomeroy had come up with some kind of scheme, he most likely wouldn't reveal it all. Still, Morgan was certain that Skousen knew more than he was telling. "You mean he just told you to go up to Ashby's place, kill the two Indians, and then rape the mother and the oldest daughter? And he gave you no explanation at all? I find that a tad hard to believe, shit ball."

Skousen looked into Morgan's cold, hard gray eyes, and he shivered. "I don't know everything, you understand," Skousen stammered. "But he told me a little."

"Then suppose you tell me and Big Horse before

the three of us're too goddamn old to do anything about it."

"Well, he said that we should go up there and kill the two savages . . ." He screamed again as Big Horse whacked off another toe.

"You best watch your mouth, white man," Big Horse said evenly.

Skousen had to sit rigid, unspeaking, for a few minutes, until the new flames of pain were down to embers. "We were supposed to kill the two Shoshonis, then do what we wanted with the old lady. Vic, he decided to add to things a little by gettin' that little bitch into things."

"Nice to know he could at least pretend to think," Morgan said dryly. Then he asked, "But if it was his idea, why was it you tryin' to soil that little girl?" His voice had taken on a hard edge.

Skousen gulped. "I paid him for the privilege," he admitted defensively.

Morgan shook his head in disgust. "Then what?" he asked, fighting back his anger again.

"Then we was supposed to kill the old lady and leave the body there in the house. It was supposed to look like either friends of those two red . . . Shoshonis or a war party from an unfriendly tribe had been there. It was supposed to look like the others killed the two men you sent there."

"Why would Shoshonis kill other Shoshonis?" Morgan asked. "It doesn't make any sense at all that Pomeroy'd set it up that way. Of course, there's been no proof that I know of that he's sane anyway."

"He said something about how he'd see how much ruckus was kicked up before he decided which story to tell. I gather that he figured the Shoshonis'd be mad because of all the killin's and that they might be angry when two of them were forced into standing guard over a white family while their own families were in trouble."

"That makes at least a little sense." He paused. "What about the kids?"

"We were supposed to take the three of 'em out somewhere and kill 'em. Then we were to cut 'em up a little."

"Yeah, so it looked like Shoshonis or Arapahos did it," Big Horse interjected.

"Yeah. Then Vic got him the notion to sink our pizzles in that little . . ."

Morgan smashed Skousen in the face, breaking his nose and splattering blood all over the front of Skousen's uniform. "Whatever filth you shit balls devised is best left unsaid," he said icily.

Skousen moaned. He thought he could feel the broken bones in his face shifting painfully. "Yeah, sure, sorry." He did not sound sincere. "Anyway, he got the notion to take her, and then leave her there with the old lady."

"What was the purpose of all this?" Morgan asked.

Skousen shrugged. "I don't know. I really don't. The lieutenant only told us as much as he thought we needed to know, and no more."

"I have a theory, Buck," Big Horse said quietly. When he sensed he had Morgan's attention—seeing as how he was behind Morgan—he continued, "I think he planned it so that it looked like an Indian raid. Didn't matter to him much which tribes or tribes. All he wanted was to be able to report that the agency was under Indian attack, that a number of white people had been killed, women ravished, children taken off into

242

the night by 'savages' bent on all manner of deviltry. Then he could take to the field with colors flying.

"It'd help, too, I suppose, that all the other murders and mutilations had been reported. He most likely has reported them as Arapaho depredations rather than the work of white men. Once he was in the field, he could legally lay waste to any Indians he found, friendly or not. He'd get promoted and moved to better duty as a goddamn hero."

Morgan had been watching Skousen's face while Big Horse had been expounding his theory. He saw signs— one of the few kinds of signs he could read—that Skousen believed what Big Horse was saying was true. It seemed the way he looked that Skousen did have knowledge of all this from Pomeroy.

Still, something bothered Morgan. It all fit pretty well, except for . . . and that was the trouble; he didn't know what didn't fit. "You know why the killings have stepped up lately, shit ball?" he asked as something squirmed around in his mind, trying to coalesce.

"I ain't sure, but I think it's got something to do with that new lieutenant," Skousen said softly, trying not to jostle his fractured facial bones.

"Whitehill?"

"Yeah. Lieutenant Pomeroy didn't tell me this, but I've thought about it some and it seems logical."

"What is it?" Morgan asked. Only the overall grimness of the conversation had kept him from laughing at Skousen's last statement.

"I figured Lieutenant Pomeroy had this whole thing concocted for quite a spell."

That made another little bell go off in Morgan's brain, but he left it alone for now, wanting it to grow into something substantial.

"Then Lieutenant Whitehill showed up. I think his orders were to take command of Camp Brown soon."

"That's good from Pomeroy's standpoint," Big Horse said. "It's what he wanted all along."

"But he wants to go out a hero," Morgan said. "He doesn't want to go out as a first lieutenant with three, four years here and nothin' to show for it. So I think he pushed things, ordered more killings, came up with the scheme about Ashby's family and all. Since he was still in command and the boiling point had almost been reached, he'd have an excuse to go into the field, like you said. And in doing it, he'd have Lieutenant Whitehill along with him to report his prowess to higher-ups. It wouldn't have to be just his word for it."

"Lovely feller," Big Horse commented.

Something still tugged at Morgan's brain. He rose and paced a little, absentmindedly slapping the blade of his knife against his thigh. Finally, he stopped and whirled on Skousen. "Is Pomeroy behind the depredations of Murdock and his murderous band?" he asked.

Skousen looked shocked. "Why do you ask that?" he countered.

"Couple of reasons. One is something he said the other day when we were at the agency. Damn, what were the words?" He paced again in thought. "Yeah, that's it," he finally said. "He said something about not allowing me and Big Horse—but me in particular—to get in the way of things. He said he didn't want me roaming the reservation chasing men who were trying to help. Something about them helping his command in its rightful duties or something like that."

"So?" Skousen asked.

"So, that sounds to me like he's behind the Mur-

244

dock raids. He has to be. It's the only goddamn thing that fits. Especially since you said a few minutes ago that you thought Pomeroy had this larger scheme in motion for some time." Morgan glared at Skousen. "So, shit ball, did I hit it right?"

Skousen could only gulp and nod. And then whistle in pain.

Chapter 30

Morgan, Big Horse, and Rough Wolf rode out the next morning. The two Shoshoni were painted and had on their best war shirts. Each carried a lance and a shield; a bow and a quiver of arrows was slung across each man's back, almost resting on his pony's rump. Each also carried two six-guns and had a Winchester in a saddle scabbard. Morgan had his two Smith and Wessons, as well as his Winchester rifle and the shotgun he had taken from Foster's saloon in Flat Fork. That seemed like such a long time ago, Morgan thought.

They left the village heading west—the direction in which Murdock and his band of marauders had gone after their lightning-fast raid on the village. Morgan had thought to ask just before the council had broken up the night before if the Shoshoni were sure it had been Murdock.

Washakie nodded gravely. "He is the one who wears the necklace made of ears and fingers of the People. And when he shot at people, he laughed. It sounded crazy, that laugh."

Morgan had said nothing. It was Murdock; there could be no doubt about it.

They picked up the killers' trail just outside the village and followed it. Either Big Horse or Rough Wolf would check occasionally to make sure they were still on track. The trail cut southwest after a few miles, surprising them. Morgan stopped, and the others did likewise. "You sure, Big Horse?" he asked.

The big Shoshoni nodded. "There's no doubt."

"Then what's he tryin' to do?" Morgan mused. "I could understand if he cut north to go around the far side of Washakie's village, or maybe even raided another village. I could understand if he turned due east here so he could make it back to Flat Fork. But the only thing in this direction is . . ." Morgan's words stumbled to a halt. "Jesus, you don't think he's connected with Ashby, do you?"

Big Horse shook his head. "I've known Orv Ashby for some time, and I'd stake my life that he had nothing to do with this. But what about the army?"

"I expect we need to pay Commander Shit Ball a little visit," he said tightly.

Big Horse nodded. "My thoughts, too." He paused. "By the way, do you know there's someone following us?"

"No," Morgan said, surprised. He looked back but saw nothing. "You know who?"

"Can't tell. He's one of the People, though."

"You sure? I don't see anybody out there."

"It's a good thing you've let me and Rough Wolf do the tracking," Big Horse said with a laugh. It was one of the other things about Big Horse that Morgan liked. He could almost always find humor in a situation, even a gloomy or dangerous one.

"I told you I wasn't a tracker," Morgan said a little defensively.

"How the hell do you catch any outlaws anyway?"

Morgan's face darkened. "The ones I'm after usually leave an easy trail to follow."

"Oh?" He knew white men were worse than children in covering their trail, but still, Morgan's statement sounded like too much to believe.

"There's bloodshed and dead bodies wherever they go," Morgan said sourly.

"Not much different than here in some ways," Big Horse said drolly. He sighed. "What do you want to do about our friend back there?"

Morgan shrugged. "He look like he's going to cause us any trouble?"

"No. I'll tell you what I think, though."

"I'm surprised you haven't done so already," Morgan said, trying to revive whatever little humor he had in him today.

"Eat shit. I think it's one of the boys. One who isn't old enough to go to war, yet old enough to feel his blood sing with the medicine and the power of his ancestors. One who would've been laughed at had he asked the council for permission to go."

"So what do we do about him?"

Big Horse shrugged. "Depends on several things."

"Such as?"

"Which one of the boys it is. Some I wouldn't mind having along. There're plenty of others I wouldn't want to even attend my burial. It also depends on whether you want him to ride alone out there and maybe get killed if Murdock and his scum cut back toward the village. It depends on whether you want a boy standing next to you in battle, if that's what it comes to. And you and I both know Murdock will never give up without a fight. This is one goddamn outlaw you're not going to be able to arrest."

"I know." Morgan pulled off his hat and ran a shirt sleeve across his sweating forehead. "Well, I think the first thing we ought to do is find out who the little bastard is."

"So we lay him a little trap?"

Morgan nodded.

Not far on, they came to Bighorn Draw. It was almost always devoid of water, other than perhaps a few stagnant pools, except when it rained hard. It was dry now; the area hadn't seen rain in several days, a strange thing since this was supposed to be the rainy season.

The three men rode down into the draw. All dismounted and loosened their saddles to let the horses breath. Then Big Horse and Rough Wolf had a short, quiet chat in Shoshoni. Just after that, Rough Wolf disappeared. That was the only way Morgan could describe it. He was looking at the two Shoshoni, turned around for a moment, and when he did, Rough Wolf was no longer anywhere in sight. Morgan sighed and shrugged.

Ten minutes later, Morgan heard a short, sharp squawk. He reached for a pistol, but then saw Big Horse sitting there calmly. The Shoshoni grinned and winked. "Rough Wolf has just encountered our tracker."

Rough Wolf half slid, half jumped down into the draw, holding a youth by the shirt.

"Rabbit Tail," Morgan said, "why're you following us?"

"That white man, he killed my friend Yellow Wing. I want to avenge my friend's death."

When Big Horse had finished translating for him, Morgan said, "Do you think you're up to the task?"

The youth bobbed his head when Big Horse translated.

"What do you think, Big Horse?" Morgan asked. "He one of the ones you might be willing to have fight at your side?"

Big Horse studied the boy for a few moments. Then he spoke in Shoshoni to the youth and waited for a reply. Turning to Morgan, Big Horse said, "He will come with us."

Morgan nodded. "What was that last bit about?"

"I told him that you are the war chief of this raiding party. As such, you are to be obeyed immediately and without question. If he doesn't, I told him I'll send him back. He agreed."

"Why didn't you tell him you were the war chief?" Morgan asked. "He'd be more likely to take orders from you than from me."

"Bullshit. You're big medicine among the whites. All the People believe that. That's why Curly Bull keeps ruffling your feathers. He's trying to knock you down a peg or two so he can strut around. But he can't do it because you have strong medicine."

"Right now I'd rather have a strong left arm."

"Your shoulder still bothering you?"

Morgan nodded. "It doesn't hurt so much as it just don't work right."

Big Horse grinned. "You get in the middle of a battle and you'll forget all about how that shoulder doesn't work right. You might regret it later, but you'll never know it while you're fighting."

Morgan nodded, knowing the truth of it. He had experienced it before, and he figured Big Horse had, too. "Does Rabbit Tail have any weapons?" he asked.

"Not much. His small bow and some arrows. A knife. That's about it."

"Does he know how to use a pistol?"

Big Horse shrugged. "It doesn't much matter, does it? I'm not giving up mine, and Rough Wolf feels the same, I'm sure. And I really doubt you'll hand over one of those Smith and Wessons to a boy."

"I've got extra," Morgan said. "Skousen's .36 Colt. I picked it up after I handcuffed him and shoved it in my saddlebags. I found half a box of shells for it, too."

"Well, even if he doesn't know how to use it," Big Horse said, "having it might keep him out of trouble. Hell, it might get him in trouble."

"You're a big goddamn help," Morgan said dryly. He got the pistol and the shells, then called to Rabbit Tail. He handed the youth the pistol. With Big Horse translating, he asked, "You know how to fire one of these?"

Rabbit Tail's head bobbed.

"I think you're full of shit, but we don't have the time to quibble about it." He showed Rabbit Tail how to load the pistol and how to eject the spent shells. "Since you don't have a holster, you'll have to stick it in your belt. And because of that, you only load five chambers. Leave the hammer on the empty chamber."

"Why?" Rabbit Tail asked, puzzled. Here was a weapon that would fire many times, yet he was not allowed to use its full power. That made no sense to him.

"Because if you don't, the first time you hit a good

bump or something on your pony, you're going to ensure that you never become a man."

"Oh," Rabbit Tail said with a gulp.

"All right, boys, let's get going," Morgan announced.

They still rode southwest, growing ever nearer to the agency and Camp Brown. Within an hour, Big Horse pointed. "See that, Buck?" he asked.

Morgan nodded. He had seen the cloud of dust. "Is it coming or going?"

They all stopped, and Big Horse shaded his eyes with his hand. After a minute or two of observation, he said, "Coming this way."

Morgan wondered as he and his small group started riding again whether it was Murdock and his gang or Pomeroy and his soldiers. It could even be Ashby, with some soldiers as an escort.

Morgan let his anger steep in the heat of his blood. Most of his anger was directed at himself. He wasn't sure what he could have done to prevent many of the deaths of the past month, but he figured he should have been able to do something.

The cloud of dust grew more substantial, until it eventually formed a light tan spot over several bouncing figures. It took a little longer to reveal that the figures wore what appeared to be blue.

Morgan pulled up. "This is far enough," he said. "If that's really Pomeroy and his men, I'd just as soon they come to us."

None of the others said anything. They just spread out a little, with Morgan and Big Horse in the center, with Rabbit Tail on Big Horse's right, and Rough Wolf on Morgans left. Then they waited. Morgan pulled out

252

a plug of tobacco and cut off a chunk. He shoved it in his mouth and began chewing.

It was not long before the figures heading toward Morgan's small group became recognizable figures. First Lt. Dexter Pomeroy was indeed in the lead. He had Second Lt. Virgil Whitehill and ten enlisted men with him.

The military procession came to a halt perhaps twenty feet from Morgan and his men. The troops formed ranks in a semicircle around Morgan's men.

"Marshal Morgan," Pomeroy said pompously, "I hearby place you under military arrest. You will give up your weapons and come along peacefully or you'll suffer the consequences."

Chapter 31

Morgan laughed loud and hard. It was a relief after days of tension. "You are one strange son of a bitch, Lieutenant," he said, still chuckling.

Pomeroy glowered.

"And not only are you strange, shit ball, you're also under arrest, for various and sundry crimes against the U.S. government."

"Like what?" Pomeroy asked, sneering.

"Like ordering the murders of numerous Indians under your charge and care. Like trying to foment war between the Shoshoni and the Arapaho, something with which you expected to cover yourself in glory and attain higher rank. Like ordering the rape and murder of an Indian agent's family."

Lieutenant Whitehill's eyes bulged and widened as the list grew. The soldiers also were looking at each other in wonder. Some seemed to be sick, as if they had had a part in all this and were now regretting it— or regretting the possibility of getting caught.

"Like directing a criminal enterprise," Morgan continued. "Like interfering with an Indian agent performing his work. Like interfering with a deputy U.S.

marshal performing his duties." He stopped to take a breath. "I've got some others, if you care for me to list them."

"Do you have any proof of these claims, Marshal?" Lieutenant Whitehill asked.

"I do. And what I don't have I should be able to get in the next day or so. I've even got a witness."

"Oh?"

"Private Lee Skousen. He was one of the shit balls sent out to rape and murder Mr. Ashby's family."

"In addition to being an insufferable bastard, you're also a lying, cheating, and interfering son of a bitch, Morgan," Pomeroy said. He drew in a long breath, blew it out, and then sneered. "Arrest him, men," he ordered. "And the others with him. If any of them resists, shoot him down." He puffed out his chest, arrogant in his power and authority.

"You men stand fast," Whitehill suddenly ordered. He edged his horse up alongside Pomeroy's and stopped with his horse's head about even with Pomeroy's left leg. Whitehill had his Colt pistol in hand. It was cocked and brushing the back of Pomeroy's head.

Whitehill looked at Morgan. "Are they obeying my orders?" he asked.

"Seem to be—so far."

"Goddammit, I order you men to arrest that marshal and his accomplices. Now!" Pomeroy screeched.

"As I said, men, stand fast," Whitehill repeated. "I am hereby taking over command of Camp Brown and all its personnel."

"By whose authority?" Pomeroy demanded.

"By my authority. I am scheduled to take command in two weeks. This just moves it up."

"I'll have you hanged for this!" Pomeroy almost

screamed. "You son of a bitch. I will. You have no right to take my command. I'll kill you for this."

"I have every right to do so. Regulations allow the next in line to assume command if the current post commander is too ill to retain his position, if he is incapacitated or is physically or mentally incapable of handling the duties of his position."

"None of those things apply to me, *Second* Lieutenant," Pomeroy said with a smirk.

"Well, sir, I am not sufficiently educated to determine your mental state, though I would venture to say that you are as crazy as a bedbug. As for the rest, I think—no, I'm certain—that you are physically unable to handle your duties."

"You're the one who's crazy here. I'm as fit as anyone on the post."

"You were." Then Whitehill lambasted Pomeroy a good shot on the side of the head with his pistol barrel. Pomeroy fell off the side of his horse and hit the dirt hard. Blood coated the side of his head.

Whitehill moved his horse back a little and then turned to face the men of his new command. "Johnson, O'Reilly, pick up Lieutenant Pomeroy and cart him back to the camp. Bring him to Dr. Snyder. If the doctor asks you what happened, tell him that you know nothing and that I'll fill him in later—if I feel like it."

He paused, thinking for a few moments. "I don't know if any of you others are involved in Lieutenant Pomeroy's schemes and machinations, but if you were, I'll ferret you out as sure as I'm standing here. It would go easier on you to confess your involvement and make a clean breast of it. Then I can—and will—help you. Refuse, and you are found out, and your punishment will be more severe." He sat there a few moments more, looking over his troops.

As the two soldiers dismounted to retrieve Pomeroy, Whitehill turned his horse until he was facing Morgan again. He moved closer, stopping ten feet away.

"He's my prisoner, Lieutenant," Morgan said.

"The army has first dibs on him, Marshal. If there's anything left of the sorry son of a bitch when the army gets done with him, you can have him."

"You sure you're going to be able to keep him locked up? He's got plenty of friends around here, it seems. Or at least many acquaintances."

"I'm aware of all that—now."

"Don't be so hard on yourself, Lieutenant. You've only been here a week or two. Hell, a man can't learn everything about the place where he does his job or the people he's forced to deal with. Not in a million years, and certainly not in a couple of weeks."

"Thank you, Marshal." He sighed. It had been a hell of a day so far. "I take it your and your men are hunting for Murdock."

"Yes," Morgan said sharply. Seeing Whitehill's look of surprise, Morgan added. "Murdock and his men rode through Washakie's village first thing yesterday. Killed three people. With Two Wounds, Old Belly, and Red Hand killed at Ashby's, it was a mighty poor day for a heap of people."

Whitehill nodded. "Yes, yes, it most certainly was."

"You seen Murdock lately?"

"Not exactly. But a work detail said they spotted them—at least they thought it was them—camped several miles from the camp, some ways up into the Wind River Mountains, on the north fork of the Little Wind."

"Obliged, Lieutenant," Morgan said. "But I figure we ought to be gettin' back on the trail. Time's a-wasting."

"Do you and your men want our help?" Whitehill asked, almost embarrassed by making the offer after all that had gone on with Pomeroy.

"No, though I'm obliged for the offer. The best thing you can do to help is to stay out of the way. And make sure you ferret out Pomeroy's helpers."

"Are you sure?" Whitehill asked rather skeptically. "It doesn't look like you have much of a fighting force with you." He pointed to Rabbit Tail.

"We'll do all right, I expect."

"Jesus, Marshal, why'd you bring a boy with you?"

Morgan's temper flared, but he forced it back down. It was, now that he thought about it, quite a reasonable question. One normally did not go on the warpath with boys. "He followed us out but stuck far enough behind that we didn't know about it until we were too far from the village to make it worthwhile to send or escort him back there."

"He must be quite skilled if he trailed you unfound for some miles when you have two Shoshoni warriors with you."

Morgan was about to say something when he slapped his mouth shut. He turned to Big Horse. The big Shoshoni sat there, looking as innocent as a choirboy, gazing toward the heavens. "You knew he was there the whole goddamn time, didn't you, you son of a bitch?" Morgan said.

"Of course I did. Trouble was, I didn't believe you were anywhere near as bad at reading sign as you said all those times. But damn if you ain't."

"I ought to arrest you, dammit all." Then he

grinned. "I guess we can't all be perfect," he said. Then he laughed. "Again, I'm obliged for your offer, Lieutenant, but I'll respectfully turn you down."

Whitehill nodded. "Well, then, Marshal, my command won't interfere in this business. I'll see to that." He grinned a little. "From the looks of it, it's more marshal business than army business anyway."

"That it is." He touched his heels to the horse's flanks and trotted off with his three companions.

They moved at a quick pace, heading for the agency in general. Just before getting there, they turned northwest a little, moving to the Little Wind River, which they planned to follow until they reached Murdock's camp. If he was still there.

Morgan felt a sense of urgency—or maybe it was expectation. He was sure a battle was imminent and he was prepared for it. More than prepared; he looked forward to it.

Half a mile or so away, they saw a solitary figure racing toward them.

"That's Orv," Big Horse said.

Morgan wasn't sure whether to believe Big Horse. He had always thought he had good eyesight, but Big Horse's abilities seemed almost beyond belief. However, within a few moments, he, too, was fairly certain it was Ashby. He grinned, thinking he had figured Big Horse out. The Shoshoni's eyesight was no better than his own. His power lay in his willingness to hazard a guess earlier than everyone else. He simply deduced who might be coming from that direction and guess it was that person unless there was something to lead him to believe differently.

Morgan picked up his speed a little more, and before

259

long he was slowing again, with the galloping Orville Ashby closing the gap fast.

Ashby pulled to a stop, his horse sweating and foamy and his own face flushed with perspiration. He waved a piece of paper and shouted frantically, "I found this in my house. What's this all about? What, what?"

"Damn, Orv, calm down," Morgan said.

"How the hell can I calm down when I come home after a week and find a letter from my wife telling me she's gone off to live with the Shoshonis?" he demanded.

"It's not as bad as all that," Big Horse said in mock offense.

"Like hell."

"Come on, Orv, relax a little. Let's squat here a bit and we can bring you up-to-date."

Ashby looked skeptical, but he nodded. When they were all sitting, passing a canteen around, Ashby demanded, "Well, what's going on?"

"There was trouble at the agency, Orv," Morgan said. "Old Belly and Red Hand were killed, and we thought your family might be in danger there. So we brought them to Washakie's village."

"And they're supposed to be safe in a Shoshoni village?" Ashby almost screeched.

"I'm offended," Big Horse said, not meaning it.

Ashby glanced at him. "You know what I mean."

"Look, Orv, I don't want to give you all the particulars. Grace'll do that. But right now she's safe, as are the youngsters. We all found out that Private Skousen is mixed up in the whole thing, and that Pomeroy was, if not the mastermind, at least the key player in the Murdock raids and the killings of the Shoshonis."

"That sounds farfetched."

"I know," Morgan agreed. "It's true, though. Lieutenant Whitehill took over command from Pomeroy, and had Pomeroy arrested."

"Jesus."

"Yeah. How about you, Orv? You come up with anything?"

"Huh?" Ashby seemed in a daze. "Yeah. Oh, yeah," he said, regaining his sense. "Thoughts of my family have made me a little absentminded, I guess." He drank from the canteen and then handed it to Rabbit Tail. "Well, as we suspected, that wire from Floyd was phony. I sent a wire from one of Hogg's stage stations and waited for a reply. It was a couple of days in coming. I don't know if some of the lines were down or whether Floyd was just too busy to get to it."

He took another sip of water. "Regardless, he was shocked—and I daresay a little irritated—at Pomeroy's presumptuousness. He did, by the way, say you are to arrest him if you deem it necessary and that he would worry about the ramifications."

"I tried arresting him, but Lieutenant Whitehill claimed Pomeroy as his prisoner." He sighed. "Well, me and my friends here have business to attend to. Take your time out to the village. Your family's safe. And give our regards to Whitehill if you pass him and his men on the road."

Chapter 32

Morgan and his companions hit the Little Wind River and began following it into the foothills of the Wind River Mountains, and then higher.

The sullen, lead-gray skies that had been with the small group since they had left finally split and poured out their contents. There was little thunder and only an occasional flicker of lightning.

"This rain's going to make it harder to find those bastards, Buck," Big Horse said.

Morgan nodded as he shrugged on a slicker. The three Indians pulled blankets around them. The rain, the low-hanging clouds, and the fog would make it almost impossible to see smoke or even firelight. The weather also would mask sounds—both their own, which was good, and Murdock's men's, which was not good.

Rough Wolf edged up to the two. "You wait here. I go there," he said, his English poor and heavily accented.

Big Horse looked at Rough Wolf and then asked him to explain in Shoshoni.

When Rough Wolf did so Big Horse turned to Morgan. "Rough Wolf says we should wait here while he goes ahead to scout. I think it's a good idea."

"Can he find them without being seen or heard?" Morgan asked quietly.

"Rough Wolf's one of the best at such things," Big Horse answered. "Hell, I'd thought of doing it myself, but I'd only wind up walking right into the middle of their camp or they'd hear me coming and shoot me dead."

Morgan nodded. "Sounds good to me. Let's pull in over there." He pointed to a stand of trees against a sharp cliff with a large overhang. Between the outcropping of stone and the trees, they should be out of the weather.

Big Horse spoke to Rough Wolf in Shoshoni for a few moments. Then Rough Wolf nodded and rode off, his pony walking slowly. It made the bow and quiver slung across Rough Wolf's back shift rhythmically on the horse's rump.

"We might as well build a fire," Morgan said. "I could use some coffee."

"Good idea," Big Horse agreed. "Rabbit Tail, gather wood."

Morgan looked at Big Horse sharply, ready to say something. But the look in Big Horse's eyes made him keep his silence. When Rabbit Tail had wandered off a little ways Big Horse said, "It's our way, Buck. It's no insult to Rabbit Tail. He is expected to do such things on his first war party. Maybe others, too. But if he draws blood this time, he'll be looked at with more favor by the others. Then he can call himself a warrior—and be treated like one."

Morgan nodded. He was not all that concerned

about how Rabbit Tail was being treated. He had just thought it curious.

Soon the three had a fire going and coffee being made. They waited, grateful for the cover they had, not envying Rough Wolf at all. The latter showed up, appearing as if by magic, a little over an hour later.

Morgan was startled by Rough Wolf's sudden appearance, but he covered it quickly. "Come, have coffee," he said.

Rough Wolf nodded and pulled his tin mug from a bag hanging from his saddlehorn. He filled it and drank a little, savoring the coffee. The day had turned cool with the rain—and with the rise in elevation—and the hot liquid felt good to all of them inside.

After a little while Morgan finally asked, "Did you find them?"

Rough Wolf nodded. "Seven that I could count," he said in Shoshoni, while Big Horse translated for Morgan. "There might be a lot more. I'm not sure. They're in a canyon a couple of miles upriver. They look like they've decided to make a comfortable camp, like they plan to wait for someone who isn't supposed to come for another couple of days."

"They on the alert?" Morgan asked.

"Didn't seem to be, partly because of where they are."

"What's that mean?"

"The canyon they're in is off the trail on a very small trail. It's almost impossible to see, since the mouth of the canyon is covered by trees and shrubs."

"Did nature put them there?" Morgan asked.

"Some of them. Murdock's men added some." Rough Wolf sipped more coffee, then he said, "Since they're in such a spot I think they figure they're well protected. And so they don't have to be on the alert."

"Can we get in there easily enough?"

Rough Wolf shrugged. "Might be hard. They're in a cave maybe twenty feet up a rocky slope. However, as soon as you get in the canyon, the trail is off to the left. It goes down an almost sheer cliff. And it's in full view of the men in the cave. Even if they're not paying too much attention, they're bound to spot us if we all try going down there together."

"Take them at night?" Morgan asked hopefully.

"Only if you're crazy," Rough Wolf responded. There was no smile accompanying the statement.

"Any ideas on how we can get down there?"

Rough Wolf shrugged again. "Alone, any of us could do it. Like I did before. But four? Not impossible, but not too likely either." He did grin then, just a little. "Of course, if only Shoshonis were to take the trail, there'd be no problem."

"You're saying I'm clumsy because I'm a white man?" Morgan demanded angrily.

"You should know better than to insult a friend, Rough Wolf," Big Horse said. "I am Shoshoni, but I'm no better than Buck in creeping up on people." He thought a minute, as Rough Wolf and Morgan glared at each other over the fire. "What direction does the cave mouth face?" he asked Rough Wolf.

"Southeast," Rough Wolf responded. "Why?"

Big Horse nodded, a little excited. "Then we go down there just after dawn."

"Why?" Rough Wolf said. He was good at stalking and other such arts, but strategy was not Rough Wolf's forte.

"Because the sun'll be in their eyes," Morgan said with a nod, understanding immediately.

"Exactly," Big Horse said. "Let's move on up there as close as we can today and then wait the night out."

"Can we find our way up to the canyon mouth at night, Rough Wolf?" Morgan asked thoughtfully, deciding to put aside his anger for the moment.

"I think so. Why?"

Morgan waved a hand at their surroundings. "This here's a nice little place to stay. We have cover, wood, some forage for the horses. We have a fire going and coffee made. Why not just stay here overnight? We can be reasonably comfortable. Just before dawn, we head for the canyon.

"I think I like that idea," Big Horse said. "How about you, Rough Wolf?"

Rough Wolf nodded.

"Good," Big Horse said. "Then it's settled." He did not consider asking the boy about it, and Rabbit Tail was not bothered by not being asked. It was the way of things.

"Can we take them once we get into that canyon, Rough Wolf?" Morgan asked suddenly.

Rough Wolf nodded again. "I think so. If we can get in there, we can take them. There's a small, clear area in front of their cave, but if they're inside—where they've made their camp—they can't see very well to either flank. Plus there are enough trees and rocks around the open area to give good cover."

"Sounds all right," Morgan said. He rose and unsaddled his horse and groomed it. Then he stretched out on his bedroll against the cliff wall. The others soon followed suit.

Morgan awoke hungry some hours later. The sun

had gone down, but clouds covered the moon and there was a thick mist in the air. He stoked up the fire and put more wood on. He made fresh coffee and set that on the fire to heat. He threw some bacon in an old black skillet and some beans in a small, battered pot.

By that time, Rough Wolf was awake and had slipped into the bushes. Within minutes, Big Horse and Rabbit Tail also woke. No one said anything. They just took care of their personal business and then squatted at the fire and had some coffee. Before long the food was ready, and they ate quickly.

Still without speaking, they mounted their horses and rode off into the thick blackness of the night. They moved slowly, letting the horses pick their way on the rocky track. Rough Wolf was in the lead, since he was the only one who even had an inkling of where they were heading.

With a whisper, Rough Wolf at last called a halt. The whispered word was passed back from man to man, since no one could really see the others.

"Is this it?" Morgan asked. He was in the rear, with Rabbit Tail just ahead of him, then Big Horse.

"Yes." The word went from mouth to mouth.

"We'll wait here for a little while," Rough Wolf said. They moved into the trees alongside the trail, deep enough that they would not be seen from the trail.

Dawn was beginning to edge into the land, and the sky had turned from pitch black to a faded, dirty gray. It wasn't much light, but it was enough for them to dismount and tie their horses off for a while.

"You think the horses can make their way down there, Rough Wolf?" Morgan asked.

"The trail's wide enough," Rough Wolf answered. "But I think we should go on foot."

"Why?"

"The horses are large, perhaps large enough to be seen. They're also noisy. And clumsy."

Morgan nodded. "Makes sense."

"Rabbit Tail," Big Horse said, "you will stay here and watch the horses."

"But . . ." Rabbit Tail stopped, then set his face. "The war leader has not said that," he said in Shoshoni.

Big Horse's face colored in anger, but then he composed himself and almost smiled. He translated for Morgan.

The lawman looked at the boy. "You'll stay here with the horses, Rabbit Tail." he said.

The boy didn't like it when Big Horse translated, but he accepted it. After all, the leader of this war party had told him to do it, and do it he must.

Half an hour later, with the dull light of a cloudy day covering them, Rough Wolf rose. "Now's the time," he said in Shoshoni. Morgan did not need that to be translated.

Leaving their slicker or blankets behind, the three well-armed adults pushed through a thick curtain of brush and tree branches. Straight ahead was a wall of stone, but to the left a trail headed downward. The trail was perhaps four feet wide, large enough to allow horses, and even loaded pack mules, but was much too narrow to permit wagons.

As soon as each man went far enough down the trail to get beyond the stone wall, they stopped and looked down at the small canyon. Dull grayish-red light splashed across the rocky slopes opposite them.

Rough Wolf pointed to a substantial cave across from them. "That's where they camp."

"Great," Morgan hissed. "Now get your ass movin' before we get stuck here."

Rough Wolf glared at him for a few moments, then turned and moved on.

It was a hard trek, what with all the loose chunks of rock and the slickness of the mud from last night's rain. Morgan was glad that the rain had stopped. Looking down, they all could see the heavy coat of fog in the canyon bottom. There was no fog this high, and the sun peeking through the clouds cast an eerie light on the fog below, and on the cave.

Eventually they made the floor of the canyon. The fog was not as thick, but they did not know whether it was because they were in the midst of it or because the sun was burning it off.

They pressed ahead, slowly, since it was very difficult to see down here. When they came to the open meadow area they backed up in a hurry. There they took positions behind trees and boulders. Then they hunkered down to wait.

Chapter 33

When the fog had dissipated enough for the men to see the cave there seemed to be little or no activity in or around it. Morgan turned his head at the sound of an owl. Such a bird should not be awake at this hour. Then Morgan noticed that it was Big Horse who had made the sound. Big Horse was pointing to his left.

Del Murdock and eight men were riding toward the start of the trail, ready to head up it.

"Dammit to hell," Morgan muttered. He jumped up and began running, leaping over rocks and logs, dodging trees and boulders. By the time he reached the small path through the trees that led to the trail up the mountain, three men were already heading up the mountain trail.

Morgan jacked a round into the chamber of his Winchester, brought the gun up, and fired. One of the outlaws fell. Suddenly Morgan saw two more men drop from their horses, both pincushioned with arrows. He fired the Winchester again but missed.

By that time, the three outlaws on the trail were heading up as fast as they dared. All the other outlaws had slipped off their horses and melted into the trees and rocks across the little path from Morgan.

"Rough Wolf!" Morgan shouted. "Up the hill." He pointed.

Seeing the three outlaws riding as fast as they dared up the hill, Rough Wolf charged toward the bottom of the trail. Then he was moving upward, loping with strong, sure strides. Bullets began kicking up dust or ricocheting off rocks, but none seemed to hit him. The three outlaws disappeared over the rim of the canyon, while Rough Wolf was a little more than halfway up.

Morgan turned his attentions back to the pines all around him. Everything was quiet now. Even the birds had stopped singing. A soft, pattering rain began.

"What now, chief?" Big Horse asked a bit sarcastically from his position a little to Morgan's right.

"Hell if I know. You see who it was made it up the trail?"

"One of them was Murdock, I think. I'm not sure of the others."

"Well, we aren't going to get those miscreants while we sit here on our asses." Morgan rose and headed to his left a little before crossing the path. He stopped, back against a tree trunk, and waited, trying to hear something that might indicate where the outlaws were. He noticed that Big Horse had done the same farther down the path. From here on, though, he figured they'd each be on their own. The trees and brush here were too thick to allow them to work closely together.

With a shrug, Morgan began moving on, slowly and warily. He carried the Winchester in his left hand. In his right he now had one of his Smith and Wessons, thumb on the hammer though the pistol was not cocked.

He stopped every few steps to wait and listen. A few minutes later, the sound of gunshots came from up on the canyon rim. Morgan winced, hoping that neither Rough Wolf nor Rabbit Tail had been hurt in that short gunbattle.

Morgan moved on, wondering where Big Horse was. He would surely hate to shoot Big Horse by mistake—or be shot accidentally by his friend. Suddenly, his hat flew off, and he saw a puff of gun smoke tangled in the trees. He dropped to one knee, Smith and Wesson cocked and extended. He fired once at the spot where the puff of powder smoke had come from. He heard nothing and figured that the man had moved immediately after shooting.

Morgan did that, too, even as the thoughts ran through his mind.

An eerie, keening sound filtered through the lodgepole pines and Douglas firs, startling Morgan for a moment. Then he realized it was Big Horse. He figured that if Big Horse couldn't kill someone with a gun or a bow, that sound might be enough to induce a heart attack.

Morgan moved a little more to his left and slipped from tree to tree. He was tired of the waiting and the skulking around. If someone was going to kill him, let him have his shot. If he missed, perhaps Morgan could pinpoint him and remove him. He moved at an oblique angle toward the place where the gunshot had come from.

Suddenly he froze. Something ahead had caught his attention, but he was not sure what. He waited, listening to the soft patter of the rain. Again he saw something, and finally he realized it was a shirt. He moved on, the little noise he was making masked by the gentle rain.

He stopped five feet from a fat, wheezing bag of a man who was hunched behind a little rock, trying to hide his obese form. "Hey, shit ball," Morgan called out softly, "you're under arrest."

Morgan could not believe a man of Al Oberman's extreme girth could move so fast. Still, the fat man could not outroll or dodge a bullet. Morgan emptied his Smith and Wesson into the fat carcass. Then he swiftly moved several feet to his right in case someone was trying to home in on his gun smoke.

No shots were coming, though, and Morgan took the time to reload his Smith and Wesson. Finally, he went forward again and checked on Oberman. The fat outlaw was quite dead, with four bullet holes. Just for an added precaution, he took Oberman's rifle and pistol and heaved them into the forest.

Once more, Morgan began his stalking through the evergreen forest. He was sweating despite the cool rain, and he wiped his face and eyes regularly on a shirt sleeve, wishing he had retrieved his hat. As battered and full of holes as it was, it would still be better than no hat at all.

Big Horse's high-pitched war cry echoed through the forest again, sending a chill up Morgan's spine. He wondered how Big Horse was faring, though he assumed that the Shoshoni was doing just fine for himself.

Big Horse had moved off almost parallel to the small path. He moved silently through the trees, his keen eyes searching, searching. He had often suspected that he had lost some his powers to smell when he was in the white man's school in Saint Louis. The few people

273

he had mentioned it to told him he was crazy. Still, he was certain that he could not smell as well as he had before. He wished now that he had regained that facility. It most likely would help, since outlaws like these rarely bathed. He resigned himself to having to use only his eyesight, and maybe his hearing a little.

His eyesight was more than enough when he spotted a blue shirt and a speck of white face. He readied his bow and waited for a time, wanting to make sure he was not seeing his friend Morgan. While waiting, he heard the gunfire up on the rim, and he pushed the thought of it away. He would worry later whether Rabbit Tail and Rough Wolf had been killed, or had killed the outlaws.

The gunfire from the rim made the man in the blue shirt jump, and it was enough to tell Big Horse that it was not Morgan there. He loosed three arrows in the span of a heartbeat. All three found their target.

The outlaw stood gargling and choking, trying frantically to pull the arrow out of his neck, which it had gone through from side to side. Another arrow had gone through his upper arm and into the chest cavity on the side, pinning the left arm there. The third had hit several inches below the second, but hadn't hit the arm, instead going straight into the body near the lowest ribs. The man finally fell.

Big Horse wove through the forest and retrieved his arrows, taking little care in their removal. As a result, several chunks of flesh were pulled from the outlaw's body. The outlaw did not feel any of it.

The Shoshoni made a short war cry of victory over the body of his enemy, and with a grim smile took the man's scalp. Then he moved through the trees again.

A few minutes later, he heard another gunshot, this

one much closer, followed immediately by another. Then there was silence. Some minutes later, Big Horse heard four gunshots, one right after the other. He worried about Morgan and hoped it was the lawman doing the shooting.

Big Horse shrugged. He could do nothing to change it either way. He would press on, heading slowly in Morgan's direction, to see if he could help the marshal. Suddenly, he was face to face with a white man almost as large as he.

Both were startled, but Big Horse recovered a heartbeat faster. He wrenched out his tomahawk, and as the white man began bringing his pistol to bear, Big Horse brought the tomahawk down on the man's forehead, splitting his head like a ripe melon.

Big Horse kept his grip on the tomahawk as the outlaw went down without a sound, blood welling out of the ghastly chasm in his forehead and head. Once again, Big Horse took the scalp—a small one this time, in deference to the damage done to the man's hair by the tomahawk—and crowed in victory. He turned and headed in the general vicinity in which he thought he would find Morgan.

The lawman still moved warily through the trees, seeking another outlaw, though not even sure there was another outlaw here and alive. He found out there was at least one more when a bullet banged off the edge of his left hip, barely missing the bone.

Morgan flopped down to the damp ground and slithered through the soaked pine needles until he was behind a substantial tree. He rose, pistol out and ready, while he waited. He hoped the outlaw had seen him fall and would think him dead. He might even move in a little to try to steal from the body. These outlaws seemed the type to rob the dead.

His patience was rewarded as he spotted a man weaving through the trees. When the man came to something of a very small open space Morgan stepped out from behind the tree, hoping he would not regret this. In his mood, under these circumstances, he would feel perfectly justified in shooting the man down. But he figured he ought to try bringing him in.

"You're under arrest, shit ball," he said. He stood sideways to the outlaw, Smith and Wesson at the end of a long, brawny arm. It was pointed at the outlaw's head.

"Hey now, Marshal," the man said, "I don't want no trouble. I surely don't. I'm just an innocent feller got caught up in something that ain't my business and which I don't want no connection with."

"You're full of shit. Now drop that piece or I drop you." Morgan saw another figure moving behind the outlaw. He shifted his pistol a bit, ready to blast who-ever it was.

Big Horse moved between the trees, bow nocked and ready to fire. That surprised Morgan. "This man's mine, Big Horse," he said sharply. "I've got him un-der control. You can put that bow away now."

Morgan was beginning to think that Big Horse had gone crazy. Why else would he still be stalking for-ward? Then the outlaw moved, bringing his pistol up fast and snapping off two quick shots. Morgan felt one of the bullets skim around the side of his thigh.

At the same time that the outlaw fired, Big Horse released an arrow, and then another one almost im-mediately after. Morgan was stunned by the speed with which Big Horse fired, but he had no time to worry about it. In the space of an eye blink, the outlaw had fired twice, Big Horse had fired twice, and Morgan had fired twice.

Morgan saw the outlaw go down, and he whirled in Big Horse's direction, crouching at the same time. Big Horse was walking nonchalantly toward him. Morgan slowly rose and looked around. Another outlaw lay dead with two arrows sticking up out of his body. Morgan breathed a sigh of relief.

"I hope that's the last of them," Morgan said with feeling.

"I think it is. You got two, I take it?"

Morgan nodded. "How about you?"

"Three counting this one," Big Horse said as he jerked the arrows out of the man's body. He pulled his knife and looked at Morgan. "You mind?" he asked.

Morgan shook his head. He had never understood why people—white or red—scalped. It didn't make any sense to him.

Big Horse put his bloody trophies away. "Let's see," he said, "you got two, I got three, and we got three on the path; that's eight."

"And three made it up the trail."

"Eleven," Big Horse said. "Rough Wolf miscounted."

"I hope not by any more," Morgan said.

"Don't judge him too harshly, Buck. There could've been a hundred men in that cave and we might've only seen five or six."

"I know. I'm not complaining about his counting, just hopin' there aren't any more of these bastards out here." Morgan shook his head. "Well, let's get up the trail and see if everyone's all right up there. I've been a little worried since I heard the gunfire up that way."

"Me, too." Big Horse paused. "Let's see if we can rustle up a couple of the outlaws' horses. I don't fancy the idea of walking up that goddamn trail."

Morgan nodded, and the two headed toward the old path. They found the horses calmly cropping grass not far from the cave. Morgan and Big Horse pulled themselves into saddles and then rode up the trail as quickly as they dared.

Chapter 34

At the top, Morgan and Big Horse found Rough Wolf dead, struck by three bullets. They also found a dead outlaw, his chest pierced by three arrows.

But mostly they found a wide-eyed, angry, and wounded Rabbit Tail. The boy's face was enraged, and though he had a bullet in his arm, he was still busy trying to calm down the horses. The animals had not liked all the activity and the gunfire. Morgan and Big Horse helped out and quickly got the horses settled.

The three of them sat. "What happened, Rabbit Tail?" Morgan asked.

Big Horse translated as the boy spoke. "I heard guns from down below, so I went to take a look. Next I saw three riders coming hard up the hill. They almost ran me over, but I got out of the way. One—a man with a necklace of fingers and ears—saw me and fired at me twice, but his horse was skittish, so he missed."

Rabbit Tail paused, thinking back to what had happened so he would be sure to get it right. "I ducked into the trees away from our horses. They tried to follow at first, but the trees were too thick. The next thing I saw was Rough Wolf coming out of the canyon. He fired three arrows, hitting the one that's dead over there. But then the other two fired at him. I saw him go down. Then the outlaws galloped off. I think they were afraid there were more of the People here.''

"A reasonable thought on their part," Morgan said quietly. "You did well, boy, you really did. That was smart to go away from the horses so those shit balls wouldn't find them. I suspect their horses are more than half played out after a fast ride up that trail.''

Rabbit Tail beamed but said nothing, not even when Big Horse winked at him.

"Well, boy," Morgan said, "I best take a look at that arm.''

"We'll need to get on the trail right away, won't we?'' the boy protested.

"We will soon enough. Those shit balls can't hide anymore. They won't get far." He smiled at the boy. "I think you're just scared of old Dr. Morgan.''

Rabbit Tail got angry, but then laughed. "Maybe I am.''

"We'll need a fire first," Big Horse said. "Come, Rabbit Tail, I'll help you look for wood. You," he said to Morgan, "take a look at your own wounds.''

"Getting mighty bossy here, aren't you, chief?''

"Somebody has to do it." Big Horse and Rabbit Tail walked off. While they were gone, Morgan got a small bottle of whiskey from his saddlebags. He almost always carried one, mostly for medicinal purposes like these, but it was often a good thing to have a few snorts handy.

He slid his pants down. As he expected, both wounds looked superficial. He squatted, gritted his teeth, then poured a little whiskey on each. It stung like hell, and he winced. There had been times, like this one, when

280

Morgan thought the fixing up of the wound was worse than having gotten it in the first place.

Morgan was just buckling on his gunbelt when the two Shoshoni returned. Soon there was a small fire going. Without a word, Big Horse took his knife and put the blade in the flames. Rabbit Tail saw it and gulped.

"All right, son," Morgan said. "Best make yourself comfortable as you can."

With wide, frightened eyes, the boy lay on the ground. Morgan cut open his sleeve, then gently lifted the arm and looked at it.

"Well, the bullet's still in there, but I don't know how the hell it didn't come out. You're lucky it didn't break the bone or hit the artery."

"Can you get it out?" Rabbit Tail asked nervously.

"Easy." Morgan grabbed Rabbit Tail's good arm and pulled him up until the boy was sitting. "Here," he said, "feel this." He gently guided Rabbit Tail's hand to the back side of the upper arm. "Feel that?"

Rabbit Tail nodded and grinned. "That's the bullet?"

"Yep. Unless you have some kind of strange growth in your arm." He smiled. "You do know I'll have to cut the arm to get the bullet out, don't you?"

The boy nodded nervously.

"It shouldn't hurt too much. But what I'm going to have you do is lay down on your belly so I have a clear space for cutting and such. Big Horse'll give you a stick to bite on. He'll also be here, if you need to squeeze his hand."

Rabbit Tail was crying a little. It seemed to Morgan that Rabbit Tail had been holding it in for a while. He did look abashed, though.

"Don't worry about the tears, son," Morgan said softly. "There's no shame in it."

Big Horse nodded at the boy in agreement.

"All right, Rabbit Tail, roll over and get comfortable." Morgan got the whiskey and poured a little over his knife blade, then over his hands. "Keep that blade," he said, pointing to the one in the fire, "handy. I figure we're going to need it."

"That's why it's there."

"Keep a good grip on him, too," Morgan said, nonplussed. "I can't have him thrashing around while I'm cutting him."

"Damn, Buck, you think I've never helped cut a bullet or arrowhead out of someone before?"

Morgan grinned ruefully. "Sorry. I'm not thinking. Usually when I get stuck doing something like this I've got a bunch of people around me who don't know their asses from a cave."

Big Horse nodded. He jammed a stick between Rabbit Tail's jaws and then placed a big, strong hand on Rabbit Tail's back. His other hand gripped Rabbit Tail just above the elbow.

"Here goes, son," Morgan said. He gingerly slit the skin of Rabbit Tail's arm and then cut a little deeper, through the flesh. Rabbit Tail squirmed like an eel, but he really couldn't move much, especially the arm. Big Horse was making sure of that.

"Got you, you little bastard," Morgan said as he pulled the bullet out with two grimy fingers. He dropped the bullet, grabbed the bottle, and poured some whiskey in the gash.

Rabbit Tail sucked in a breath and all his muscles tensed.

"Almost done, boy," Morgan said soothingly. He

282

turned and grabbed Big Horse's red-hot blade. Without warning, he set the hot metal on the wound.

Rabbit Tail stiffened even more, and then he relaxed completely—into unconsciousness.

Morgan pulled the blade away and stuck it in the fire again. "Best turn him over and make sure he didn't swallow his tongue or anything," Morgan said.

Big Horse gently rolled the boy onto his back and forced his jaws open. "Seems to be fine."

Morgan nodded. He pulled the knife out of the fire again. With a small grin, he said, "Well, this one ought to be a hell of a lot easier."

That done, Morgan bandaged the arm with an old shirt he had in his saddlebags. He also fashioned a makeshift sling to keep the arm from being jostled.

When Morgan finished up on Rabbit Tail, Big Horse skinned the two rabbits he had shot while he and Rabbit Tail had been out looking for firewood. He jabbed green sticks through the skinned and gutted rabbits and hung them over the fire. Morgan made the coffee. Then both sat back, leaning against wet logs. Morgan picked up the bottle of whiskey. "Want a dose?" he asked.

Big Horse nodded. "Don't mind if I do." He took the bottle Morgan held out and drank half of what was left. Morgan took the bottle back and finished it off.

"What happens now, Buck?" Big Horse asked.

"We take care of Rabbit Tail first. Then we get him back to the village. Rough Wolf's body, too," he said.

"And then?"

"Depends which way Murdock and whoever the other one was go."

"Was one of the men you killed down there Nordmeyer?"

Morgan shook his head. "No. You?"

"Nope."

Morgan nodded. "That must've been him with Murdock."

"My thoughts, too."

They ate in silence, finishing just about the time Rabbit Tail came to. "Hungry?" Morgan asked.

"A little."

Big Horse handed him a piece of meat on a knife. The boy took it and ate gingerly, as if he was afraid the food would do something strange and terrible to his stomach.

After Rabbit Tail had eaten Morgan asked, "You think you can travel some, boy?"

Rabbit Tail nodded. "We're going back to the village?" he asked.

"You are. Me and Big Horse'll drop you off and leave Rough Wolf to get a proper funeral and burying."

"What about you and Big Horse?"

"We still have business to tend to."

"I want to go."

"No," Morgan said flatly. "We were damn fools for taking you in the first place. You almost got yourself killed. There'll be plenty of time when you're older that you can do that."

"You're wounded, too."

"Not as bad as you are. I can get around on my leg well enough. What're you going to do if you need to shoot a gun or a bow?"

Rabbit Tail shrugged.

"Don't worry about it, Rabbit Tail," Big Horse said. "You have gained honors."

"How?" Rabbit Tail asked sullenly.

"No horses were taken from us. You were wounded while keeping the ponies safe, even as Rough Wolf died to save the ponies."

The boy was only partially assuaged.

"We best get moving," Morgan said, getting to his feet.

They saddled their horses. When that was done Big Horse placed Rough Wolf's body across the dead man's horse. Just before leaving, Big Horse walked up to where Rabbit Tail was sitting on his pony. Big Horse had a rope tied to the horses he and Morgan had ridden up the trail. Big Horse handed Rabbit Tail the rope.

The boy took it without comment or question. Like so many other things, he was expected to care for the stolen horses as well as his own. It annoyed him now, since he really only had the use of one arm. He decided he could hold his reins plus the rope to the other horses in one hand. But still, his wounded arm ached like nothing he had ever experienced before. He wanted nothing more than to be allowed to go back to sleep, a nap from which he hoped he could awaken completely recovered.

"How do you like your new horses, Rabbit Tail?" Big Horse asked.

"Eh? What?"

"I asked you how you like your new horses." He jerked his chin in the direction of the outlaws' horses.

"Mine?" he asked, face beaming.

"Yours," Big Horse said.

They took their time, but they did not dally, either. The trip out was somewhat easier, since it was mostly downhill instead of up. But most importantly, they were making the journey in the daylight.

Once they hit the scrub desert beyond the foothills of the Wind River Mountains, they opened up some, putting the ponies into a brisk trot. It was only mid-afternoon, and Morgan thought there might be a chance he could get back on Murdock's trail before the daylight was gone.

Morgan was running out of energy, though, by the time they reached the village. Even though his two wounds were relatively minor, he had lost some blood, and it was barely a week and a half since he had been wounded in the shoulder. All the wounds were taking their toll on him.

He was surprised to see Orv Ashby there. But he was really surprised to see Ashby's family still in the village. Morgan asked Ashby about it.

He laughed. "They were treated so well that they have made many new friends here." He shook his head in amazement. "So Grace said she wanted to stay a little longer."

Chapter 35

Screams woke Washakie's village. Morgan and Cloud Woman rushed out of their lodge. A woman named Red Moon stumbled into the camp. She was screaming, and she was covered with blood. Her sister, Antelope, rushed out and grabbed her. It was as if Red Moon suddenly knew she could collapse; she went down in a heap, pulling Antelope with her.

Shoshoni rushed to the two women, shouting questions. Red Moon was babbling, but even the Shoshoni could not understand what she was saying.

Finally, at Washakie's request, Morgan fired off two quick shots from one of his Smith and Wessons. That quieted the crowd enough for Washakie to shout, "Bring Red Moon into my lodge."

That was done, and then all the warriors filed in, filling every inch of the large tepee. The women and the children stayed outside, pressing as close as they could get to the skin lodge to hear what was happening inside.

Big Horse sat down on Washakie's right side and Morgan sat on Big Horse's right, near enough that the big Shoshoni could translate for him.

"Where's Orv?" Big Horse asked Morgan when the lodge was full.

"He told me last night he wanted to get back to the agency as soon as possible," Morgan responded. "So he planned to leave a couple hours before dawn. I heard him shooing his family out of my lodge sometime this mornin', but I was beat and didn't pay much attention."

It took some time for Antelope to calm her sister down and they could determine that none of her injuries seemed mortal. Then Washakie said, "Tell us what happened."

"We were camped on the Little Wind, in the big bend it makes. Big Heart wanted to hunt, for we were low on meat. Yesterday afternoon, men came. White men." She would not look at Morgan.

"How many men?" Big Horse asked.

"Six, I think. Maybe seven."

"Did one of them wear a string around his neck with human ears and fingers?" Big Horse asked.

"No."

Morgan was dumb struck. He had been certain it was Murdock and Nordmeyer, the only two who apparently had escaped. "Jesus," he muttered, "that's all we need—another band of white outlaws raiding Shoshoni camps."

"Then what happened?" Big Horse asked.

"They killed Big Heart and the two youngest, Puma and Brown Arm, and shot me. I fell and pretended to be dead. When they weren't looking I crawled to the riverbank. I stayed behind some reeds there and watched. They captured Laughing Elk." She paused for a drink of water from a gourd spoon.

"Who's Laughing Elk?" Morgan asked.

288

"Red Moon's daughter," Big Horse responded. "She's about fifteen winters."

Morgan nodded, a sick knot in his stomach.

"Each of them took Laughing Elk." Red Moon was crying heavily now, and her words were said with much wailing. "Two of them twice that I saw. When it got dark I ran as long as I could, then walked through the night to get here."

"What did these men look like?" Big Horse asked.

"They all looked like him," Red Moon said, pointing to Morgan.

"There are differences among even the white people. Stop being angry at our brother and think what these men looked like."

"One I saw was very vicious when he took Laughing Elk. He looked nice, though, before that. Neat, clean, all the hair gone from his face."

"Shit," Morgan breathed. "That's Ward Haggerty."

Big Horse nodded. "Any others you can remember?" he asked.

"One I didn't see at all. Another was tall and very thin. He had hair on his upper lip. Another was short and plump. He looked funny. Two looked much alike. Maybe they were brothers. Fairly tall, dark hair, funny noses."

"Good God," Morgan muttered again. He reached into his shirt pocket and pulled out some papers. While everyone waited, wondering what he was up to, Morgan sorted through the papers and pulled out two. He handed those to Big Horse. "Ask Red Moon if those are the two men," he said.

While Big Horse conversed quickly with Red Moon

289

and showed her the pictures, Morgan absentmindedly shoved the other papers away.

Red Moon nodded vigorously.

Big Horse handed the papers back to Morgan. "You don't need that translated, do you?" he asked grimly.

"Nope."

"You know them?"

Morgan nodded. "You remember the time Foster told us about some of Murdock's men? I mentioned that I had been tracking these two and their brothers before I got here?"

"Yes. Are they the ones?"

"Yes. Kevin and Jess Spangler."

"This isn't good, my friend," Big Horse said solemnly. He sounded a little worried.

"It sure as hell . . ." He paused, and then snapped, "Let's get out of here." He rose.

Big Horse followed him, and they shoved their way through the milling mob of women and children. Morgan spotted Cloud Woman. "Go saddle my horse. Now!" he told her.

She looked at him in question, but then turned and ran for their lodge.

"You better get your horse, too."

"You mind telling me what this is all about?" Big Horse asked sharply.

"Orv Ashby. Him and his family're ridin' out that way heading for the agency. There's every chance they'll ride right into the shit balls' camp."

"Damn." He paused. "But don't you think the outlaws'll be gone by now?"

"It's likely. But what if they're not? We can't take that chance."

Minutes later, Morgan was on his horse. He had

just explained to Cloud Woman where he was going and why. "There's a strong possibility that he's safe," Morgan finished. "And if that's true, the outlaws'll probably have moved on. If that's the case, I'm going to follow them." He kissed her and then climbed into the saddle.

Big Horse was waiting for him, and the two swatted their horses, galloping out of the village. Less than an hour later, they came on Ashby's party. With the agent were his wife, his three children, and three Shoshoni warriors acting as an escort.

"What's wrong?" Ashby asked as Morgan and Big Horse rode up and stopped just in front of Ashby. He looked worried.

Morgan explained it. Then Morgan pointed. "The place it happened is a mile or so that way," he said.

"Dear Lord," Ashby gasped.

"Right. I want you to turn back, Orv," Morgan said. "Head back to the village."

"But I must get back to . . ."

"I know," Morgan interjected. "But unless you want to risk your wife's life, and the lives of your children, you'll turn back."

"Do you think those outlaws are still there?"

Morgan shrugged. "There's no tellin' without ridin' over that way. Which me and Big Horse plan to do."

"But what if they're not there?" Ashby asked. "I'll have wasted several hours of traveling time."

"Just because they're not there doesn't mean they're not somewhere around here. I think it'll be safer in the village, and it's closer than the agency. You push those horses a little and you can make it back there pretty quick."

"What'll you do after you get to the spot?"

"Depends on what we find. I expect the outlaws are gone, and if so, I'll head out after them straight off."

Ashby stood thoughtfully a few moments, then nodded. "We'll turn back."

"Good," Morgan said. He leaned close to Ashby so he would not be overheard. "Did your wife explain everything?"

Ashby nodded, but anger clouded his face.

"How're she and Bonnie handling it?"

"Well enough under the circumstances."

"How about you?"

Ashby smile weakly. "The same," he said. "It's not easy living with the knowledge some men tried to . . ."

"No need to talk about it," Morgan said calmly. "Just remember, though, Grace and Bonnie are countin' on you. You have to be strong enough to get them through all the shame and hurt. You can't do that by showin' any weakness."

Ashby nodded, his face etched with determination. "You're right, and I know it. I've tried to be optimistic about all this. It's hard, but I think I've pulled it off so far."

Morgan nodded. "All right then, you best get movin'. The sooner you get going, the quicker you'll be in the village."

Morgan and Big Horse watched as Ashby and his party turned and began riding slowly back the way they had come. Then the two trotted off, slowing only when they were a hundred yards or so from the campsite. At about fifty yards they dismounted and, using their horses for protection, moved ever closer.

There was no one living at the campsite. The three bodies had been picked at by the scavengers of several sorts, and they were a gruesome sight.

Big Horse was already poking around the area, looking for tracks or sign of any kind. Finally, he told Morgan, "Murdock's been here. Either that or someone's got his horse."

"You sure?" Morgan asked skeptically.

Big Horse nodded. "What I'd like to know," he said, "is what the hell he was doin' here."

"Me, too. I got my suspicions, though."

"So, tell it."

Morgan kneaded his wounded shoulder, trying to get a little more movement out of it. "I think Murdock and the shit balls he had with him in the canyon were supposed to meet more men here. Or somewhere near here. The ones he was to meet got here first and found Big Heart and his family. They killed Big Heart and had some fun with Laughing Elk," he added, throat constricting at the very thought. "Then Murdock and Nordmeyer came along. I expect they stayed the night, abusing the girl, then rode on to Flat Fork."

"But why would they meet here?" Big Horse asked. "Why didn't the new men just wait in Flat Fork?"

"Well, since I'm guessin' on all this anyway, I'd say it was because they all planned on going on another raid."

"Would've been a hell of a big raid."

"Since Murdock had the stones to raid Washakie's village with only seven or eight men, he certainly would be willing to try it with fifteen or so. He'd be smart enough to know that Washakie' would have the village on alert now, which is why he'd want a much larger force than last time. And Murdock's crazy enough to try it."

"That'd seem to cover all the particulars, wouldn't it? Except for where they are now."

"You checked for sign. Didn't you find anything? I'd wager they headed for Flat Fork this morning."

"Why?"

"Where else're they going to go? Murdock lost a good portion of his gang in Flat Fork a few days ago. Yesterday he lost another batch of men. He needs more gunmen, and he won't be able to get them anywhere else but Flat Fork."

"So we head for Flat Fork?"

Morgan shook his head. "I," he said, emphasizing the word, "will head for Flat Fork. You will head for Washakie's village."

"You aren't leaving me out of this," Big Horse said.

"Yes, I am. I used to tell Two Wounds this all the time. You—or any Shoshoni—would be dead a minute after you got into Flat Fork. Those shit balls'd use you for target shooting. Besides, I'm afraid Murdock might be really crazy now after his losses. There's a chance he might hire damn near everyone in Flat Fork and take an army out to decimate Shoshoni villages. If that's true, the People'll need you more than I would."

"I hate when your reasoning is impeccable, you white-eyed devil, you." He sighed and held out his hand. "You watch your ass, white man."

"You too."

Chapter 36

Shotgun in hand, Morgan pushed through the doors and into the Bighorn Saloon. Everyone looked up at him, but he focused directly on Del Murdock and the two Spangler brothers. Between Murdock and Kevin Spangler was Laughing Elk. She was naked, as far as Morgan could see, and had a rope around her neck. She looked frightened and battered. Five other outlaws also sat at the table.

The bartender started to bend, and Morgan figured he was going for a scattergun, so Morgan fired one barrel of his shotgun. The bartender went down. Morgan turned back to face the table of outlaws and calmly reloaded the weapon.

"Let the girl go, shit ball," Morgan said in a raspy voice. His rage was at full boil just beneath the surface. Controlled, it might make him invincible—or so he thought.

"You talkin' to me, tin star?" Murdock asked.

"Ah, yes, with all the shit balls sitting at your table, you might be confused as to which one I was addressing. In this case, yes, it was you."

Murdock laughed a little. "She-it, Marshal," he

said, "you want to poke an Injun bitch, go out and get your own." His companions thought this hilarious.

Morgan shifted ever so slightly to his right and unloaded both barrels of buckshot into the two men sitting at the end of the table. Morgan did not know either of them, but they fell in bloody, shredded clumps.

Morgan looked back at Murdock, whose face had stiffened in anger and, possibly, some fear. "You Spangler boys, how'd you get mixed up with shit ball there?" he asked as he reloaded his shotgun again.

"We ain't tellin' you shit," Kevin Spangler snapped.

"No harm in tellin' him, Kev," Murdock said. "He ain't gonna be alive long enough to make use of any of the information. Go on and tell him."

"We're cousins," Kevin Spangler said. "Once some asshole of a lawman killed . . ." His eyes got very wide. "You were the son of a bitch killed our brothers," he said quietly.

"Yep. And unless you and your shit-ball friends here want to end up like them, I'd suggest you toss your guns down now and give yourselves up."

"Sure, Marshal. Sure," Kevin Spangler said unctuously. He began rising slowly from his chair. Then, suddenly, there was a six-gun in his hand.

Morgan didn't hesitate. He loosed both barrels of the shotgun. Kevin Spangler took a full load of buckshot in the chest and went down, his pistol clattering across the floor. The other blast hit nothing but wall, as everyone else at the table began moving.

Murdock shoved straight back and then rose, kicking the chair away from him. As he moved, he kept his grip on the rope around Laughing Elk's neck. She was pulled up and backward, until her back bounced up against Murdock's front. He dropped the rope and swept his left hand around her, holding her in place with a hand cupping the girl's right breast. It was obvious now that she was entirely naked. With his other hand, Murdock pulled a pistol and started firing at Morgan.

Morgan dropped to one knee. He figured his main target now was Nordmeyer, who probably was the most dangerous of the men right at the moment. Morgan felt the cold calmness spreading through him like it always did at such times. He brought the Smith and Wesson up in his right hand and fired twice. One bullet clipped Nordmeyer, who was moving to his own right. The other missed entirely.

Cursing himself, Morgan fired again. This time he hit Nordmeyer in the side, and he figured he had punctured one of his lungs.

At the same time, though, Morgan's hat went sailing off, apparently from a shot coming from his right. Morgan flopped down on his belly and then rolled a few times, once more coming up on one knee.

Jess Spangler was slumped half across the table, dead. Morgan wondered about that for less than a heartbeat. Then he swung to his left. As he did, he heard gunfire behind him, and he wondered what that was all about. He could not take the time to see, though. He quickly drilled Haggerty, who had gotten tangled up in his chair. He saw another unknown outlaw was also down.

Morgan almost jumped out of his skin when he heard, "You all right, Marshal?" He was about to turn and see who was addressing him when a bullet caught him high up on the left side, only a couple of inches from where he had been shot not long before. The impact knocked him flat.

He pushed up quickly, ignoring the blood seeping into his shirt and even his vest. He cocked the Smith and Wesson and aimed it at Murdock, who was still holding Laughing Elk in front of him with his lecherous grip. "Put the piece down and let the girl go, shit ball," he said firmly.

Murdock laughed. It was a strange, warbling, maniacal sound. "Just try'n shoot me while I got this here little redskin piece in front of me."

"I will, if you insist."

He laughed again. He thumbed back the hammer of his Colt and let it drop. All he got was a click. Panic spreading across his face, he kept firing and firing. "Shit!" he screamed. He threw the gun away and pulled a knife. He moved the knife blade around till it was resting on Laughing Elk's throat. "Back the hell up, lawman," he snarled. "Back the hell up or I'll cut her good."

Morgan fired, and the bullet smacked Murdock in the left eye, less than four inches from Laughing Elk's head. The outlaw spun away, his knife nicking Laughing Elk's throat.

"Come, girl," Morgan said quietly. "Come. It's all right."

Laughing Elk hesitated only a moment. She had been treated disgustingly by Murdock and his men, and this tall white man with the shiny star had just killed many of the outlaws. She had heard about the man with the star. He was a chief and had big medicine among his people, and she thought she could trust him. She ran swiftly toward him. "Get behind me," he said, not even sure she understood. He gave her a gentle push where he wanted her to go.

He was fairly certain that no one would be causing him trouble—at least not the ones in front of him. He half turned, eyes widening in surprise when he saw the storekeeper with a pistol in his hand.

"Mr. Applegate," Morgan said. "I'm obliged."

"It was the least I could do, Marshal," Applegate said.

Morgan nodded. "See that shit ball just to our left there?" When Applegate nodded Morgan said, "Please ask him—politely of course—if we might borrow his long coat to cover this poor child."

"Sure can. Yep. Goddamn, sure enough," the man said nervously, tearing off his coat before Applegate had even looked at him.

"Thank you," Applegate said sarcastically as he took the coat. He came forward and handed it to the girl. He tried not to look at her, but he couldn't help himself. She was so beautiful, with smooth, dusky skin, small, high breasts, and a perfect oval face. He gulped hard when he gave her the coat.

With Laughing Elk attired after a fashion, Morgan went forth to see about his and Applegate's handiwork. He thought he had heard some groans from over where Jess Spangler lay, and he headed that way.

Suddenly there was a commotion outside. People began screaming, and many of them began running. Above it all, Morgan could hear a war cry or two.

Then Big Horse was standing in the doorway, filling a good portion of it. He had a war club in one hand and a pistol in the other. "Looks like I got here a wee bit too late," he announced, sounding disappointed.

"What the hell . . ." Morgan started.

"I got a couple of the boys from the village and we came to see if you needed some help."

"A couple of Shoshonis sent all those people fleeing?" Morgan asked skeptically.

"Well, a little more than a couple. Twenty-six, to be exact." He laughed.

"Very goddamn funny," Morgan said weakly. Then the blackness came over him, and he fell.

Morgan was groggy when he awoke in his lodge. At least, he thought it was his lodge. He closed his eyes again, wondering if perhaps he had dreamed up everything—the Spanglers and Cochranes, Del Murdock and his men, Washakie, Two Wounds, Big Horse, Cloud Woman.

Lord, I hope if any of this is a dream that at least Cloud Woman is real, he thought.

He opened his eyes to see Cloud Woman's worried face over him. On the other side was the large, round mug of Big Horse. He sighed in relief.

It was several more weeks before he was pretty much his normal self again, but as soon as he could get out of the robe bed, he did.

"What did I miss after I went out?" he asked Big Horse a few days later.

"Well, we found two of those 'shit balls' alive—Jess Spangler, and a fellow said his name was Ronny Cole. Apparently, your friend Mr. Applegate wasn't as efficient as some others I know."

"What happened to the two?"

"They, and Lee Skousen, plus Lieutenant Pomeroy, are now residing in the Camp Brown guardhouse,

300

awaiting you. Oh, and Lieutenant Whitehill sends his regards. As does Orv."

"They say anything to you?"

"Yeah," Big Horse said with a grin. "We encouraged them a little. You had things figured out pretty well right. It's almost as if you knew what they were planning."

"If I'd known what they were planning," Morgan said sourly, "I'd never have let any of this happen. Anything else I ought to know about?"

"Well, let's see. Rabbit Tail's wound has healed and he thinks he's something special. He's even asking to go on war parties. The store man, Mr. Applegate, has taken a shine to Laughing Elk, and claims what she went through doesn't bother him."

"She reciprocate those feelings?"

"It appears so. She was in bad shape for a little while, but Applegate practically moved in with her. I think he really helped her get over things."

"He can't take her back to Flat Fork."

"Of course not. So Virg Whitehill offered him the chance to be Camp Brown's sutler."

"That it?"

"Jesus, you've only been out a couple of days. How the hell much do you think things can change?"

"Not much, I suppose."

"Sounds like you're sorry to have come out here," Big Horse said with a laugh.

"I've been in lots of better places, I can tell you that," Morgan replied. Then he looked up at Cloud Woman and grinned. "Of course," he said quietly, "there are some things to be said for being here."

FOLLOW THE SEVENTH CARRIER

TRIAL OF THE SEVENTH CARRIER   (3213, $3.95)
The enemies of freedom are on the verge of dominating the world with oil blackmail and the threat of poison gas attack. *Yonaga*'s officers lay desperate plans to strike back. Leading a ragtag fleet of revamped destroyers and a single antique WWII submarine, the great carrier must charge into a sea of blood and death in what becomes the greatest trial of the Seventh Carrier.

REVENGE OF THE SEVENTH CARRIER   (3631, $3.99)
With the help of an American carrier, *Yonaga* sails vast distances to launch a desperate surprise attack on the enemy's poison gas works. But a spy is at work. The enemy seems to know too much and a bloody battle is fought. Filled with murderous rage, *Yonaga*'s officers exact a terrible revenge.

ORDEAL OF THE SEVENTH CARRIER   (3932, $3.99)
Even as the Libyan madman calls for peaceful negotiations, an Arab battle group steams toward the shores of Japan. With good men from all over the world flocking to her colors, *Yonaga* prepares to give battle. The two forces clash off the island of Iwo Jima where it is carrier against carrier in a duel to the death — and *Yonaga,* sustaining severe damage, endures its bloodiest ordeal in the fight for freedom's cause.

*

Other Zebra Books by Peter Albano

THE YOUNG DRAGONS   (3904, $4.99)
It is June 25, 1944. American forces attack the island of Saipan. Two young fighting men on opposite sides, Michael Carpelli and Takeo Nakamura, meet in the flaming hell of battle that will inevitably bring them face-to-face in a final fight to the death. Here is the epic battle that decided the war against Japan as told by a man who was there.